ANKHARA CODES

AN ADVENTURE TO ESSENCE

ELLIE DEIGHTON

Ellie Deighton
hello@elliedeighton.com
www.ellieanndeighton.com

Publisher's Note: This is a work of fiction. Names, characters, places, and incidents are a product of the author's imagination. Locales and public names are sometimes used for atmospheric purposes. Any resemblance to actual people, living or dead, or to businesses, companies, events, institutions, or locales is completely coincidental.

Book Layout ©2017 BookDesignTemplates.com

Photography 2020 Lauren Couanon

Ordering Information:
Quantity sales. Special discounts are available on quantity purchases by corporations, associations, and others. For details, contact the "Special Sales Department" at the email address above.

Ankhara Codes/ Ellie Deighton. -- 1st ed.
ISBN 978-0-6450160-0-0

*It's not about right or wrong. Is this the path of your soul?
If yes? Act. If no? Dig deeper.*

—ELLIE DEIGHTON

CHAPTER 1

MEGAN

Three Days Prior

I wouldn't have it any other way. The rhythm of body grinding into mine. Sweet tears of pleasure landing on my hips and breasts. *Yes.* I'm lost here and I'm found here and that actually sounds like the most pretentious thing I've ever said but fuck me sideways (if you haven't already) it's true. I see him close his eyes and slow down to take a deep breath. He soaks it all in. He soaks in me. In himself. In this lust. It's art. Watching him and feeling my body respond to his deep grounding breath. My system relaxes in places I didn't know I had tension. I'm melting. Not disappearing. Letting go of the tension that has been in my body for God knows how long. Or maybe He doesn't know; maybe Satan knows. This is meant to be his playground, not that any of that guff makes sense to me. It's straight-up bullshit that this is anything less than holy.

"Ughhh." Sounds escape my throat that I've never heard before at the kiss of his cock on my cervix.

More.

I fucking love this.

He winks at me. He knows; he leans down to whisper in my ear, "Bite me." So I flip out from underneath him and he rolls, allowing me to sit on our pelvic throne. His fingers dig into the sides of my thighs. Almost my ass. *Almost gentlemanly.* I smirk. Not that I care. I want his fingers everywhere. I want him everywhere. I grind my seat on him, in circles.

"Mmmmm..." His turn to sing. With my eyes I tell him to put his arms back. To lay surrendered. To receive his heart and mine. Both penetrated. Both open. Both powerful beyond belief. As evidenced by the tears streaming down my face, I am completely stunned by the beauty of him.

"You too, love." He says it with his eyes and yet I hear him and I bring my hands to the air. I'm dancing like I imagine a priestess would dance. My hands are playing with the air around us, viscous like honey. My tears land on my breasts, swimming along my body to meet his. I can feel him all the way through me, piercing everything. My throat opens and I cry as the grief in my heart cracks open. Again. *Who is this man?* The fire inside is swallowing and birthing me at the same time. Like a tidal wave built of pleasure. If I didn't know better I'd say I was sparking. That's how it begins. Full body waves. I ripple and open my eyes to find his eyes captivated by me, and my first orgasm sings through my body. His body responds and we are truly lost now. Thighs shaking, I lean in to kiss him and find myself underneath him again. *How does he do that?* He moves with such quick grace I don't see any of it. I just land under his body, melt under his embrace and open. My heart. My eyes. My body. Open. Easy, in the face of his self-certainty. Easy, until a wound is kissed by his love and then I am frozen. Immediately noticed by him as our bodies are now merged in this telepathic knowing of one another.

He pauses. Gazes. His eyes ask me permission. I nod. The

stillness is disrupted by his penetration and I cry. Never have I known being loved like this. Never have I felt such a familiarity and connection. Never have I felt I was making love to myself in the embodiment of another. Until this. Until today.

You literally met him today you slut.

Part of me cares. Part of me is afraid of the aftermath. The shaming. The conversation. The "thanks" or "see you later", only to probably never see you again.

Fifty-one percent of me had to say "yes" for this to happen. Isn't that how it works? Just a little more yes than no and voilà, the deed is done. Not that this was like that; I wanted him. My body wanted him. My heart knew him. My soul recognised him. Assuming my soul is real. I am so in my head now. Dammit, noise. Noise noise noise. Man. Beautiful man.

Shit.

Beautiful man is staring at me.

"Are you okay?" he asks me and he really cares, it's obvious. He's really noticed. This is what it's like to be with someone else who sees it all and doesn't run. I can't believe I nearly didn't do this because of the noise. So much noise. So, so much noise. *Man. Beautiful man.* I vow to myself to never let the noise prevent my desires. A silent prayer. A-fucking-men. *Literally.*

"I keep nearly saying I love you." Okay. Not what I had expected to say. Good. Great. Surprising even myself with my outrageousness this morning.

"I have loved you a thousand lifetimes." Okay. I'm down. The awareness exists in me that this is literally insane but my desire to care is non-existent. I'm lost in him again and the flame inside me is smouldering, licking his. I can feel my body unlocking. Opening again. And unlocking this time so quickly because I can feel my heart somehow knowing itself inside his. I can feel my heart in his chest just as tangibly as his sword is between my legs, and it's a magic I thought only existed in fake movies written to make you feel shit about your love life (or lack of one). I'm in my head again.

I open my eyes and his eyes meet me. I don't ever think I'll be the same. I am lost in him and completely powerful to do everything about it.

⚜

I don't remember falling asleep and I'm not actually sure if I did. He's still here. Gently breathing. Which does make sense seeing as I'm the one in his bed. I should go. That's how this works in the movies – and, actually, in my entire friendship group, but I don't remember Josie ever telling me sex was like this before. This was... different. Primal. Emotional. I mean... God, *I cried*. So did he if I remember correctly. Like I'd ever forget. He had smiled when his tears fell. Like he was remembering something. Like he was remembering me, which, of course, makes absolutely no sense whatsoever.

I shrug myself away from these thoughts that will surely drive me crazy and lean into him to whisper good morning. Before I get the chance he opens his eyes, smiling a smile that I'm almost sure will be the death of me.

CHAPTER 2

NOAH

66 Hours Prior

*J*don't want her to leave. She's phenomenal. She looks around and rubs her face like she's trying to occupy herself while I stare at her. I'm almost trying not to, but I don't want to look away. I want to drink her in. Her hair is so black it somehow seems blue or purple. Her Bahama blue eyes. Literally – looking in her eyes is like staring into the sea around the Bahamas. They are so clear I can't tell if they are more blue or more green. I'm going to vote blue, but I'm sure they're sparkling just like the ocean glitters in sunlight. Her skin is so pale against my olive skin, and soft. So soft. *Listen to yourself, you sound like a soap opera.* I don't even know when – or if – I'll see her again. When... Well. I don't know if I will. This isn't normal. I've never felt open like this before. Not with somebody else, anyway. Definitely not with somebody else. Maybe not even with myself. Not since I was a kid. Not since... I can't remember when. Maybe actually never. Maybe something has opened that I can't close again. Not that I'd want to close it. I wonder if she realises the effect she's had on me. *You basically told her you love her, you idiot.* It's a miracle she's here and not running away from me thinking I'm some creepy stalker. *"I have loved you a thousand lifetimes."* Who says that?! I was just in the moment but in hindsight... I was on another fucking planet. *Come on,*

Noah. It's ridiculous but I actually would have been shattered if she'd left.

I've never stayed up all night with a chick BEFORE anything sexual happened. We had barely kissed until the sun came up and lust took over. It wasn't really that though. It didn't feel like lust. It felt like... more. *Love.* Surely not in less than twenty-four hours? I can't believe how comfortable and how not over-whelmed I am here with her. She's lying on her back with her eyes closed. Maybe she's pretending she can't feel me staring at her. I don't know how, but I know she can feel me. She's glow-ing in that 'I just had the best time' kinda afterglow. If I didn't have to go to see Jasper I would stare at her all day.

JASPER. I'd completely forgotten he was coming over.

"Megan. We have to move." *"We" feels good on us. Like I can breathe.* "It's seven a.m. I have plans with Jasper and, correct me if I'm wrong, but I'm pretty sure you don't want him to walk in here and see you naked."

She laughs at me and rolls over, shaking her butt at me be-fore getting up to dance around the room. *Don't do that when I have to leave, it's torture.* I want to ravish her. I want to be a gen-tleman and remind her Jasper will be here soon but she doesn't seem to care at all. In fact, I've never seen a woman like this before. A woman. Usually I don't call chicks that, but the way she holds herself is... well. She's actually just being herself. It's beautiful and strangely magnetising. I want to dance with her. *Well that's it. You have officially lost it. You want to have a morning dance with your one-night... lover?* I let out a sigh. I don't know what has come over me.

My phone buzzes and I reach over to check it and see a text from Jasper saying he'll be here in five minutes. Fifteen min-utes late. Just on his usual schedule, which usually I'm not so grateful for. Nothing about this morning feels usual. Megan is dressed now, and tying her hair up in a messy bun. I love messy buns, so of course that's what she's doing. She is perfectly imperfect.

"Thank you for a mindblowingly fun night," she whispers in my ear and then kisses me on the cheek before skipping out my room and running downstairs. I'm wondering if she makes up words all the time when I'm snapped out of my reverie by the window crashing shut downstairs. I look out my bedroom window just in time to catch a glimpse of black-blue hair disappearing over the fence. I have a whole thirty seconds to myself before Jasper crashes into my room.

"Sorry I'm late, man. Who have you been up to?" He winks at me, and I slam myself back onto my bed.

"I don't know," is all I could get together.

"You must know something to have kept her here for that long," he quips. Confused, I look up at him.

"What are you on about?"

"It's Sunday. You've been officially missing for over twenty-four hours"

I almost fall over, then I realise I can't fall over because I'm already laying down. *This is not normal. This is not normal at all.* I sit up hoping to catch the smirk I know so well on Jasper's face, but I don't see a smirk. He's frowning confusedly at me, looking at me like I've just told him the pet spider I don't have is yellow. His face is a pretty accurate representation of how I'm feeling.

We were making love for a whole day and night and neither of us even noticed. Did we? Did she? Am I the only one losing my mind here? Why did I just call sex "making love"? Have I bumped my head? Did she actually leave yesterday and I passed out in between? I pick up my phone to check the date and there it is, bright as day. Bright as Sunday morning, actually, and I couldn't even text her to see if she knew. I'd just spent twenty-four hours inside this woman and I didn't even have her full name to find her on Facebook.

You fucking idiot.

› CHAPTER 3 ‹

MEGAN

31 Hours Prior

J've gotta call Josie, she's gonna flip her shit. But I kind of don't want to. It's always me talking and her not quite being there, not quite getting it. I've never met anyone that tries so hard, anyone so ready to listen to every detail I have to share about my life. Even so, there's just something about it that leaves me unsatisfied. It's like I'm constantly having to explain details that would be obvious to her if she really got me. *Stop being such a bitch.* Nah, fuck that – I never speak poorly about her and I'm not being a bitch. I'm just confused. I don't know what's missing in our friendship. In fact, I don't know a friendship I've ever had that's been different. It's always the same. A new connection that goes deep fast, and then just fizzles. It's like I always want to go deeper but something tells me not to take them with me. So I don't. I separate. I invest less time in sharing the details. I spend more time alone and then eventually something happens and I wake up one day without a best friend. Without what feels like any friends. Lots of 'friends' but never any real friends. Never any friends I'd invite on an adventure with me if I was in a movie or a novel. I wonder what it would actually be like to take Josie on an adventure.

I can see it now. I'm driving the getaway car and the monsters are chasing us and she's telling me to slow down and be kind to them. Seriously. That girl is a walking, talking kindness machine. We'd be dead in the first three scenes.

Shaking off the thought, I head to the diner anyway. Maybe she'll be there. Maybe I'll sit alone and bathe in the memory of the ink covered blond that made my body sing in ways I didn't know I could. Tattoos do something to me and his somehow felt ancient. They electrified my body. Speaking of my body, I'm fucking starving.

"Hot chips and a beetroot smoothie, please." The waitress looks at me as if I'm bonkers and then smiles a forced smile. Weird. Jenny was usually super-sweet and I would have thought she was used to my order by now. Guess not.

The bells ring as someone opens the door and I see Josie's ponytail flick her right in the face as she searches for me. She looks frantic. Frazzled. A far cry from the sweet perfection of her usual self. Something's wrong. She catches a glimpse of me and gulps in a drink of air before making her way over. She looks relieved and devastated and mad. Her legs are trembling and she stumbles over a chair on her way over to my table.

"What was that all about?" I ask her, gesturing at the now super out-of-place chair. She looks like she's about to slap me in the face. My stomach drops. *Fuck, what have I done?*

"Josie?"

Nothing.

"Josie, what is going on? Are you okay?"

This would be a great time for the superpowers I'm sure someone had suppressed in me at birth to re-awaken and show me I'm a mind reader. *Why are you such a weirdo? That's such a weird and unhelpful thought to have right now, Megan.* Megan. Ugh. I hate this name. My name. It has never felt like my name. It feels... beige. I am anything but beige. I'm more like—

Josie slaps me across the face.

"Josie, what the...?!" I stop myself. She has tears in her eyes. I just completely zoned out and she was sitting right in front of me looking like a teenage trainwreck. I take a good look at her and begin to realise how shaken up she really is. Her hair looks like it hasn't been brushed for days. Her eyes aren't just teary, they're puffy, like she'd already been crying well before walking through the door. Her hands are shaking, and her almost always perfect nails were chipped and bitten back. Something had to be seriously wrong for her to deteriorate like this since I'd left her at James's place last night. That was less than twelve hours ago. *Did they break up? How did I not see this coming? Shit, friend award to Megan the beige. Fuck. I'm just gonna berate myself and ignore the fact that she just slapped me in public for a moment longer.*

"My mum died." She finally spoke. *Double fuck.*

Everything went into slow motion.

"What did you say?" I whispered.

I didn't want to hear what I thought I heard. I wanted to be wrong. To be so zoned out in the shit of my own brain that I'd concocted this crazy shit outside of it too.

"My mum is dead and you haven't picked up your phone for twenty-four hours."

Fuck. Twenty-four hours? How? What happened to her? What happened to me? Why isn't she home with her family? Was I drugged? No way. Last night was epic beyond comparison and I remember every fine-ass detail. This is not... This is... This can't be real.

"Josie, I..."

"Next time you decide to go AWOL—" She stops and just starts shaking her head and focusing on breathing. "What am I going to do, Megan? They killed her. She was my mum. And they just killed her like it meant nothing. Right there on our living room floor. I mean. Bransen is a mess. Dad won't even speak to me. He's just lying on the bedroom floor as if she's gonna come home and trip over him when she walks through the door, like that way he won't miss it. And—"

This time I cut her off.

"Josie, stop. Go back to the beginning. Is your mum really... is Mrs Jo really... dead?"

My head is spinning so fast all I can see is her dark chocolate eyes and how melted in sadness they are.

"She's dead, Megan. They killed her."

"Who are you talking about? Who killed her?"

"Witches. Witches killed my mum."

*

All I can do is stare at her. My head is spinning a hundred miles an hour and my mind is moving faster. Mrs Jo's death was shock enough. Serena. Serena is her real name, but James and I call her Mrs Jo, short for Josie. *Called* her... Past tense. Past tense. She's dead. Josie's mum is dead and I'm just sitting here blankly staring at her in shock. Witches. Had she really said witches? I don't want to ask. I feel crazy. Witches aren't even real. Are they? Far out. This is too far out. My hands are tingling. I was joking about the superpower thing. My hands can't actually be tingling. Mrs Jo can't really be dead. And even if she is, it's definitely NOT because of witches. But the look in Josie's eyes tells me she believes what she's saying. She believes every word. While I was wrapped up in the most blissful sex marathon of my life, Josie's family had been ripped apart. This couldn't be real.

"Snap out of it, Megan, you're ready for this." A voice whispered behind me. I jump and spun around as fast as I could but there was no one there. There wasn't even anyone at the tables be-

hind us. My chips and smoothie arrive and I look around and realise the only other people here are the waitress and the chef, Paddy. Even he looked concerned, and he's literally the bubbliest human I've ever met. Usually you can't get to your seat without copping at least three of his dad jokes and today he hadn't said a word. I'd been too self absorbed in my pleasure to notice. *You should be ashamed of yourself.* Crap. Josie. Ten points to beige Megan. I have to ask though.

"Hey Jenny," I call out to her as she walks away, "where is everyone?"

She looks around cautiously before lowering her voice and answering.

"Hiding."

Hiding? Before I even register that's what she'd said she's gone. Straight back into the kitchen. I take a look at Josie and come back to her. She needs her friend right now. She's completely freaking out and yet somehow still sitting there just staring at me with those big puffy eyes and teary cheeks. I reach out and take her hand and it startles her.

"Come on," I say to her as gently and sturdily as I can manage. "Let's get you out of here."

She nods and wraps her arms around mine with a sniffle as I stand up. I leave enough for a tip on the table. I haven't even touched the food but my appetite is gone and we are out the door before I even think of it. I've just got to get her home and so I can figure out what the fuck is going on.

I have said "fuck" a lot for a Sunday morning, but fuck. It's like a ghost town out here. Was I on such an orgasmic afterglow that I just hadn't noticed anything before? Sex could be like that. Real sex. Real pleasure. It's like a drug and the good stuff is blinding. *Love is blinding.* That's why I have a three time rule. Three times and then onto the next one. That way I could keep it about me and not get attached to them. Sometimes I could even get away before they attached to me. *Two more with inky blonde.*

Josie's squeeze of my arm tightened my stomach and snapped me straight back to reality. How on earth am I thinking about a guy right now when my best friend's mum just died in some supernatural shit show? We've arrived at her street and she's pointing and staring at the road in front of her house. Burn marks covered the road and... Wait.

"They're burnt symbols" I say to Josie under my breath.

"And look. That's who they're looking for. I think it says Angela?" She points to the only symbols on the road I can understand. They're words. All I can make out is: *We'll find you An****a.* It could say "Angela". But it's smudged over, and my intuition is screaming at me to run. *RUN RUN RUN.* Frozen still, I continue to stand on the road with Josie clinging to my arm.

"Maybe they were looking for this Angela person and mum got in the way?" she croaks. I can tell she's doing that thing where she tries to figure out the answer to something so she doesn't have to feel. She's going to have to feel this eventually, and even now her emotions are leaking through. This is not the kinda thing she can just 'tough guy' through. *I'll be here when she needs me. I can help her with this.*

"We'll figure this out Josie," I promise. An overwhelming burning sensation ripples through my body and I hurl all over the kerb. *Fuck.* I feel sick to the stomach thinking about it, but we are going to find something wacky here. I can feel it in my bones.

"Whoever this 'maybe Angela' person is has answers and I'm gonna find them. If it's the last thing I ever do, Megan, I'm gonna find them," Josie declares to me like a vow.

I'm nodding, but something tells me this isn't going to be that simple.

Curiosity overtakes me and I kneel down to touch the burn marks.

"Ahhhhh what the!" Searing pain rips through my wrist as though I'm being branded. Josie gasps as I pull up my sleeve and we see it.

I've been marked.

The same black mark that was on the road is etched into my wrist, and when I look back down to the road, there's nothing there. No scorch marks. No trace of anything other than the same old road I'd seen a million times on my way to Josie's house.

"I told you. You're ready."

I look up at Josie. "Did you hear that?" I ask.

"Hear what?" She looks at me with confusion and fear all over her face.

"Nothing," I say. But it wasn't nothing. It was the same voice I'd heard at the diner. The same voice I'd thought was whispering into my ear from right behind me. *Who are you?* I say in my mind, wondering if that's where the voice had actually come from.

"Come home," it replies. *"We need to talk."*

I gulp. This is not how I expected my Sunday morning to turn out. And this is definitely not beige.

Fuck.

CHAPTER 4

MEGAN

31 Hours Prior

*I*t's an old and rusty-looking and ancient feeling and it feels new at the same time. None of it makes sense. It feels powerful. The mark is still burning on my skin. A strange, curved cross I've never seen before, branding me like a cow being claimed by a cruel owner. *Claimed.* The word scares me. Is that what's happened? Has someone claimed me?

My mind is racing a million miles an hour as I make my way home from Josie's. It felt awful to leave her, but I had to. I have to know what this voice wants. Who it is. What it means. I know I can help Josie if I can just get some clarity. Answers. She needs answers and this is the best clue I've got.

I charge through the front door and race straight up the stairs. I don't know why, but I just feel like my bedroom is the place to be.

"Good to see you make an appearance!" Dad is sitting in his reading chair, laughing at me under his breath. I'm so lucky to have him. Both of my parents actually. They are so relaxed with me. Perhaps a side-effect of adoption. Adoptive parents go one of two ways in my experience - they either over-possess you and push you away, or they over-trust you in an effort to win you over. My parents were definitely the latter. I had a loose leash. *Still a leash.* I'm seventeen. Well, tomorrow I will be.

Rules suck, but they also give me a sense of normalcy. Today I'm grateful I didn't have to come home to a series of questions about where I'd been. Get home early Sunday nights for family dinner and always be ready for school. They were the two rules. I landed a sweet deal when they chose to make me their daughter. They worry about me, I can tell by the way they look at me, especially Mum. She always has this look on her face like something is about to go wrong. I wonder if she knows about Mrs Jo. I wonder if Dad does. I decide I don't want to be the one that tells them. I can't deal with that right now, so I close my bedroom door and take a breath.

Okay voice in my head. I'm here. I'm alone. Let's have it.

I wait for what seems like an eternity to finally hear the raspy voice. It sounds like an old person. So old I couldn't even tell if it was a man or woman speaking.

"Uncover me."

What? "Uncover yourself."

The voice chuckles. You know, as creepy voices in your head do.

"I'm going to need your help, dear."

Dear? Better than slave I guess. Maybe they haven't claimed me. Maybe this is a friend, not a foe. An ally. One way to find out.

"Okay. What do you need?"

"Take this cloth off me." I look around the room. Cloth. Cloth. Cloth... I don't have any pieces of cloth anywhere. There has to be something. I bet there's something obvious I'm overlooking right in—

"Oh!"

Could it really be? This would officially put me in the weird and wonderful – but mostly weird – monster film scenario. My crystal ball. Mum had bought it for me years ago and I never used it, but for some reason it always felt right to keep it out on display on my dresser. Well, almost on display. It's covered by a black cloth that is looking grey from all the dust. There's nothing else in the room it could be, so I move towards it.

Heat waves pulse out towards me. And I can *feel* them. Like actually feel them, the same way you feel the ripples of the ocean push up into your legs when you stand at the seashore. *This couldn't get any weirder.* My heart is slamming in my chest and I can feel little beads of sweat rolling down the sides of my face despite it being autumn. I reach out towards the cloth and see my fingers shaking. Black nail polish chipped on two of my fingers. *Dammit.* I'd been biting my nails without even realising. I take a deep breath and yank the cloth off, then gasp. Right there in front of me is the clear crystal ball I know so well. I've had it for years, it is so familiar – except it isn't. Never before have I seen green mist inside the sphere. Part of me thinks this is next level cool, and part of me wants a damn good explanation for what has become a quantumly inexplicable day. And it wasn't even lunchtime yet.

"*Thank you.*" In my awe at the green mist, I'd totally forgotten the ball was talking to me. At least, I think it was.

"Who are you? Are you a crystal ball? Like a genie?"

The voice chuckles again. "No dear, nothing quite so fairytale as that. I'm your grandmother."

I'm sorry. Who what now? I close my eyes. *I am actually losing my mind. Maybe I was drugged last night with some sort of psychedelic. Maybe I'm on mushrooms and they're so good I forgot I had them.* I opened my eyes to look at the crystal ball again and gasp. The green mist is still there but in the centre of it is the most ancient looking woman I've ever seen. *My grandmother, who I've never met, coming to me in a crystal ball. Perfect.*

I don't know anything about my birth mother and father.

I don't know anything about that part of my life. I'd been one of the lucky ones, being adopted so young I could barely even remember the orphanage – just some of the kids I'd stayed in touch with over the years, but those memories were more of after. Of comparing adoptive families to see who got lucky and who didn't. I definitely did, but I didn't know anything about my ancestors. I had just assumed I didn't have any living.

"You're my grandmother?"

"Yes."

"How are you talking to me from the inside of a ball? Is this some sort of Facetime device I don't know about? Creepy, by the way, if you'd like some feedback. Unexpected. A bit rough arriving unannounced after seventeen years, don't you think?" *I have so many questions.* "How do I even know you're telling me the truth?"

"Let me see. It's your birthday tomorrow, and you have a new tattoo to remember it by. Judging by our family history of strong-willed women, I'd say you hate the name Megan, and probably have a sense of it not belonging to you. Despite being young in years, you hold a wisdom you can't explain and to which your friends can't relate. You make love to older men in an attempt to connect with someone operating on your wavelength. It's usually not worth it in the long run. You are deeply connected to your pleasure body, and are able to speak of and experience desire in a way your friends don't even know to daydream about. And despite this being the strangest and most unsettling day of your life, you're grounded in your body. Your breath is relatively steady. Your heart has raced and slowed much more efficiently than the average person's would. Even amidst the chaos, desire is on your mind. The last boy you met is on your mind, but your loyalty has you here, pursuing the only clue you had to help a friend in desperate need of saving

– because, deep down, you wish someone had been able to be that for you on the days you needed it, before your new family took you in. You are fast becoming the woman you needed as a child, and you don't have the context to understand why you are wired like that. You just are and that's that. You haven't wasted energy on the hope of figuring out the root of why you are how you are, because the path of figuring that out is a calling you've been ignoring until today."

Woah.

"How did I do?" *Really fucking well, Granny.* That still doesn't prove that you're *my* grandma though.

"I... What are you doing here? Why now? Where have you been? What happened to Mrs Jo? Did you have something to do with that? Do you know who did? How do you know me so well without even knowing me?" She's either psychic or a stalker. I haven't decided yet.

"It's in your blood, and me coming to you now is written in your destiny."

I can't explain it but it feels true. I can *feel* her. My mind wants to make sense of it all but my body... my body is sold. My body just wants to know what's next.

I have a feeling things are about to get hot in here.

CHAPTER 5

DJEN

Eleven Hours Prior

"You broke the law." He looks at me in exasperation. I've put him in an awful position but I can't bring myself to care. I had to protect her. Our species depended upon it. Our legacy.

"Jate…"

"Save it, Djen. The only thing that matters is that she is safe. It is done. We must keep this between us, or I will be forced to act to the fullest extent of the law. Please. The Higher Council is forgiving, but the Royal Council cannot know of this. I can't lose you too. Not yet."

As our leader, it is his job to keep The People safe. It is also his job to uphold the law that I have willingly and knowingly broken. The Forsaken are after my granddaughter and I couldn't leave her roaming about in the unknown. She has no idea what her birthday is going to reveal to her. None, and I have to know she will at least make it to then to awaken to her true self. This is why the Higher Council will forgive my law breaking - they are, after all, the spirits of our ancestors. They want to see her safely home too. The Royal Council, however, the board of witches set to protect our people and palace, are not so connected. As fear has penetrated our land and people so too has it penetrated our council. Their focus is on the law. It is black and white, but our predicament is not. They would have my seat at the table for this breach of conduct, if not my head. Fortunately, it is only us of royal blood who communicate with the Higher Council directly - Jate, myself, and when she's ready, my granddaughter will too.

Already she is so open. She's initiated herself into her essence in more ways at her age than most humans do over their whole life. More even than some witches. But she really has no idea. Tomorrow she will find out her true roots. Her family history. She will know me as her blood. Hear of her mother and father. Eventually, she'll find out about her brother too, though I hope that information could be saved for another day. His casting out from our people and his intentions for them would be a pain to her heart. His rejection of the Higher Council still pained my own.

"She's strong," I say to him softly, yet fiercely. "I have full confidence in her ability to fulfil the prophecy."

"She's a girl." He sits at his desk on his big leather chair and places his head in his hands. He hasn't seen her. In fact, he hasn't seen her in sixteen years. *Almost seventeen.* That's what she'd said. She's almost seventeen. That was the problem. The legal age of contact for adopted witches was seventeen. That was the law I had broken, though these were extreme circumstances. Not every adopted child has an army searching for them – let alone the Forsaken, an army that doesn't abide by the Law of Heart as we do. All they care for is the power that comes with the current predicament on Earth, and ensuring that the prophecy that will require they share that power isn't fulfilled. Our Law kept us in alignment with the Higher. Without it, we weren't much different from them. We're all afraid. Change is imminent. We had lived like this for two thousand years. Separate from the rest of forgotten humanity. Separate from our own people, because of blood. A hundred years ago, we had received the knowledge that a member of our family would be the breaker of this age. That, finally, a child would be born who could re-awaken the planet to themselves. Re-awaken the witch in all. Ignite the power that exists in all beings, despite their forgetting, despite their sleeping existence. I never in a million years would have wished this for my granddaughter, though speaking to her has re-assured me the ancestors have chosen wisely. She really could be the one to do this. I can feel it in my bones. The power in her is uncanny, unlike anything I have witnessed, with the exception of her brother... but her energy was so different. Skavari is wild and untamed; well-trained in the arts and focus, but emotionally unstable. Choosing to become Forsaken in the pursuit of what he believes to be a more powerful life. He doesn't believe in re-awakening all humans. He wants power to stay in the lineage, and in the lineage only. Ankhara, though... *I wonder if I should call her Megan...* she is different. She will not stand with her brother. Already I had seen her so loyally choose her heart. That was the leader we needed.

"She's a woman, Jate. And more fierce than we have ever had to handle." He looks up at me, his hands still wrapped around his face. Half caressing himself, half holding himself together. This hasn't been easy on him, especially since Ang had passed. Losing her... Well, we had almost lost him. It was this day, this child, that had given him the hope to live on. She hasn't seen him in sixteen years, but *Megan* still has complete hold of her father's heart. I can see in his eyes that nothing scares him more.

"She's my child, and it is time for her to come home." He stands and ushers me out of his chamber. "Come, she is arriving tomorrow, and everything will change. We must rest while we still can."

As the light switches off and the door closes behind him, I sigh. He's right. Tomorrow will change the trajectory of our family forever. For that, a good night's sleep is in order, so I let him lead me up the staircase to my living quarters.

"Goodnight, mother," he whispers as he kisses me on the head. I squeeze his shoulder and nod farewell. *Rest.* I will it to him through my eyes. He gets the message and turns toward his own bedroom. This could be the last full night of sleep in our time. I want to make sure he takes it.

CHAPTER 6

MEGAN

Eight Hours Prior

All I want to do is climb out my window and into his. I can feel his fingers etched into my hips. I can smell him. Taste him. *Mmm.* I knew sex was medicine, but before Noah I'd always felt this sense of obligation about it. Like an obligation to share what I was doing and to help my lover open to the same places. Riding the waves of orgasmic bliss wasn't as juicy when your partner didn't know where you were. I didn't feel that with him. Not even in the slightest. His body immediately settled into its nature. I could tell from his facial expressions that he hadn't experienced his own pleasure like that before. The shocked eyes with a hint of fear were the tell-tale sign of the first time a man orgasmed with his whole body. Such a brief moment of fear, and then the animal awakens and the hunger for the beloved was like that for a God or Goddess. I can't imagine there could possibly be anything on earth more beautiful.

Snap out of it. My best friend's mum died today and I'm lying in bed fantasising over my latest sexual conquest. Classic me. In my defence, something about Noah was different, and every other part of my day had been a mind-blowing shit show. Murderous "witches". Speaking smoke that turned out to potentially be my grandmother. Inside a freaking crystal ball that I honestly left on display because I enjoyed the way I could see my face reflect in it. Even so, it had been covered for years, and I'd still abandoned Josie in her hour of grief to come home and speak into it. Not that I knew that's what I was doing. My mind was racing. If I focused on the mind-blowing sex, at least I could calm down for a hot minute for a moment of normalcy. If I focused on the rest... well. Was I actually losing my mind? I mean, I'd always known I wasn't "normal", but I never thought anyone else was either. I think people just forget how to express themselves somewhere along the way. That's the difference. Noah expressed himself. I want to immerse myself in a whole world of that, but the old lady's voice is in the forefront of my awareness: *"Whatever you do, don't leave. Don't go outside. It's unsafe in ways you'd never imagine. I'm sorry I can't tell you more. I shouldn't even be speaking with you."* Way to be vague, lady. Way to be fucking vague. And ruin my sex life while you're at it. My pussy won't stand for this for much longer.

"I'll go tomorrow." Talking to myself calms me down. It feels weird knowing that tomorrow I'm meant to be celebrating my birthday and meanwhile the whole of Fairfield is indoors having a collective panic attack about a fantasy freak murder. Fair enough, it was weird – but come on. Witches? Real witches? And what of this supposed tattoo on my wrist? Marks do not just appear on people's bodies like that. Old mate crystal granny could have told me what the fuck that was about. In fact, if she really is my grandma, there are about a thousand things I'd rather she'd told me other than "it's dangerous to go outside". I have so many questions. How about... where are my mother and father? Are they alive? Who are they? Did they give me away because they had to or because that was what they really wanted? Was I a mistake? Was I... did I have siblings? *Woah, I hadn't even thought of that yet.* Is there a secret sister or brother that I've never been told about? *Surely Mum and Dad would have mentioned that.* Where does she live? How the fuck did she get in that crystal ball? Is this a conspiracy I don't know about – did Mum give me that thing so that she could spy on me? Am I being punked?

I'd been so shocked by her existence – and, you know, the talking green mist inside the inanimate object – that, I hadn't asked her anything I really needed to know. It hurt my heart in ways I never wanted to talk about that my parents had left me. I was grateful, don't get me wrong; my adoptive parents are fucking awesome. I could not have struck more gold than I did the day they chose me. That didn't change the fact that I'd always wondered. I'd always known, even before they told me after my twelfth birthday. "You're becoming a woman now," they'd said. They were worried puberty would make it obvious to me that I didn't really look like them. I mean, these boobs are definitely not from those bloodlines. I am *blessed.* And, quite frankly right now, cursed.

I roll over on the bed to pick up my phone but there's nothing on it. I can't believe I haven't heard from Josie. Text, call, nothing. Not even a status update or an insta-story for her fifty thousand followers. I don't think she's ever not shared something with them. She even posted a story when she lost her virginity. She was grounded for two months but she gained the street cred that gave her social media queen status. It won't take long for people to start asking questions.

Noah. Why had I not even gotten his number? I could have written mine in lipstick in his bathroom. *Idiot.* I guess I'll have to do what I always do – hope I bump into him again. Or not. Maybe continuing to dally with this one was a bit dangerous. I could already feel myself loving him after just one sexual encounter, which is the kinda love-addict behaviour that I usually find so repulsive in the dating scene. Here I am. A love addict alone in my bedroom fantasising about a stranger. I don't even know his last name.

"Fuck this." Sometimes I talk to myself to snap out of things and ground. Other times I'm more like a closet inspirational speaker. "Megan Fay Birchfield. You are a strong, sexually alive, heart-driven, independent, lit-as-fuck woman. You do not sit in confusion. Confusion is the enemy of your destiny. You act. You go for what you want, no fucks given. You are NOT a beige-ass victim. Though sometimes, it's okay for a moment, 'cause God didn't give you ego-trumping superpowers for breakfast and you're still in training with those. Get your sulky ass up and go get the D."

Yup. There she is.

I jump out the window without a second thought.

The streets were quiet and dark. Like, next-level dark. Somehow even the majority of the streetlights were out. People had drawn their curtains. I know these people. They don't do that here. I've never even ventured out of our house with a key because we don't need to lock the front door in this neighbourhood. It's G-rated suburbia. We have street parties. Unknowns are spotted in town within fifteen minutes. Yet something was really spooking everyone. It couldn't possibly be the witch thing, but people are weird when they're scared. I get that. Once I hid under my bed for twelve hours because I thought I saw a black figure floating outside my second-floor bedroom window. Actual bonkers. Maybe I just flip over the edge today. I don't care. I want to climb into Noah's bed and taste the saltiness of him. *He might have another woman in his bed. It's true.*

He might. He might have a girlfriend. He might live with his mum. He might have a little sister who sleeps in his bed when she has a nightmare. He might just straight-up tell me to fuck off.

Tell me all you want, the way you moaned last night won't be something you'll be forgetting this lifetime. He'll want me. And if he doesn't, quite frankly, he can suck my dick with his idiocy.

Something I'll never understand is why people are so weird with their desire. You like it. You don't like it. You love it. You hate it. Say it OUT LOUD. So many of my friends complain to me about their sex life but if I asked them what their vagina looked like they'd spit their drink in my face. They don't know. And the guys? So afraid of not doing a good job, not getting good feedback, that they miss the point of what a real good job is. Which is... real. That's all great sex is. When what you're giving and receiving between the sheets is as real as the thoughts you can't control in your sleep.

"Noah, I hope you're fucking real," I said out loud to myself. A prayer from my heart to the powers that be, or really, to the heart of Noah.

It's cold outside. I find myself hugging my arms to my body. I can't shake the eerie feeling that I'm being watched. Weird, with all the windows covered, that I feel like that. "Just one more block." Even talking to myself isn't making me feel better. I've been so caught up in the chaos of me that I've forgotten I'm walking alone in the same streets a group of murderers could be walking.

"Whatever you do, stay inside." She had like two minutes with me. She wouldn't have said that if there wasn't a reason.

I run the rest of the way to his front yard and go around the side to jump the same fence I had earlier that day. On a scale of one to ten, how creepy bad or fantasy good does a guy find a woman crawling in through his window? Is that like, next-level one-night-stand error indicator or sex dream come true? I'm about to find out.

His bathroom light is on. *Well. At least you're up.* My window climbing skills are a true gift; I'm in through his window without him even hearing, and then there he is. Standing by his bed, hair wet from the shower, still wrapped in a towel, looking down at something. He has his back to me. *You have a beautiful back.* I'm just about to attempt a hello when he turns around and jumps, dropping his phone. *That's what you were looking down at.* I hope he wasn't texting a girlfriend.

"Crap! Shit. Fuck." A quick symphony of my favourite words spill out of his mouth as he sees me, dropping his phone and wincing as it lands on his foot. Then his eyes relax in recognition of me.

"It's you." *Me? Me as in "the phenomenal woman who blew your mind last night", or me as in, "call her that because you can't remember her name?"*

"Fancy seeing you here." Really, Megan? Beige.

He laughs and shakes his head.

"Any other way you'd like to blow my mind in the next twenty-four hours? Best warn me now because I'm not sure I can take any more surprises." Wow. He likes me. And he's *fun*. I can be fun...

"Right now, all I want to do is rip off that towel and make sure you're so covered in me you need another one of those showers in the morning."

To his credit, it only took him about three seconds to drop the towel and throw me onto the bed. Thirty seconds to rip off my tank top. After that, though, he is entirely the gentleman. His weight on my body is so familiar. I want all of him. All of it. Whatever that looks like. He looks to me for permission before gently kissing my stomach and caressing my jeans down with his hands. His breath is slow and deep and it reminds me to be present with mine also. I love a lover whose presence brings me to me. His expert hands effortlessly undo my button and zipper and the unravelling torture of him teasing me with my own clothing begins. More slowly than I've ever been undressed, he slips my jeans off over my feet, never completely removing his touch from me. He leaves my underwear and crawls back up, kissing my body from my ankles to my knees, to my thighs to my... oh, straight over to my stomach, ribs and sternum. Yum. This guy knows how to warm a woman up. By the time he gets to my neck I can already feel the lace of my G-string wet with my dripping. I am opening like a freaking flower. *Fuck me.* He nibbles my ear lobe. *Fuck me.* Lacing his fingers through my hair he pauses, body pressed on mine, to look at me.

"Morgan." His voice is like velvet chocolate. "My last name. So you can let me know in advance next time."

Noah Morgan wants there to be a next time. Again. And we haven't even gotten past the entree yet.

"Next time you can come to me," I reply.

He smiles and presses his lips to mine. Candy. He tastes like candy and smells like freshly sea-salted earth. What kind of potion makes him smell so good? I need that brand in my life. My mind is silenced as I lose myself in his kiss. Our bodies entwine as I wrap my legs around him and he loses his hands in the darkness of my hair. He pulls it at just the right level – enough to make my head roll back, not enough to trigger real pain. Enough to make my eyes roll back into my head as he kisses and licks my neck.

"May I?" he asks, and I know he means my breasts. I nod. I want him in every inch of me. My mouth starts watering just as his lips sweep over my left nipple and his hand firmly holds my vulva. A moment of honouring before—

The glass of his window cracks and jolts us out of our trance. In a fraction of a second he flips himself into a fighting stance by the bed while somehow managing to throw his shirt at me to cover myself. We aren't alone anymore. Three black-hooded creatures stand by the window on broken glass.

"Megan. Put that on and stay behind me." I blink. Put what on? The shirt. Got it. I nod to myself and put it on somehow without tangling myself in it. It hangs like a dress on my body and I am glad for it. I don't want these freaks to see me so openly. Whoever they are, they don't look friendly.

"You don't want to do this." Noah is speaking to them. Does he know who they are? Are we about to be the next murder victims? These guys don't look like witches, but they're creepy enough and they definitely weren't meant to be here ruining the oasis of my day.

"Just give us the girl and we won't hurt you, mortal." *Mortal? All humans are mortal. These guys are either idiots or something I don't know exists. This is exactly what crystal granny warned me about. She said I wouldn't understand.*

"The only way to her is through me." He is literally protecting me like a knight in shining armour. Pretty impressive considering he's standing in front of them naked with half a hard-on. I'll thank him for it later. Right now I need to focus on getting the fuck out of here. Preferably not alone. I scan the room for something I can hold onto but the only things I within reach are his phone and a book on his bedside table. Excellent luck. Not. Picking them up feels like a better option than being empty-handed, though, so I do – about half a second before the two Hoods on the left charge at Noah. The third leaps towards me. *Fuck, fuck, fuck, think, think, think...* I flip up the control centre on Noah's phone and flick the torch light on, straight in my attacker's eyes. He yelps and dodges to the right of me, unbalanced enough that I get a kick into his side. He falls into the bathroom door frame and I jump off the bed and swing the door closed, hitting what I'm pretty sure is his face. I brace myself against the door, expecting him to try and get out. At least if I can keep him in there Noah only has two creeps to deal with. *Noah!* I'd almost forgotten the others were here. I look to him. This is the first time I actually *see* him. Noah is weaving in between the two hooded figures, graceful as a dancer, like he's done this a thousand times before. *That explains why he's so shredded.* His body is as beautiful as his movement. These hooded guys are clearly surprised and way less prepared than he. He has the element of surprise, yet I can tell that the advantage is waning. They're beginning to gather themselves and I have no idea how long he can keep this up. Naked. His still-naked cock is flying around with the rest of him. He is an artist, a dancer, a warrior, a servant. *Help me.* He looks at me, confused, as if expecting me to know what to do right now. *How on earth am I supposed to know what to do?* Frantic and determined, I look around for creative inspiration. There must be something... ah ha! Fairly certain that my bathroom friend was unconscious, I sprint to the far corner of the room. The others, focused on Noah, don't seem to notice me, though I'm not looking back to see what they're doing. I'm laser-focused on the wooden pole I've spotted leaning on his desk. *How had I not noticed this before?* I guess I was distracted by a different pole... one that is now flying through the wind in a fight to protect me. Me. They wanted *me.* I don't have time or bandwidth to think about that right now. I just need to help Noah get us out of here. I pick up the pole and plunge into the air with it, making the strangest war cry I've ever heard. I whack one of the Hoods in the shoulder blade and throw him completely off balance. Somehow I've caught him by surprise. I also catch a smirk from Noah. He's impressed. *Not the point right now.* Something slams me across the face.

Fuck.

I'm so caught up in celebrating my one blow to the enemy and Noah's approval that I've missed the part where the Hood I hit turns right back around to punch me in the face. I've never been punched in the face before and I decide right now that I don't fucking like it. That shit *hurts.* It also lights a fire in my belly, a primal rage I've only ever tapped into in the bedroom. *Technically, we're still in his bedroom* I think to myself, before swinging the pole straight into the ribs of my second assailant. I have no idea how I'm managing to land my blows. I've never been trained in any sort of fighting, but something comes over me. My reflexes move my body before I have the chance to think. The wooden pole in my hand feels like a wizard's staff, like it has a mind of its own, and all I can think about is what it will feel like when I walk out of this place. The rest is a blur and before I know it Noah is next to me, taking over. His opponent is down and out and he's come to finish the job. Noah throws the last Hood against the wall and he lands in a heap on the floor. With a quick look to me to check I'm okay, he runs to his bedside table and pulls ropes out of the drawer. I would have so enjoyed finding out about those in a different context. He proceeds to tie up each of the Hoods in quick succession. My bathroom friend is lying in a pool of his own blood; it appears I broke his nose when I slammed the door on his face. Oops. It is brutal to see. It doesn't matter that he'd been attacking me; this was a person, and I'd hurt him. I feel sick to my stomach and am about to drop to my knees when Noah grabs me.

"Not yet, Princess."

Did he seriously just call me Princess?

Before I have a chance to complain he has dragged me down the staircase to his laundry cupboard. He opens it and begins filling a duffle bag with what looks like Buffy the Vampire Slayer's secret stash of weapons. *Dude, what the fuck? No, better question: who the fuck are you?*

"Here." He hands me a blade, curved like a crescent moon. "Use it like this." He quickly demonstrated a graceful slicing motion. "Not like this," stabbing the air in a way that makes me feel awkward just looking at him. Overwhelmed as I am, I'm glad he showed me. I definitely would have been a stabber.

"Thanks." I want to ask him what the fuck is going on, but I don't seem to be able to speak properly. I'm in awe of him, and completely shocked. I can hear my blood pounding in my ears.

He grabs my shoulders gently and looks me dead in the eyes. "I know this doesn't make any sense right now, and I promise I'll explain everything. Right now, I just need to get you home safe. One step at a time. Okay?"

"Okay, but—"

"Hey." His eyes are softly holding me. "Do you trust me?"

Trust him? He's just saved my life and it doesn't seem like I have a whole lot of healthy options right now, but for whatever reason, my heart feels sure of him. I feel confident that he would do absolutely whatever he could or needed to do to keep me safe. He is a warrior in an arena I didn't think existed anymore. This world of witches and hooded assailants and having fighters for lovers. He'd get me home. Then I could worry about what was next. Then I would ask what was really going on. Then I'd need answers. *One step at a time.* "Yes. Somehow I do."

He nods and takes my hand. "Come with me then." I nod with a start and grip the blade in my hand with a tight wrist.

"And keep your grip loose on that." He speaks to me as though he knows every move my body is making and it baffles me. I loosen my grip and move my wrist and it feels stronger, like somehow in the loosening I have more control. I look at him but his focus is elsewhere. We move swiftly in the dark. Alert. Focused. He is focused on our path, looking around like they do in the movies when the agents are on a secret mission and they don't want to get caught by the enemy. *Are we on some sort of mission? Is that why the crystal granny didn't want me to go outside? She wanted me around for something else?* All I can focus on is putting one foot in front of the other. I trust Noah but it doesn't mean my mind isn't spinning. None of this is real to me yet. I still feel like I'm playing some sort of extravagant scavenger hunt game with my new lover friend. Extreme sports date night. That would have been a lot simpler.

✳

Before I know it we're in the bushes out front of my house. *How do you know where I live?*

"You need your crystal ball." He's looking at me with an apology in his eyes. There is so much more to this then what I have been let into. "I'll come with you. I don't want you out of my sight."

"Okay." Honestly, I don't know what else to say. I do know that I don't want to be out of his sight either. Whoever those Hoods were, they might have killed Mrs Jo and they might've killed me. If they really want me for something I do not want to be around when they find me and I definitely don't want to be alone if they do. Noah is very welcome here as far as I am concerned, at least until I have more answers.

We walk in through the usually unlocked door using the spare key. In the whole of my almost seventeen years I can only once remember using the key to enter this house. At the time there were a bunch of kidnappings happening interstate and Mum was crazy highly strung. Is it locked now because of Mrs Jo? I have to ask.

"Mum?" I lead Noah into the living room but no one is in there. My parents have a very basic, organised social life. Sunday night is not a night they go out. My stomach drops. "Dad?" Tears fill my eyes. *I don't think I can take any more weirdness right now. Where are you?* I run upstairs hesitantly but I need to know. They wouldn't just leave. They wouldn't just leave me here. They couldn't. Not today. Not on the eve of my birthday. They wouldn't. They just literally would not do this. I check Dad's reading room first. Nothing. Their bedroom. Nothing. Tears are falling like a waterfall now. Unstoppable. This day has just been too much and this is the final straw. Noah walks in and gently asks permission before touching my shoulder and kneeling down to be at eye level with me. I hadn't even realised I had dropped to my knees on their bedroom floor.

"If they're not here and there's no sign of a struggle, that's a good thing." Something inside me snaps. That rage I'd touched earlier turns on like a fire hydrant and there is nothing I could do to turn it off, even if I wanted to. Let's be clear. I don't want to. It is all I can do not to explode out of my trembling skin.

"You are going to explain yourself to me right now. All of it. Who the fuck are you? How do you know where I live? Where did you learn to fight like a Japanese ninja? How do you know about my crystal ball? What have you done to my parents?" That last one is a low blow but I don't care. I'm teetering on the edge. Less than two hours ago I'd been about to make love to this man, and now here I am with him in my parents' bedroom, which would be weird even if they weren't missing and we hadn't just been attacked by three hooded figures who wanted *me*, only to find out that he wasn't at all who I'd thought he was. *This is why you don't go home with strangers, Megan you idiot. You might find out they're actually already stalking you and going to kidnap your parents.*

"I don't know where your parents are. I can guess. I want to tell you everything. I do. I will. I just can't afford to waste time when you aren't safe yet. We need to get you home. Once we're there, we'll be secure and I can tell you everything in the peace of your own bedroom. This is... this is not your true home. I know you don't know, but I know you *know*. I know deep down you've always known, and now you're seventeen you're going to find out everything. They'll tell you the whole prophecy. It will all make sense by morning, but please, come with me now. Let me do my job." He is exasperated and calm at the same time. Something about this is unsettling to him too. Like he doesn't know the full story himself but just needs to play his part and figure it out later. I don't know how I know that but I just do. I know he wants this to be over as much as I do.

"Last night. When I met you at James's and we... Did you know? Did you know this was all going to happen? Did you already know who I was? You seducing me with those eyes and your... was that just part of some grand plan to get me to trust you so you could take me home to wherever you think that is?" I so desperately want him to say no, but I don't know how that can be possible. There is that grief flashing in his eyes again. *This hurts him too.*

"Yes. And no." He looks confused, like a puppy overwhelmed with choices. "I didn't know it was you. I wouldn't have... I've broken the law by... I didn't know it was you."

Broken the law? Wouldn't have what? Wouldn't have fucked me? If he knew what?

"All I knew was that I was here to rescue Princess Ankhara of the People. I was told I would know who she was by her mark. A mark I didn't see until you swung that pole, by the way." He gestures to my wrist. "I didn't know... My job is to get you home safely. And I would appreciate it if you could keep our interactions discreet.. Connecting with the Princess in that way, with anyone in the Royal family unless royally invited... I could lose more than my job if... I could lose my life. And you would lose the respect of your People. I'm sorry." He sobers in a moment, as though he's just realised where we are. "We need to leave." He jolts up at the speed of lightning pulling me up with him. "Now Princess. They're here."

CHAPTER 7

NOAH

One Hour Prior

*I*n less than three minutes we gather the crystal ball and leave the house. There is a letter, too, on Ankhara's bed and I feel such relief for her. She deserves the full truth, and she deserves to hear it from those closest to her. From those who had known her all her adopted life. I don't know where her adoptive parents might be; I only hope that they have taken the initiative to journey to our home and let us know the Princess had left their home. To have left a letter means their leaving was likely a choice, rather than a forced exit, but there is something about it that just doesn't feel quite right. The eeriness of the empty house had reverberated through me, and even though the Hoods had arrived in pursuit of us and not before, something is off. I can't put my finger on it but I don't have the space for that right now either. Another mystery for a later puzzle. Right now, *Megan* is about to receive the prophecy and she doesn't even know it.

We arrive at a safe house a few blocks over after losing the Hoods. I've been planting these spaces all over the town in the past weeks in preparation for this day. I was hoping things would go a lot more smoothly, and that I wouldn't break the law making it happen, but at least we're here now. We can rest. Pause. She can digest, and the prophecy will help her do that.

The sun is almost rising. Almost. The light is coming over the horizon but the sky above us is dark. *At the rising of the sun, the dawn of the passage birth, the hedonist will receive the words to awaken, or not, human earth.* It is coming, any minute now.

She is beautiful in ways I didn't know existed. The way she moves. The way her body floats seamlessly through her surroundings. She is holding the crystal ball, rolling it over in her hands, kneeling, the letter on the floor in front of her. On the envelope are three words: *For Our Daughter.* As if they'd expected perhaps someone else to find it. There is a blank, almost emotionless expression on her face as she stares, contemplating. She looks numb, but I know she is anything but. Grief, anger, desperation and loneliness vibrate through her body. I want to hold her. I want to tell her everything is going to be okay. But I've lied to her without even knowing. I've become a man I don't want to be without intending it. I had been so drawn to her, and I had done my due diligence and checked her wrist to find no mark, so I'd thought it would be okay. *Idiot.* Now here we are, alone in a safe house, having made love and broken at least four laws that could have me executed, and I can't even tell her the whole truth. They'd have my head for that too. *She has to unveil this.* The prophecy clearly states that she had to receive this information for herself in her own time and readiness. I can't throw it at her, it would do more harm than good, so I bear witness to her. There's nothing I can say, nothing I can do now beyond keeping her safe. She is the vessel for a revolution she doesn't know of yet, and she's a girl whose entire world just got flipped upside down. Her best friend's mum just died, a grief that will compound when she learns she died in the Forsaken's pursuit of her. In Skavari's pursuit of her. Her parents are missing, and she has no idea whether or when or how she will see them again. What concerns me the most is that neither do I. I've received no word from headquarters with regards to their appearance. There haven't been any orders to bring them in. Either they left of their own volition or someone has made it look that way. Top that all off with me, a guy she doesn't logically know, seducing her and making love to her, almost twice, and then announcing that he's some warrior for the people for whom she is a princess.

She's having a rough night, and I could not possibly be more in love with her. I sigh. That is going to have to be a dry pill that I swallow. There is nothing I can do to change the law, and nothing I can do to have her fall in trust with me again.

CHAPTER 8

PRINCESS ANKHARA

Now

I want to open it. I don't. I want the ball to speak. I don't. I want Noah to touch me, to hold me. I don't. I want to run. Hide. Scream. Cry. Ask questions. I don't. All of it and none of it. Completely overwhelmed, I sit here staring at this letter in the hope clarity will come. It doesn't. And I know it won't. I know I have to feel it first. I don't want to. I don't care. I want to make all of this go away so that I can return to the ignorant blissfulness that was Noah's body merging with mine, pre-hooded creeps. Pre-finding out Mrs Jo had been murdered. I want to return to that first night with him where everything had felt magic. I also want to return to my homecoming yesterday, where I'd skipped over spending time with Mum and Dad and told them I was missing dinner because I didn't feel well. *What if I had just talked to them about my crystal ball?* For all I knew, they didn't know. Or maybe they knew it all along. Maybe anything. Part of me hopes the answers are contained in the envelope in front of me. Part of me hopes it contains money and a plane ticket to meet them on a spontaneous holiday that I know in a million years they would never take.

This letter holds the truth. My truth. *Their* truth of my life. I don't know how to feel about it, and I don't know how to express my feelings in front of *him*. I look at him out of the corner of my eye. *Yup, he's still watching me.* He's so present to me I feel awkward. I almost get up to take the letter to the bathroom with me when something clicks inside me. My heart kicks into gear. *If you can orgasm and cry with him, you can be in this in front of him.* But he lied to me. *No, he found out about you too late, and doesn't know how to communicate with you.* He's repulsed by me. *He's repulsed by the law.* What law? *I guess we'll find out.* It was true. I love speaking with my heart. He can hold this. Whatever this is, he can hold me in this. And he never will if I don't let him. I have to let him.

So I let go. I take a deep breath and close my eyes and feel the energy in my body. This primal desire mixed with fear and grief and longing. Desperation. I'm desperate for him. Desperate for answers. Desperate for the truth. The unfiltered rawness that comes with the real truth. That I am now allowing through my body. Tears come and my body writhes in response to all the feeling. Such deep intense feeling that feels like it has been sitting in my DNA for lifetimes. And as I feel it all and my body moves through waves, he silently watches. His breath deepening reminds me to stay connected to mine as I feel, and his non-judgement gives me permission to feel more deeply. Completely unfiltered, I roll around on the floor, wailing, hissing, sobbing, hiding, opening. And he watches. He allows the unfolding of me and so do I. We take turns mirroring permission to one another until we lock eyes. *Hold me.* I almost beg him, and he knows. Slowly.... gently... cautiously he approaches me. Asking questions with his body and receiving answers from mine. Slowly I melt into his lap, asking him to see me. To witness me and hold the entirety of this experience of meeting who I was for the first honest time. And he does. Time melts. I melt, and I don't remember falling asleep until waking up tells me I did.

Waking up in his arms is new. It's different. There is an openness from both of us. I can feel the awe in him and I feel such deep love and thankfulness for him. Then I remember. *The letter!* And I jolt up, shocking him into a fighting position.

"Relax. There's no threat. I just want to open this." I gesture towards the letter and his shoulders relax. He exhales deeply and invites my body to do the same. Having felt my nervous system in its full spectrum, I now feel open and clear. There is the faintest hint of fear, but it now feels more like an excited anticipation of a new world. My future is about to take an unexpected direction, and part of me knows there is something about the unexpected that is magic. I am excited for a letter that had moments ago debilitated me. I know I haven't slept long as the sun is only just peaking over the horizon now. I can feel rays of light cracking in through the window and caressing my skin. It's time.

I take a deep breath and pick it up. Mum's handwriting. Of course she was the one to communicate. Dad communicated with his eyes, Mum with her words. I open it and slide the folded letter out between my now steady fingers. Unfolded, it reads:

Our Darling Daughter Megan,

We are so sorry to leave you in the shock of waking to what must be a whole new world, but I fear we must. I'm writing this because I fear the coming of your 17th birthday. We knew, when we received the blessing that was you, that something big would come for you on this day. We were warned that something or someone would come to mean you harm, and in that, we knew that to keep you safe we might have to say goodbye. None of that changed the way we instantly fell in love with you when we saw you for the first time. You were an angel to bless our world of humanness with such grace and a love that I have never known, and neither has your father I promise you.

At this moment, as I write this, you are with your friends, having what I hope is the most memorable night, for this may be your final night of ignorant bliss with them. Oh honey, I wish I could hold you and tell you everything is going to be okay, but the truth is, this is just the beginning. You are about to be called to a task that no other can achieve, and the weight of that fate will be a lonely one for you to bear. If you are reading this, it means my preferred choice of speaking to you in person has been taken away from me. I couldn't have you finding out the truth from another. It is sad enough to me that you may be reading this alone. Please, before anything else, know that I speak for both your father and I when I say, we love you. With all that we are, we love you and it kills us to know there is no way we can be with you now, in your time of greatest need. Know that no matter where you are or what you are facing, we will always be with you and you will always have your gifts from us inside.

In October of 2004 we received a letter. It held within its pages a story of another time. Another place. Another world. One of angels, witches and magic... of all the things we believed were real as children, but had squashed in us as adults. Slowly, we began to remember a world we had both long forgotten. At first, we thought the letter was a beautifully written practical joke played on us at random, but letters kept coming, telling us of a child who would need support and safety that only the human world could offer. Your father and I had been try-ing for years but, as you know, never conceived a full term pregnancy, and we were desperately looking for a gateway to a family when one day a letter came with three men and a babe. A child, guarded fiercely by three warriors who informed us their King and Queen were seeking a safe haven for this child to be raised in normality. Sweetheart, this child, was you.

Officially, you are Princess Ankhara, Sacred Heart of the People and Awakener of the Sleeping. Destined to awaken greatness in those around you. Destined to awaken magic in humanity. This is you.

We've seen these qualities in you and, honey, I want you to know we are already SO proud of you. This journey you are about to go on, to meet your true family and live out your destiny, will take you away from us for a time, perhaps even forever. For that we ache, but, in our hearts of hearts, we understand now that this was our true calling. That you being the woman you are could be the final and only thing we co-create on this planet and for that, we would give our lives over and over again.

I fear if you are reading this, then we may have done that exact thing. We may no longer be walking this Earth with you. I want you to know we are both alive in this. We made this decision effortlessly the moment we saw you and we wouldn't change a second of it. My only wish is that I could be there to see you fulfil your destiny, but rest assured my sweet, sweet girl, we will be with you, no matter how or where.

Finally, you have a brother. We do not know much of him but we do know, you cannot trust him. He is your heart's poison and will be the key to your undoing if you let him. Trust your family and your guardians. Do NOT trust your brother. I understand you will be angry and curious about him, but please, consult your heart before taking any action with him.

I'm sorry we couldn't tell you sooner. I'm not a single bit sorry for the life we have shared with you, and the freedom from responsibility you were gifted as a result of this journey we've taken together.

Grace be with you. Follow your heart, always.

Love,

Mum & Dad

PS. Marry when you meet a man who gives the same reverence in his eyes that I do. Marry when your heart couldn't possibly bear the alternative. Marry when you would rather die than forsaken your beloved. That will be Him.

The last part is scrawled in my dad's handwriting. Of course he had managed to get that in there. I smile, in a moment where smiling would have otherwise felt impossible. That was his gift.

"Thanks Dad," I whisper. I would do anything in this moment to see the look in his eyes of him hearing me, but I know he did.

Then I remember. *Ankhara. I am Princess Ankhara.* It hadn't fully registered when Noah had called me Princess earlier. It hadn't even fully registered reading Mum's words, until now. I'm a Princess. What does that mean? What is this destiny they were talking about? And a brother. I have a brother, who by the sound of it, is more like an evil brother I'm going to wish I didn't have?

I look up at Noah and find him sitting patiently, waiting for me to speak. I think he wants to know if I am okay. Strangely, I am.

"I actually feel relieved."

He looks surprised to hear me speak and even more startled by my words.

"I always knew Megan wasn't me. I couldn't explain it. But I always knew. She never felt like *mine.* I didn't believe it, and to be fair, I've always been a bit of a princess. I struggle being told what to do."

I'm trying to lighten the situation with my humour. It's almost working. He smiles a smile that doesn't reach his eyes but I can feel him feel me trying and that is the most important thing to me. He just sits in stillness, awaiting my every move. Silently watching.

I look him in the eye and ask, "Are you a guardian?"

He looks startled and calm at the same time.. It baffles me. "Yes, Princess, I am."

"Can you please stop calling me that? I don't want to feel separate or above you," I almost beg him. I feel so completely desperate, like he is the last thing in the world I have a genuine, untainted connection to and I don't want that to be ruined.

"I can if you order me to." He smiles, a challenge. I like it.

"I officially order you to never call me Princess. Ever." *That felt good.*

"What shall I call you?" he asks, and I have to pause. What *should* he call me? Megan isn't my name, but Ankhara doesn't feel like mine yet either. Like maybe when I meet my family the name will feel right, but until then.. *Annie.*

"Annie. Yes. Annie."

"Okay. It's nice to meet you Annie." He means it. I can tell by the look in his eyes, there's a sense of relief in him that I've eliminated the formality. I don't want to be formal with him. Despite all this chaos and unknown confusion, I want to be rolling around with him. On the floor by the fire, in the sheets, on a grass hill, everywhere. I just want to relish that morsel of sweet desire that even the smell of him inspires in me. I love him. It doesn't make sense. None of it does, but that almost makes it better. *At least if it doesn't make sense it fits in with the rest of your world.* I'm just about to lose myself to thoughts of him when the crystal ball starts glowing on the floor before me.

"What is...." I begin, but as soon as I look directly at the light I am mesmerised. I become speechless.

"The Prophecy." I can hear Noah whispering beside me but it feels as though he were miles and miles away. Everything is dissolving into a distant presence as the light grows brighter and a white smoke begins to swirl inside the crystal. I wonder if I should be grabbing a pen and paper to write this down but I can't bring myself to move. I am lost in presence to the light and smoke, and my reflection peering back at me between the two. I look different. Somehow older. It's my birthday but this is more than that. There is an age that only the wisdom of experience can give you. *How is this only just the beginning?*

I barely have a moment to notice myself before the reflection disappears and the ball begins speaking, this time without a face, and in a voice that holds a thousand years of wisdom.

> *"A thousand years,*
> *Or a thousand more*
> *Will mark the descendants calling;*
>
> *A thousand hours,*
> *Through lands of powers*
> *Will produce the rise or falling.*
>
> *A single chance,*
> *A lover's dance,*
> *To shed sin from perception.*
>
> *A rain and sun,*
> *Elemental one*
> *Will lead from imperfection.*
>
> *And if she choose*
> *To light the path,*
> *The world will need the dagger.*
>
> *And if she won't*
> *Ignite the path,*
> *The world will surely stagger*
>
> *Into the night*

Of darkened soul,
With no hope of a morning;

Into the night
Without the stones,
And death will need no warning.

As hearts will beat
And tears will keep
Locked up with all the windows,

Extremes will melt,
Only numbness felt,
Innocence lost in the limbo.

Innocent child,
A woman now,
Ready and falling in love;

The time has come
To choose the one
Your destiny sent from above.

Your hedonist heart
Free from fear of sin
Is key to unlocking your calling;

Follow your heart,
Forget the art
And Be to cease the falling."

"And so it begins." Noah speaks so softly it's like a gentle river across my skin. I nod to him, wordlessly.

And so it is.

I hadn't registered the pain in the moment, but in this pause the burning on my arm becomes inescapable. I look to it and there, on my skin, right below the mark I'd already received as a surprise gift, is a series of numbers. I don't fully understand the prophecy I've just received, but it appears we had a thousand hours to fulfil it.

CHAPTER 9

JORDHANA

999 Hours Left

I had forgotten what it felt like to be this alive. To be breathing, moving and sighing the fire inside me was a gift. Two thousand years is a long time to be frozen. Mine was a cruel fate; despite being frozen in physical body, my spirit had been alive and free to wander for many, many long years. It is a strange thing to be turned to stone and to still have thought. It is even stranger to be turned to stone and still have an alive, emotional body with no avenue of expression beyond the spirit realm. Witnessing my body, frozen, stolen in time, was a challenge beyond my wildest imagination. I hadn't known it would be like that, and I wonder: had I been better informed, would I have chosen a different path? Was I truly as noble as this fate made me appear? I would never know. I would never again have that choice. For that, at least, I can allow a sense of peace to ripple through me.

In the dawn of the sleeping times, a wise man and a warrior had come to me. Unlike most who approached me, they meant absolutely no harm. In fact, they came to request my help and service. They had come to ask if I would bear The Dagger. I hadn't known what they were asking, but I'd felt the desperation in their lungs when they breathed the words. Lungs are my flavour. They are my language. I can tell the entire emotionality of a being based on the essence of their breath. These humans were desperate. In need of a cure humanity had forsaken, so that dragons alone could provide it. We dragons are creatures of integrity. We protect that which is of value to us, and we honour each warrior that comes to us. We honour each being, attacking only in response to attack. We do not instigate war. We are a peaceful community, treasuring that which we have in the hope of one day re-populating our species, depleted by so much misunderstanding. This was why we had been chosen. We were of an integrity that could not be disputed by any species. This is why the wise man and the warrior approached me on this very day, two thousand years ago. This is why The Dagger had been placed in my heart, to await the princess who would live to save – or not save – The Sleeping. The princess whose destiny would be to remind the world of magic. I could feel her in each moment. The strength. The courage. Also the recklessness. The sacred rebel. The hedonist. I could feel her with such clarity, in such detail. I could feel the way she looked at her guardian and the integrity with which she saw him as her equal. I could feel the way she held reverence for her adoptive parents and curiosity about her biological family. I could feel the way this world surprised her mind-body and fell like a relief upon her Spirit. She was coming home in ways she'd never come home, as she'd never known who to come home to. Feeling her gave me a great hope, although under the relief and above the remembering I sensed in her a deep rebellion against her path. I sensed an anger that couldn't find a window. I sensed the frustration that beat through her insides, the deep rage at never having been told the truth. I could sense the grief in the heart of the girl inside, the girl who had been lied to by everyone she had ever loved. I could hear the thoughts unconsciously bouncing and slowly building power. It scared me. It scared me how deeply it pierced and how much power I could feel in every inch of it. It wasn't the power that scared me. It was the different flavours of it, and not knowing which flavour she would choose. I didn't know if there was more power in the animal desire to fight or if the heart would win. Either the sacred or childish rebel would be victorious and the consequence of her choice was my heart. If she chose us, if she chose her people, we'd finally be free. And not only us – that freedom would expand throughout the entirety of Earth. Every species would be touched by her action. If she didn't, if she chose to leave, to discard her role and rebel with her brother, it would cost all beings their magic. If she said no to her destiny, we would lose our essence – and, by extension, our legacy. If she came to take The Dagger's power for herself, she would never access her true power. Even worse for me, if she never accessed her true power, it would mean a half-death for me. I would turn to stone forever, and this time there would be no chance of escape.

CHAPTER 10

ANKHARA

997 Hours Left

It's a strange feeling, this moving tattoo. It almost burns. Almost hurts. And almost feels like it is meant to be there.

I look up at Noah, expecting puppy dog eyes, and meet the eyes of a warrior. Something has turned on inside him that I don't think I'd ever understand. I'm no warrior. A rebel, sure. A bit stupidly courageous sometimes, sure. But a warrior? Definitely not my flavour. Warriors are loyal, consistently brave, fight for a cause. I never know what I'm fighting for, I just have this deep urge to fight. I guess now I have a cause. Not that I understand it at all.

"That's how long you have to fulfil the prophecy." Noah speaks softly but fiercely. *Is it really just me that has to do this?*

"And I have to do it alone? I don't even understand a quarter of what that all meant. I don't even know where to begin." This has been such a confusing, worldview-shattering thirty-six hours. *It concerns me that I feel no sense of this getting any less weird. Buckle up, "Princess". Woah. That has a whole new meaning now.* I get lost in my thoughts for a moment and don't notice that he's gotten up and started gathering things.

"Yes," he says as he opens drawers and zips up our bags full of goodies. They probably aren't goodies, but it feels nice to think of it that way. "And no. Djen will help you. She's the matriarch of your family. Your grandmother, actually. She and your father will sit and serve you however they can, but your grandmother is the one who will be able to open a communication channel with you wherever you are. She'll be your primary."

All this language that doesn't seem real to me. *A grandmother. My father.* I want to ask if I'll be meeting my mother but the thought of it evokes such sadness in my body I already know the answer. My mother is gone. I won't be meeting her. *At least I'll get to feel her.*

"I'm not really sure what to do with myself." Anger. Sadness. Relief. Fear. I actually just want a hug. Part of me is excited about going to this other world and meeting family and what sounded like magic. Part of me wants to curl up into a ball in the hopes that Noah might wrap me up and hold me. I have a feeling neither would be that simple, and that I'll regret not making the choice to be held here, but I also know that if I stop now I might not get back up. "Okay. Okay, I'm ready." *As I'll ever be.* I stand up awkwardly, but certain,

"I'll get you home safe before you know it."

Okay my warrior sex god guardian. Take me home before I realise how insane this all is.

He reaches over to put a rucksack on me and secure the dagger in my hand again. He bends my wrist back and forth, reminding me to hold it loosely.

"Come, Ankhara. It is time for you to meet your destiny."

Well fuck fuck fuck here we go.

"Yes, here we go," he smiles and turns towards the door of our so-called safe house. I don't feel safe though, I feel like everything is about to change. He continues speaking while I do my best to stay focused on holding the dagger in my hand loosely. I keep involuntarily tightening my grip. "You're about to get a bit of a taste of what life on the run feels like."

"Excuse me?" Life on the run sounds like no life for a would-be Princess. Life on the run sounds awful. Limiting. It makes even my freedom feel like a trap.

"You're being hunted by the enemies of The People, Annie. I don't know why exactly, but something has shifted. They can sense you now and they are hot on our tale. Maybe it's the awareness of our world you are re-gaining, maybe it's your birthday, maybe it's the activation of the prophecy. Hell, maybe it's all of the above but for whatever reason, they seem to know where you are."

My mind is racing though I don't see anything to do but formulate a plan. I need to do something. "Okay, so what's the plan?"

"You move quickly, don't you?" He raises his eyebrows at me as though he's impressed. "Okay, then. Quick it is. We're going to move quickly. We're going to stop for nothing. Not for food, not for water. We are going to race as quickly as we can first through to the border of this town so we can get ourselves in the cover of the forest. Once we're in the forest, we will have a bit of a journey before us." He looks frustrated and I want to wipe the look of concern off his face.

"What are you worried for?"

He squishes his face and shakes his head. "Once upon a time we could portal with our magic, but that is a gift our people no longer have the strength for. We have to make our way by foot."

"Well I didn't think we were going to fly there."

He laughs for a moment before his face is flooded with seriousness and the warrior in him takes over. "This is serious, Annie. These.. creatures. They will not hesitate to murder you. You are what competes them for their energy and power. You are the representation of hope to our people. To all people. That means those who'd prefer that hope doesn't exist... Well, you can imagine how they feel towards you. You must be ready to strike to kill. You cannot afford to hesitate."

Phwoar. Okay. Intense. I'm fine. I'm not fine.

"I'm not killing anybody, are you kidding me? Do I look like a murderer to you?!" I throw my arms about in exasperation and he ducks, narrowly avoiding the swing of my dagger-wielding arm.

"Jeepers, Ankhara, you're gonna take my head off if you keep waving around like that."

Oops.

He sighs. "Of course, you don't look like a murderer. This is not your heart, killing. Fighting for what you love, though, can you do that? Can you fight to protect those you love? Because their world will be impacted by this too. I'm sad to say it already has."

"Mrs Jo..." Pain strikes my chest as I realise what he's telling me.

"I'm afraid so." He confirms my fears and tears well up in my eyes and begin spilling over my face.

"I don't know if I can do this, Noah. Two days ago I was just a normal teenage girl going to normal teenage parties doing normal teenage things and now, you're telling me that I'm responsible for my best friend's mums' death—"

He grabs my chin softly with his fingers and pulls my glance up to his. "This is in no way your fault, Ankhara." His voice runs over me like warm honey and my breath softens. If I didn't know any better I'd say his eyes were telling me his heart was broken at the thought of me blaming myself. "This is simply your destiny, and mine is to guide you home. Will you let me?"

I nod. He's right. It's not my fault. *It just feels like it is.* I push my shoulders back and gesture towards the door. I may not be ready, but I'm as ready as I'll ever be, and the longer we wait, the more tense I'm going to get. "Let's go."

Within moments of the words leaving my mouth Noah has us outside and running. Part of me wants to slow down. The streets are somehow dark and quiet, even though it's morning. Running through them feels loud and obvious. *Who's the trained warrior here, Ankhara?* I'm going to have to keep trying that name on for size but the voice in my head is right this time. Noah is trained for this. I'm pulled out of my daze by Noah's cry.

"Annie, move!" I duck just in time as three Hoods come hurtling out of the front yard to our left. As if they were hiding in the middle of suburbia, the creeps. I don't have time to internally criticise them anymore before they begin throwing blows. Again, just like in Noah's bedroom, two lunge for him and one surges towards me. I'm almost offended that I'm not perceived as a threat until I realise, I'm really not. I am zero per cent trained for this, holding a weapon I have no idea what to do with.

Just as I am about to be on the receiving end of the Hood's blow, Noah wipes him out from behind. He has taken out his assailants and knifed mine in the back before I had even blinked and he continues towards me without hesitation, looking me up and down and then looking around us before reaching out for my arm.

"Run, Ankhara, they will be the first of many. Run!" He really doesn't have to tell me twice. As soon as he touches me we began running again. Adrenalin has well and truly kicked in. Relief and dread simultaneously flood me as we near the entrance to the forest. It is thick and dark and will provide good cover, but that also makes me think it will provide cover for these creeps chasing us. I shiver as I run and shake off the thought.

"Keep your weapon drawn and ready." Noah barely pants as he speaks, despite the fact we are running. I am already out of breath but before I even have the time to stress we plunge into the forest and darkness consumes us.

✦

Hours. For hours we have run through the forest darkness. Attack after attack after attack. Some Hoods. Some... creatures. Some I had killed, though it didn't feel like it. It felt as though they had killed themselves the moment they had attacked us. We were such a team. Despite me having no training, Noah and I had fought together like geniuses. It was like we were connected in some way, like a sixth sense. *That is stupid, you just got lucky.* I decide that it's not murder if someone leaps at me with a weapon, and in all the chaos and exhaustion I feel no guilt. I feel curiosity.

"Are you okay?" Noah's voice pierces the sense of being overwhelmed that is beginning to flood me.

"Okay? Yeah. I'm okay. Obviously I'm okay. I killed..." I look down at my knife to see black and blue blood mixed with the red I was expecting. "Something. I killed a few somethings. But I'm okay. Is something wrong? Why are we stopping?"

"We're here." I take a deep breath and look around but it makes no sense to me.

"What do you mean we're here?" There is nothing but silence around us. Nothing that is, except for more grass and more trees.

"Just because you can't see it yet, doesn't mean we aren't here. Can you feel it?" He places his hand on my heart and I jump, then soften, closing my eyes. "We're safe here, Annie. We've made it. Feel."

And I do. I let go of the tension I am holding and I surrender into feeling. At first, I feel nothing, and then, a buzzing. A tingling sensation, like there's a field of electricity that my mind and eyes cannot see, and yet, it's here. I can feel it. "Woah. What is that? Why couldn't I see it before?"

"Because to see our world would break your definitions," he explains. "Sad as it is, your definitions are what project the human realm as separate to ours, and so it is. But you aren't human, Annie. You can feel it, you've just forgotten how."

"Isn't that just the same in all of us? Why can't we all remember?"

"Because they've spent lifetimes forgetting. Humans more so than any other species. More than even just forgetting, many even fear magic, disbelieving ."

"I get it now. I mean, I can see how true that is *now*. But why? Why did we start forgetting? Why are we afraid of ourselves?"

He looks around as if to suggest we should keep moving.

"Please. Just tell me the story. Tell me one story that will make at least some of this make sense to me." I beg him with my voice, eyes and body. I am begging for a morsel of orientation, and whilst I'm not sure that's what another other-worldly story will give me, I'm willing to try.

Noah's connection to me prevails over his mind telling us to move forward. He takes my hand and sits with me on a fallen log.

"One story." He nods and I close my eyes to drink in his voice.

"Many, many moons ago, your family gave all the original earth's people the gift of themselves. They gave them the gift of remembering their magic. There was a great gathering, where all creatures of all the lands came forth to remember their true nature and purpose here in this life, and your ancestors taught them how. Your ancestors gave them the toolkit to their intuition, the key to their spirit guidance, the gateway to their heart's calling, and soon after receiving the wisdom themselves, they opened the codes for all.

"And for a time, they followed just that. The original earth was a place of heart. You will love the stories, An — Princess, just wait until you may read them. Many years of beauty followed. A time known as the walking remembrance. I only wish... well. It didn't last.

"Two thousand years ago, the royal family gave birth to twins, the son and daughter of our people as they were seen, and as they aged, tension grew between them. The son, Juce, did not take well to sharing the seat of power. He wanted it to himself and, in an effort to keep the throne, he killed his sister, Anastasia, after she bore her first child. The legends of Anastasia tell of the sweetest heart a girl could express. She was kind, a true leader, and the people adored her even as she grew into a young woman. She was twice the leader Juce would ever be, and yet the seeds of fear Juce planted spread. He shared tales of a dominating legacy, of a select few who would share the throne in the form of magical powers, and it was these seeds of fear implanted in our people that grew. He set homes on fire and banned the use of magic. He burned our people as a show, to discourage any magical use. The appearance of the earth entities – the fae, the nymphs, the dragons, the tree folk – only led to their death, and, despite their immense power, Juce's manipulation proved more insidious.

"Eventually the earth folk retreated into their own dimensions and made themselves invisible to all humans, discerned only by those who maintained a connection to their magic. The world as we knew it, a place of harmony and wisdom and shared magic, was gone. In less than a decade he obliterated the earth we once knew, rewriting history and planting seeds of false religions to inspire more forgetting. It was a living horror story with no escape.

"Our legend tells that your uncles came together and prayed. They sat in a circle, in devotion to a higher purpose, seeking guidance. It is said that they prayed for hours and hours without avail, and yet their hope was sung true. They held hope that if they persisted, help would come – and it did. It was in that circle that the spirit of Anastasia appeared for the first time. As she came forth, she shared a prophecy – *your* prophecy – that one day an opportunity would arise for the royal descendants to seek redemption on their ancestors' behalf. Details of the prophecy were shared only in secret, and a resistance was born to maintain hope through the royal lineage and offer refuge from the ears of Juce and his informants.

"That was also the time of the Higher Council. Prior to this... horror, our people had been led by heart and heart alone. There had been no higher guidance necessary. Everyone was connected. Can you imagine...?"

Noah looked at me with such desperation I almost shed a tear.

"Never mind... My point is this. The Higher Council were brought together and welcomed to earth by your ancestor Anastasia as a line of hope for our people as they waited out the prophecy. Generations passed and Juce's reign ended, though the fear he had produced in our people did not. The royal family, and only the royal family knew the details of the prophecy and maintained a line of communication with the Higher Council. They are like — the ultimate spirit guides, I think those of your world would call them. The royal family are trained in communicating with them from a young age, yourself and Skavari excluded, as the prophecy foretold one of you would be born with the twin spirit of Juce and the other the twin spirit of Anastasia." He looks at me as if waiting for me to say something.

"That's you, Princess Ankhara. You are the heart of Anastasia, unique in essence of course, though here to share those same gifts of love. You are here to create the next great gathering. Through the expression of your heart, it is said that all beings on earth will hear the invitation to come home to their magic, and you will rule a peaceful land once more upon the defeat of your brother and the retrieval of The Dagger."

I have so many questions, but I just stand in shock, listening to him speak. Staring at his beautiful, salty lips, I can't help but want them on me, and yet my body and mind fail me. I can't move. I don't know what to say. I've been awake to this world for a whole five minutes and I feel like I have mountains crashing and crumbling over my shoulders. I didn't sign up for this. I didn't learn about this in calculus. Though, I guess on some strange level I did. What he said was true, I could feel the resonance in my hips and I could see the truth vibrating off his lips. At the very least, he believes it. He believes in me.

"And what am I supposed to do with that exactly?" I ask, exasperated and proud that I've actually managed to get words out of my mouth.

"Simply move one step at a time. And the next step is to welcome you home." He smiles and holds his hand out to me, "Are you ready?"

I gulp. *Come on then, we've made it this far. Take that hand of miracles.* I take a deep breath and nod, accepting the outstretched hand that really means accepting something so much bigger. "Let's go home then."

His smile grows as my hand finds its place wrapped in his.

"Wait, is there a castle in this place you call home?"

He looks ahead and braces his weapon in his other hand, and chuckles. "You have no idea what you are in for." He speaks under his breath, then casts a circle with our hands and declares the space before us will show us home.

"What are you —"

Before I get the words out I turn and look at the land before us. The forest we'd been running through is gone. The land behind us looks the same, but outstretched before us is a land of rolling green hills. At least, a land of what would have been rolling green hills had the grass been alive. Instead, it is mostly dead and sandy. There, on the other side of the rolling lands stands a palace ground like nothing I have ever seen. I've seen pictures of Hogwarts and old castles in England but this... This is next level. I can't see the end of it. I can barely tell which part is the beginning and, if not for the giant flags either side of the most enormous gate-like doors, I wouldn't have noticed the entrance. Even from this distance they are huge.

"Welcome home, Princess."

CHAPTER 11

NOAH

973 Hours Left

*F*inally.

My only thought when we finally arrive at the gates is *finally*. We've made it. All day and all night fighting off Hoods and demons to arrive here. I look at the Princess and felt a strange sense of pride. She is an actual gangsta and she has no idea. The way she lunged straight at her attackers with no training makes her a chaotic weapon. Once she's had some training, she'll be lethal. We are both completely covered in dirt and blood, a mixture of demons', Hoods' and each other's.

She is so alive with adrenalin and magic, not that she understands the magic part yet. She is one of the most powerful people alive. One of the only ones who has maintained their power. It's baffling to me that she's not realised who she is sooner, or at least had an inkling. She's a natural, but the look in her eyes tells me she is freaking out right now. *Fair enough, babe. BABE?! No, Noah. Don't even think-call her that. You're going to have to pretend you barely know her now.*

"It's... this is my home?" I've never known that someone could sound so formidable and uncertain in the same moment. She looks at me, ordering an answer with desperation in her eyes.

"Yes, Princess – and I'm afraid I'll have to call you 'Princess' here. I fear I could lose far more than my rank if I do not." *Trust me, it's as weird for me as it is you.* I could stare at the way her hair tickles her cheek all day. Even covered in mess she's beautiful. Perhaps even more beautiful. She is wearing her spirit right in front of me.

"Only until I change that stupid law." She's got no fucking idea what she's about to walk into, but I appreciate the sentiment. "Let's go meet the fam, shall we?"

Just as she says this, the palace gates begin to open to reveal a row of shields and soldiers. I kneel forward before her and bow my head.

"I present to you Princess Ankhara, Sacred Heart of the People, Awakener of the Sleeping and Warrior of the Spirit." It feels weird presenting her like that, like an object for their affection.

"Let me through you idiots, she's my granddaughter," comes a woman's voice I know to belong to Djen. The soldiers part and she races through, somehow still the most graceful woman I've ever seen even in her desperate plunge through the crowd. As soon as she sees Annie tears spring to her eyes and she gasps, hand to her heart. "It's really you," she almost whispers, but the world is so quiet every word reverberates around and through us.

"Somebody better tell me what the fuck is going on because I am about to lose my goddamn mind." *Ankhara* is a force to be reckoned with.

Djen smiles, and that is the moment I notice Jate appear farther behind.

"That's my girl" he says, a smile on his face. "Welcome home, Ankhara. It's a delight to my heart to have you back."

Let the games begin.

CHAPTER 12

ANKHARA

901 Hours Left

Waking up in so much fluff is still a shock to me. This place, everything about it is so... extra. We have extra pillows. Extra food. Extra staff. Extra bedrooms. Extra. There's also extra separation. I can imagine that growing up here would have been both exhilarating and frightening. I've been daydreaming about that a lot. What would it have been like to sleep with a servant keeping guard at my door, and my parents a hundred feet away in their own bedroom, guarded by their own servant? They call them guardians but really, they feel like servants – they don't have freedom, they're slaves to our protection and to our causes. Our cause... what even is that? We've been tossing and turning and discussing and dissecting this prophecy for three days now. Three days of waking up in extra fluff. Three days of getting absolutely nowhere with this prophecy. All Djen – *my grandmother* – will say is that our ancestors had enrolled a dragon in giving humanity a chance for magic to return one day and... that was it. She doesn't know where the dragon is. She doesn't know what The Dagger – this supposed magical knife that had been stuck into this poor-ass dragon's heart – even looks like. For a prophecy everyone was making such a big deal over, everyone sure was clueless. I feel useless, attending my weapons training with the royal guard, courtesy of this Royal Council that I am already so not a fan of, every afternoon after a long morning of reading books in search of clues and getting nowhere. I don't even know what I'm training for.

No one has told me anything about my brother and no one will speak about it. They're all so focused on the prophecy they seem to forget that I haven't been here for sixteen-and-a-half years. They seem to forget that they don't know me, their child and granddaughter, and that I don't know them, that I don't know what happened to my mother, that no one will talk to me about my own brother... it's so weird. They're all so focused on the task at hand they've forgotten I'm a human – and I've forgotten it is okay to speak my voice and remind them. In the wake of all this change I've become a flavour of numb I've never lived. I am quiet. Cautious. Unsure of myself.

Fuck that.

I roll out of bed and stand up in the fancy silk pyjamas they'd given me. That wasn't all I'd been given. I also have a walk-in robe the Kardashians would envy and a weapons vault that the FBI would be jealous of. *This whole place is ridiculous.*

There is a knock on the door and at my call a guardian enters with my breakfast, just as I'd requested. *At least I can have what I want.* That is one good thing about this place. I never have to cook anything and I can literally ask for whatever food I think of. Which would be great, if I had a healthy appetite to eat it with. Numbness was not conducive to phenomenal appetite. I am lost in my thoughts when I look up and notice the guardian still standing there staring at me. *Dude, that's weird. I'm in my bedroom, stop staring at me.*

That is when I realise it's him.

"Noah!" I gasp. "I can't tell you what a relief it is to see you, this place is awful, no one will speak to me about anything real, everyone is talking about prophecy this and prophecy that and training this and you must prepare for that but no one will even meet me as their family. I feel so disconnected from everyone here." *Everyone except you.* He looks at me like a scared boy I've shocked with too much information. Right. Formality. "I'm sorry. It's been a lot. How are you?" *Fuck this, I don't want to know how you are, I want to break shit.*

"I'm very well thank you, Princess. I'm very pleased to have you home." There is sadness in his eyes as he looks at me. It's like words are coming out of his mouth but they aren't what he actually means. *Hold me.* That is what he really wants to say. *I'm sorry I'm not holding you.* That is what I want to hear. Not this shit.

"I don't care for your formalities, Noah. You are not my slave and I will not treat you as one. Where have you been? I thought you had left—"

"I won't ever leave you if I have a choice about it, Annie." There is such silky smoothness in the way he speaks it makes my body move. *He called me Annie.* It makes my pelvis pulse involuntarily and I feel the ripple of his voice slither up my spine. This is the most I've felt for days, a sweet surrender to feeling that I've missed. I don't know this world. I don't know a world of being so numb to my emotional body. It doesn't make sense.

"Why won't anybody tell me where my family is?" I mean my adoptive family, but he understands. He's the only person in this place I don't have to waste my breath explaining things to.

"They don't know. We... we don't know." He hesitates in answering, and I can tell it's because he doesn't want to see my reaction. Part of him is afraid of me, like I'd caught him in a lie again. But this time he hasn't lied. "I was under the impression they'd chosen to return here when they weren't at your home and there was no sign of struggle. I was wrong. Today is the first day I've been able to find myself in your presence to speak with you. I've been trying, but they insisted I take days off. And. Well. I don't live in the palace."

He says that last bit sheepishly and I want to scream at him, *I don't live in this freaking palace either mate,* but I do now, and I see him as anything other than my mate. Unless we're talking the kind of mate you make babies with, but I'm sure as shit not ready for that. I just need practice loving someone and being loved.

"I don't wish to live here. It doesn't feel like home. I don't feel like I have permission to do anything other than train and answer questions and, honestly... well. I don't want any of this. I don't understand any of it. No one has taken the time to..." I trail off, not knowing what to say, and look at the floor by my feet. Sometimes I feel like if I look at the floor I'll find certainty. Like the Earth will ground me back into a reality I can make sense of. Sometimes it works. Today it grounds me into the reality that makes no sense because that's the reality I am in. Today it makes me cry.

I fall to my knees and let the tears I've been hiding behind my numbness for days fall. Roles collapse and he is by my side in a heartbeat, for me to collapse on him. For the first time in my life I cry without filtering for witnesses. I just cry and cry and cry and there is nothing else I can do. There is nothing else I want to do. I want to melt into the floor with my crying. I want to melt into him. More than anything I want to leave this place, to find my parents at home in the living room asking me if I'd had a good couple of days with Josie and her family. The thought of Josie only makes me cry more deeply. Sounds I've never heard escape from the depth of my lungs as I lose myself to the grief of losing Mrs Jo and leaving everything I had known

and loved in my world. Everything except Noah. Everything except this man who is currently allowing giant teardrops to fall
on his knee and slide to the ground across him. He consumes
the grief with his caress. It dissolves into him and through
him and it gives me a permission I'd never known. When the
writhing stops he brings his hand to my chest, first pausing for
a permission I gave without hesitation. His hand on my heart
pierces the last veil, one I hadn't realised I was holding. In a moment I have become his. Not his to own but his to revere. His
to share time with. His to love. His to be loved by. Just... His. A
surrender I've never known sweeps over me and I lose myself
to a grief transmuting into the greatest loving pleasure I've ever
been lost to.

CHAPTER 13

NOAH

900 Hours Left

She is the greatest pleasure I've ever known. Lost in her heart in my arms. Lost in her grief and her newfound surrender. Never have I ever seen a human express like this, let alone a woman melt to such a state in my embrace. Before my eyes she has collapsed from defiance into a vulnerability to rival that of a newborn child. She is the sweetest, most painfully beautiful thing I've ever laid my eyes on. *It is an honour to serve by loving you.* I've never loved a woman before. I mean, I loved my mother but I'd never known her. She died protecting me when I was just four years old – something I have hated and punished myself for in countless ways. Not loving a woman is one of them. I've slept with women. I've respected women. Hell, Djen is the most powerful person I've ever known – until now. This is a power I hadn't known existed. To her core she is rocked, and yet she has her glow piercing through it all. I can still feel her heart, not turned off to hide her grief. It is all here. Her anger dancing with her love and her fear dancing with her wonder. What a wonder it must be waking to this world at seventeen. What a wonder it must be to learn of magic and heroes and dragons and come to see that you're the greatest hero of our time. What a terror, to know that for your whole life we've been waiting for you, wishing for you. What a conundrum, that for your whole life the family you have loved as your own had concealed the truth from you.

She is beginning to calm. Her body is softening, her heart rate slowing with her deep breathing. Her eyes no longer dart about inwardly. Softly, she opens her eyes and looks up at me, and that is it. I know in that moment I'd never love another the way I have already come to love her. And it isn't a dance. It isn't the attraction. It's the remembering of myself when I look in her eyes and see the full spectrum of everything. The deepest, darkest pain she is afraid of, and the fiercest, strongest pleasure she is revelling in.

"I want to show you something," I say to her as softly as I can so as not to jolt her. She nods and begins to sit up, not losing contact with my skin.

I stand with her and lead her to the door. I give her a moment to change her clothes and she just rolls her eyes at me. Of course she doesn't care. She's a badass, although I knew if I say that to her she'll just say the rest of us are uptight. The thought makes me smile.

"Come on already," she urges me. It amazes me how quickly she has melted back into being her normal, not-normal self. "I want to see."

I nod and pull her through the door behind me, pausing to dodge another guardian before crossing through the empty hallway. We walk up a staircase and through the great hall before entering through a passage hidden behind a staircase and a life-size painting of a king from another time. I don't know his name, but I know the face of the entryway.

"It's in here. Everything you need to know about your bloodline is in this room. I'm sorry it has been hidden from you for so long." I gesture for her to enter but I am too slow. She is already walking, touching, scanning the bookshelves along the walls as if she can't believe what she's seeing and knows exactly where to look.

"I've dreamed of this." My eyes widen as she speaks. "This very room, I have dreamed. Such detailed dreams I always thought they had to be real and I could never put my finger on it. Countless dreams of dancing and laughing in here with the woman I dreamt to be my birth mother. She used to sit there with a huge grey feather and then I'd walk in, creeping as quietly as I could and she'd pretend she hadn't heard me until I was almost at her desk and then she'd jump up and chase me, tickling the feather up and down my back and around my neck. I'd dream it, Noah and I wasn't a baby. I was older. My whole life I had this dream." She has peaceful tears sliding down her face as she whispers, "Until I was thirteen."

Her voice breaks and a part of my heart breaks witnessing her.

"That was when she died." She didn't know, yet, but somehow, of course, she knew. "I crept into the room on the night of my thirteenth birthday and she wasn't there. I was devastated. I'd been so excited to see her and tell her I'd started bleeding on my birthday. I was so excited to tell her I'd become a woman just like her... And she was gone. She was just gone. No note. No sign of anything wrong but I knew. I knew in my heart of hearts she was never coming back. I only once had that dream again, after that, on my sixteenth birthday. I entered the room again in the dream world and spoke to what I imagined to be her spirit, and she said..." Her voice trails off and she walks behind the desk and opens the drawer. Her face breaks into an almost familiar expression of shock and sorrow and thankfulness.

"She said she wrote them all down. Every single one – she said she'd written them all down and that soon a friend would bring me to read them." She looks up at me, handwritten letters spaced out between and underneath her fingers. "She said I could lean on you. She told me you were a fruit to devour and, honestly, I'd thought I was losing my mind."

"You're a dream walker. Of course, you're a dream walker." I can't believe I hadn't thought to ask her if she knew of her gifts.

"A dream walker?" I can tell from her expression she has no idea what I'm talking about. "You mean like, a lucid dreamer type thing? I mean, I've seen that in movies and things but never thought... Well, I guess I'd wondered but I didn't actually believe it was possible. I guess there was a lot I didn't believe was possible."

She is right. There is so much to this world she doesn't know, and this is only the beginning. She has so little time to catch up on as much as possible. Soon she'll be leaving on her quest. *God, I hope I can go with her.* More than I have ever wanted anything in my life I want to go on that journey with her, but I know that even if I go, there will come a point at which I will have to leave her. *This a mission she has to complete alone.*

"Come, Ankhara. If anyone was to find us here... If anyone was to find *me* here with you... You wouldn't enjoy the consequences, let me start with that." I can tell by the deflation of her body and the way she looks at me that she can't bear the thought of leaving. I can also tell she will leave anyway. She'll do anything in her power to protect the home she's found in me. I can feel it, and I feel the same for her. "Bring your letters. You can hide them in your room. You deserve the privacy of at least that."

Relieved, she frantically gathers the letters and bundles them together with a piece of string she finds in the same drawer she'd retrieved them from.

"Fuck them if they think they're keeping this from me. I'm

getting answers today." Never have I seen such a determination of speech. I believe her every word. "And fuck them if they think they're going to stop me from spending time with you."

Fuck them. I never realised I have spent my whole life wanting to say those words. *Fuck them, my love. Let us seek the truth.*

Swiftly and quietly we sneak back to her room and I leave her there, elated that I've been able to start my day by supporting her; saddened that I don't know when I'll see her again.

CHAPTER 14

DJEN

898 Hours Left

Since Ankhara came home I have been completely engulfed in the meaning of it all; completely consumed by the prophecy and if she will fulfil it. How she can even start. How she can possibly be capable of completing the tasks she'll inevitably be unleashed upon? Underneath the fear I can hear the whispers – *of course, of course she will be able* – but my mind tells other stories. My heart is saddened that we have taken no time to connect with her. My duty tells me I don't have a choice in that. Deep down I know that is bullshit – that I was the supreme monarch and technically could do whatever I wanted – but truthfully I feel trapped, without options. As a species, we are out of options. Less than a thousand hours – that is the difference between humanity's magic being re-awoken or a child – this child, my grandchild, in her failure – being the reason magic dies with us. This family has already been through so much. Too much for one lifetime. Too much for many lifetimes. Sitting here knowing that this is the beginning of much more is a cruel way to invest my time, but the alternative is a death I cannot bear. The death of hope. If we stop, if we give up, all hope is lost. Our inaction will mean a death far greater to the world than we could fathom. I feel the truth of that and it frightens me more than anything ever has. It frightens me more than even losing my daughter had. *Impossible.* That was a pain I never thought I could overcome. In some ways I never have. I will never be okay with outliving my child. I will, however, be okay with delaying getting to know my grandchild if it means saving her life and, as a side effect, saving the world of magic. She can do it. I have to believe that to be true. I have to believe our ancestors would not have allowed this soul to be born without that true nature and purpose. I have to and I will. Ankhara is our last and only hope, and although it aches that I had been powerless to save her brother, I can do everything to prepare her until the time of her departure. I can do everything within my power to make sure she is equipped with the capability to fight her demons. *I will do everything in my power to be outlived by my granddaughter.* I pledge myself and I cry. I feel the fear of failure despite all of our best efforts, and I gather myself. I acknowledge the fucked-up-ness of where we are, and a strength is bestowed upon me. *I'm ready now.* I am ready. I really am. At this moment, I am ready to risk it all for the hope that she may make it home a second time. I am ready to risk even my own need to keep her safe so that she may live her destiny. I hate it, but I am ready for it.

It doesn't take me long to regret my surrender to that. Less than a minute after I gather myself there is an aggressive knock at my door, and half a second's pause until Ankhara bulldozes her way through the entrance to stand in front of me. There are angry tears streaming down her face and she is shaking, holding a bunch of letters in her left hand. *Where did she get those?* She is breathing so intensely I fear she might pass out and I scan the room behind her to see what she will fall on if she does. I relax slightly, seeing the couch behind her. She is still in her nightwear; I might have chuckled if she weren't so terrifying.

"When are you going to tell me the complete truth?" she

downright yells at me, slamming the letters on the desk before me. They have her handwriting. *Ang... This isn't possible.*

"How do you have these?" I ask her in my bewilderment. I'm not used to young women, or anyone for that matter, barging into my chambers with this much, or any, attitude. In a way it is refreshing. Most people treat me like a porcelain doll with no emotional capacity. It is also disconcerting.

"Never mind how I have them. How did you not give them to me? How could you not tell me she dreamt of me and wrote to me? How could you not give me the only piece of evidence that I ever existed to her?" She is completely shattered and furious about it. Shame floods my being. *She's right.* It helps that I didn't know of these letters.

"Ankhara sit down, please." She stares at me defiantly, as though sitting would be an acknowledgement of defeat, so I reassure her. "I'll answer your questions, just please, sit. I don't want to scream at my only granddaughter and I don't want her thinking the only way she can honestly speak with me is like this."

She sits. A little bewildered, a bit relieved and a lot exhausted. She's been holding this explosion in for days and we've all been oblivious in our pursuit of the prophecy.

"Okay," I say to her, feeling defeated with my abandoned granddaughter. "Where should we begin?"

"The beginning," she answers, defiant even when she's seated.

CHAPTER 15

ANKHARA

898 Hours Left

This better be fucking good.

I've never been so fucked off in my life. I've had it. Completely fed up with this half-living numbness that has lasted a full three days but feels like a full three lifetimes. I am worse than pissed. I'm devastated. These letters... they are so much more than letters. They are proof. Proof that all these years of thinking I was crazy were... well, that I wasn't. That it had really been her. That I had really had a relationship with my birth mother... dreaming or sleeping or whatever it was, it's more than I had yesterday. It is more than I ever thought I'd get to have. It is... a sense of home. She feels like a sense of home. That is why I'd always liked those dreams so much. They felt like the best kind of home. More than I've ever felt with my second family. They are my family, and I love them, but...

They aren't her.

And they never will be. No one can ever be her. No one has ever looked at me as unconditionally as her. *Except maybe Noah, which is weird.* I shake my head to shake off the thought of him. Now is definitely not the time for my hedonism, much as I'd love to taste even the edges of him again... *and stop. Stop. Stop. Stop. LATER, FANTASY LADY.*

Focus returns to my eyes and I find myself staring at crystal granny. I should probably stop calling her that, but I don't want to. It's my internal rebellion, a way I get to keep her separate from me. I get to keep her and this whole world trapped inside a crystal ball cause the me speaking to her knew nothing compared to what I do now. I have a sickening feeling that the me in this chair right now knows nothing compared to the me that will walk out of this room. It doesn't help the sweaty nausea that is already pulsing through my fucked-off body.

"...Ankhara – are you listening?" crystal granny asks me with a worried look on her face. I like that about her. It feels like she cares. Like despite all this nutty prophecy shit that has kept her from spending any sort of time with me she still wants me to sit and breathe through my fear. *She cares.* She really does care and it makes me even more afraid. *If you care so much, how come you are so obsessed over everything other than knowing me?*

"Because I don't know if I can do this if I know you." She literally replies to my thoughts and it feels strangely familiar to my body. It feels normal. My mind, however, disagrees. My mind wins.

"What the fuck was that? What was that? Did you seriously just reply to my thoughts? Now you're a mind-reader? Do you know what I'm thinking now? Have you been listening to my thoughts since I got here? Is there any aspect of my life that is actually mine?" That is the bit that confronts me. These last few days the walls of any privacy I ever thought was mine have crumbled into the black hole that is this world I was born of. I snap back into focus. *Crap, that means... Noah?*

"Yes. I know of your... affection for Noah. Yes, I hear your thoughts. Yes, I've heard a number of them since you've been here. I've tried not to, trust me. You are rather loud, dear." She smiles in a gentle way I swear only grandmothers can smile. I start breathing again and my shoulders relax. If I can dream walk, why not have a mind-reader in the family?

"Can I? Hear thoughts I mean. Could I learn? Wait. No. I don't want to be distracted by this party trick nonsense. I want you to tell me the whole story. I want the truth, unfiltered, from the beginning. From the moment I was born. I want the good bits too. Please. Not just the pain."

She nods. I can tell the mind-reading conversation is brewing for another day but right now she is all about to tell me the story of me, and I am all about to let her.

"You were born here. In this very chamber." She looks around and tears fill her eyes. She is lost in a hazy memory as she speaks. "She was beautiful. Your mother. She ran in here so, so excited that her waters were about to break and also terrified. She was like that, her magic was beyond what you could imagine. She always just knew and yet she was always so connected to the part of her that was human. She'd wanted her mum."

She looks down at me and continues.

"It helped that she had been just down the hall and your father was out. I was the nearest and next best. She was going on about ecstatic birth for about two minutes before her next contraction and that was that. She wasn't going anywhere. I called the midwives and an army of a type I hadn't witnessed in a very long time gracefully held your mother through the deepest hours of her life. She was transformed in the hours of birthing you... more so than I had remembered for myself. It was the greatest triumph of nature I had ever seen. First, you. An angel sent from the heavens. We knew. The moment we saw you we knew who you were and what you were here for. And then, your brother, Skavari, was born. Not three minutes after we met you we were saying hello to him for the first time. Your mother wouldn't let you go. Either of you. Eventually, she handed Skavari to your father, and we all sat there for hours. Just watching while your parents met the both of you. I will remember that day until I die. I've thought of it many times whilst sitting at this desk. Do you see that darker patch in the carpet just in front of you? That's the mark. The stain of her water breaking. The mark of your entry to the world. It will be over my dead body that anyone ever touches this carpet."

There is such pride and grief in her eyes as she speaks. I have no words. Only tears and the lucky ability to breathe without thinking. She continues after a brief, choked pause.

"It didn't take long for us to notice the difference in character between the two of you, or the difference in reaction our people had to you both. Your brother was... pained. He didn't interact with anyone other than you. He was fixed on you, as children usually are on their mothers, and despite the people not knowing this, their intuition turned them away from him. They loved you. They were cruel to him. It broke your mother. And Jate... he didn't know what to do with himself. He focused all of his energy on Ang and the twins. On you. You three were his entire world.

"That's why we had to do it. When you were three months old rumours of the prophecy child became inescapable. They had already been circulating for a time. We'd known before you were born who you'd be. But the people were loud, many afraid, some aggressive. One night our security was breached and a civilian made his way into your bedroom, long enough to mark your brother's face... any longer and, well, I highly doubt the two of you would be here. Definitely not Skavari. Your mother fought the intruder herself. Oh, you would have been captivated to watch her fight! She was as graceful as a dancer in the way she took down her opponents. Even your father couldn't overcome her. It was a gift. A gift that saved your lives, no doubt, and sent the palace down a very dark spiral.

"That was the first attempt on your lives. Over the coming months there were twelve more. None came so far as to breach the kitchen, but nevertheless we were living on edge. We didn't know how that first intruder had gotten through to your room, and we had no idea if he had told somebody else how to. We were all sleepless in the night, fearing the worst. Fearing your safety in your own home, in your own bed. Your mother slept in that room with you for months. There's a rocking chair, you'll see, with scratch marks from where she tried to keep herself awake. Your father tried to sleep in there too, but Ang wouldn't let him. Jate had a kingdom to run in the daytime. A people to serve. Your mother was too noble to allow the people to suffer on their behalf. The breaking point was your father falling asleep in the Royal Council. It was on that day it was decided. You were to leave. The Council voted, and to your parents' dismay, it was ordered that you would go to be with the Sleeping. We called on retired witches who had chosen to go live among the humans, and that was when we came across your adoptive parents. They had been trying for children for years, to no avail. Your mother had worked as a scribe for years and your father had baked in our grandest kitchens. They were simple, loyal folk with kind hearts and no connection to the magical world – by their own choice, mind you. In their defence, they'd all but forgotten our kind existed when we brought you to them. That's how magic works. If you separate from it, you forget it exists. Logic and reason prevail instead. It was proposed and you were removed from your parents' custody the very next day.

"I've never seen devastation like that. The look on your mother's face when you were taken from her arms. The fatigue of failure in your father's eyes. It was a tragedy – to our family and to our People – that there were so many so against the fulfilment of your destiny. Your brother, however, had a following of his own developing. In the days following the loss of you, it became obvious that the People had divided into those who believed in your destiny, and those who believed in your brother as an alternative.

"You see, a hundred years before you were born there was another prophecy. A prophecy telling of twins coming to earth to decide the destiny of all, humans and witches alike. It scared many, and was ignored by most out of fear and ignorance until you arrived. The prophecy foretold that one twin would be given the choice to save magic for the world and the other would obsessively pursue power. *One twin to free all, one twin to desire ruling. One twin to see all, one twin to be gruelling.* It was your destiny, and despite your mother's certainty that you would both see the heart of it, your people didn't leave you the space to choose. Your death was announced at your six-month anniversary, the prophecy dying with it. At least, for many years we so wanted to believe that. Skavari was a challenging child. Your parents loved him as they continued to love each other, but there was a grief that never left their eyes. You, Ankhara. Your whole life they've been missing you. Begging for your safe return home. Witch law states that an un-initiated witch is not to be contacted by our world. It also states that adopted witches are not to be contacted by the birth family until they are seventeen. I guess I broke both those laws when I came to you the day before your birthday.

"Five days ago we received word, you see, that your brother had discovered you. Your brother is well trained. A force to be reckoned with. He never believed you were dead. Never. He persistently demanded your return. Every birthday you were what he wished for. At sixteen, he declared that unless you were returned to him he would leave forever. There was something in the way he said it... your father was afraid of him. I felt it. No one dealt with Ang's passing. Not really. Not like we should have. Skavari the worst, and he did as he said. He left the day after you turned sixteen and found refuge in the Forsaken, a bunch of would-be witches choosing the lesser outcome of your prophecy – for magic to forsaken, in exchange for a short life of perceived power. They don't believe in magic for all. They don't believe in waking up the world. They believe in ruling The Sleeping, and terrorising The People. They've already begun attacking us again. He'll come for you Ankhara. Your brother will come for you, and I'm afraid it's not a reunion you could ever be ready for."

I gulp. This is not what I was expecting. This is the part where I'd believe I was being punked in a strange, strange movie. This is like a soap opera. *Evil twin fights war to keep the world small and controlled while good twin gives her life for the people.* I can see the headline already. It dawns on me that this is completely ridiculous. I had arrived in a palace, cloaked and hidden in the mountains, to find out I was the hero of a prophecy that everybody expected would fail.

"Okay, granny. So. What on earth do I need to do?"

"Well, dear. The rest of the story is long and scary, but the short of it is, you have to slay the dragon."

Dragons are real. Dragons are fucking real and I have to kill one. Of course.

"That about sums up a shit ending to a shitty story, doesn't it." I'm disappointed by the lack of originality. Long-lost child off to slay dragon and save the world. Never heard that story before.

"Well dear. I suppose it is." I don't think I can take any more so I stand and turn to walk out, still holding the letters we hadn't spoken about.

"Ankhara—" I pause and turn to look at her. "Don't tell anyone about him. Not even your father."

Noah. She's talking about Noah.

I nod, and turn again to leave.

"I'd like to hear about those letters when you forgive me enough to tell me," she almost whispers.

She didn't know.

She can't see, but I'm smiling as I walk out of the room.

She didn't know.

CHAPTER 16

NOAH

892 Hours Left

Brushing the horses is something of a therapy for me. The sounds of their tails swishing and their grumbling bellies comfort a lifetime of painful action. Whenever life becomes too much, I find myself in here loving horses. *She's too much for me.* She is all I can think about. The pain she is in. The way I feel when she's in my presence. Even when she isn't she makes my skin burn. I long for her touch and to be lost in her, in ways I've never felt even remotely. It is a mystery to me how she lives the way she does. Fearlessly emotional and forcefully truth-chasing. She won't let anything slip if she feels it was right for her or the people around her. *I wonder if that means she'll never kiss me again, or if it means she'll cast everything aside and fight for loving me.* It seems unlikely that I'll ever hold her unless she is in grave danger, something I don't wish for in the slightest. I'd do anything to keep her safe. *That includes staying away from her.* I don't want to compromise her position or her integrity before she's even had the opportunity to earn the respect of her people.

I sigh and walk over to the stable wall to hang the brush I've been using, tipping over a metal bucket that I decide would be a comfort to sit on. I sit down and pull my hair back with my hands, sighing again. I am one hundred per cent meant to be staying away from her, and I one hundred per cent want to adventure with her across her lands, and show her her mother's favourite reading place. Ang had taken me out there once when I was really young, only a couple of years into training for guardianship. She'd told me she wanted to know that her favourite spot wouldn't be forgotten. She had always favoured me and I had never known why. I wanted to ask her if she knew my mother, and the thought of it pulls me back into the memory of that day with her.

Come Noah, I need to show you something of great importance. That's what she'd said as she took my hand and walked down to the stable with me. It was such an unusual sight – a queen in a stable – but I remembered the way her hair flicked on her shoulders and the sparkle in her eyes in that place. She'd loved it. She felt so at home there, like the royalty could just melt off her and she'd happily be a stable girl, tending to horses and reading books in the forest between gathering fruit and flowers. That life would have suited her. *I bet she would have had a long and happy life.* I couldn't help but go there with my thoughts, but I wasn't distracted for long before being pulled back into the land of memories.

We rode into the forest for what felt like a whole day, but couldn't have been. The sun had been directly above us when we arrived in a clearing by the river. It was covered in purple foxglove and there were several fallen trees that offered perfect places to sit. She had gestured for me to follow her, and being together with her had felt like a distant familiarity. The boy I was had longed for his mother for as long as he could remember, and just being around her tender, loving aura had filled that void in minutes. She climbed into the hollow of a tree, which at first frightened me. *Come Noah, this is what I wanted to show you. I promise we are safe,* she had said to me, and I trusted her, so I had followed. We climbed up through the tree, arriving at an opening that extended out onto a branch. It was the perfect place. Up ahead I could see the grounds and trees and, in the distance, the palace. Below was the river, making the most serene background music. Right next to me was Ang, the Queen of all of our lands, but at that moment, she was just the mother of a friend I hadn't met yet, telling me about her daughter and how, one day, we'd be great friends and it would be my job to serve and protect her. *One day, you'll see why I had to take you here. One day, everything that has yet to happen will make sense.* Her words had confused me, although the boy I was didn't have the attention span to remain fixed on her words. That day had stayed with me always. Less than three months after she passed, I had gone almost all the way back to her spot before turning around and coming home. Something had told me it wasn't the time. Something had held me back, but now that I'd met *her*, now that I knew so much more of what she'd meant, I needed to return to that place. I needed to take Ankhara to the place her mother had begged me to one day show her, as if she somehow knew she'd never show her herself. I frown. *Did she know she wasn't going to be alive when Ankhara came home?* I shake the thought away. It is too much to contemplate today. Already I have made my way onto the breakfast shift so as to see her. Getting onto the evening shift on the same day is going to be a difficult one to explain, but with everyone so focused on the prophecy, this could be the best chance I have to take her out there, and the sooner the better. The longer I wait, the more likely it is that Skavari's friends will have descended on the place.

If I am going to honour the only wish Ang had ever asked of me, I will have to coax Ankhara out of the castle at night – which, really, is unlikely to be difficult. Sneaking past the guards, however, is a different story. And I don't have time to think about it. It has to be tonight.

"I'm sorry I almost forgot you," I whisper into the stable, and I could swear I hear her voice in the wind. *You've never forgotten, Noah. You've always remembered at exactly the right time.*

Maybe I'm imagining it; maybe I want it to be there, but the feeling of a soft touch on the back of my head confirms to me only one thing: Ang isn't here in physical form, but her spirit will live here with her people until her people are no more. Which could happen very soon... *Not if I have anything to do with it.* I'll give my life serving Ankhara if it comes to it. I'll do anything to support her following her destiny with the prophecy. I've already given her my heart. Time to risk my freedom.

My decision is made. I'm breaking Ankhara out of the castle tonight, whatever the cost.

CHAPTER 17

ANKHARA

887 Hours Left

I am sitting in my nightgown on the window seat when he sneaks in. I know it's him straight away. I can smell the saltiness of him; it reminds me of earth near the ocean. More earthy than anyone I've ever smelt. *Usually you don't remember people's smells, Ankhara. Duh.* I smile to myself and look down at the letters I am still holding. Calling myself Ankhara feels so much more... home. After seeing my name in her writing, it feels true. It feels... real. I am a princess, sitting in the window of her castle, trapped in her world full of magic she didn't know she breathed. *In love with a guardian I can't touch.* In love nonetheless. Of course, I'm thinking about him when I feel him sneak in. If I hadn't felt him, I wouldn't have known. *He's so graceful.*

"I wondered if you'd be back after the mess I was last time you were in this space." I speak to him without looking up, still captivated by the letters.

He walks into the candlelight radiating from my desk and bedside table. He could be the scruffiest, dirtiest man I'd ever laid eyes on and his good looks would still completely captivate me. He is beautiful. The kind of beautiful only men can be. Messy. Perfectly imperfect. Candlelit cheekbones. Charcoal ink on his skin looking darker and more appetising than ever in this light. He is speaking to me and he looks quite serious, but I hear no words. All I can see is his lips moving, and I want them on me. I don't care what he wants to talk about. I need him underneath me. I want to taste him again. I want to drink him in and forget this room in this palace in this underworld I've awoken to. I want to forget a world exists where I can't be with him, where I don't have the sovereignty to choose. That isn't a world I believe in and it isn't a world I want to be in.

I stand up, looking him in the eyes, mouth slightly open, and slowly begin slipping my gown off my shoulders. He swallows and catches himself. I've thrown him off guard. Really, I do care what he is here for; I just don't care about my desire *less*, like most other girls I knew would. Not me. I step towards him like an animal on the prowl. A lioness. A jaguar. Both. He is my prey. My equal. Both. My hips dance to the left as I step forward and my gown falls to the floor. *Three more steps.* He gathers himself by taking a deep breath as I move forward and my right hip calls to him. *I am like a siren singing with my body and breath, the difference being he is completely powerful in choosing to be here with me.* I am focused on nothing else in the world but him. My prize. My gallant warrior who has done nothing but honour and protect me. This man I feel I've known in lifetimes and yet have only known for days. *Two more steps.* I slip my night dress off my shoulders and allow it to crumple at my feet. To my enjoyment, he gives himself full permission to take all of me in. His eyes caress every inch of me. His smile glows as the light flickers across his face. I can see his pulse in his neck, and his fingers uncurl with his longing to touch me. I feel the longing in every inch of him as he admires me in my nakedness. Every curve is his to drink in and he allows it all to be there, a beauty before him that even I relish. *One last step.* I feel his breath touch my breasts as I lean almost into him. He is so close now

I could kiss him. I could touch him anywhere, but I hold off. I keep my eyes on his and bring his hands to the lace underwear I am pulling off, urging him with my hands to slide it down. He obliges and slowly, but surely, slides it down over the cheeks of my ass before bending down to pull it from me ever so carefully, centimetre by centimetre. My breath shakes as he bends down and kisses tenderly the space between my breasts.

My heart.

He kisses my ribs. My stomach. My hips. The soft round flesh of my womb. My pubic mound, right above my clitoris. He kisses me so softly I almost can't bear it, as he gently guides my feet through the lace G-string, one after the other. I close my eyes and bite my lip, sighing. He is a heaven I didn't know I could melt into. Before I even register him standing again, he picks me up and lays me on the bed. Just as I had relished his soft tender kisses, I relish his firm touch as he swiftly places me down and holds me there. He stands back up off the bed, fully clothed still, and holds his hand up to me.

Stay. The way he can speak to me with his eyes is my favourite thing about him. It makes my whole body shiver and relax. He walks to the door and locks it. *Ever the gentleman, Mister Morgan.*

He's wearing a white button-up shirt that perfectly shows off the colour of his skin, and now it was my turn. He smiles and winks at me as he begins to undress himself, as painfully slowly as I had. I feel myself drip onto the bed as I watch him, my legs slightly parted so he can see all of me. Still, he holds my eyes. Shirtless looks *so* good on him. The light bounces off the definition of his abdomen and chest and the beautiful 'v' that marks the path to his holy cock. I truly see him as holy. I can't imagine calling him anything else at that moment. He is holy and whole. Erotic and innocent. Vulnerable and... a man.

The man I love. It doesn't even feel weird seeing him like that. It feels natural, as though nothing else matters and nowhere else is happening. I notice everything about him. The way he smells sweet and salty and somehow feels earthy and like the ocean at the same time. The way he dances with me. He doesn't force any moment. He doesn't insist on anything I'm not already begging for with every fibre of my being. We are so connected, from our breath to our body to our thoughts, that I almost don't care when someone starts banging at my door.

Noah is on top of me now, his weight bearing down on me with a sexy flavour of familiarity and his body intricately woven into mine. He is very nearly entering me, and then not. His every motion almost enters my very wet, very open pussy.. Almost, and as soon as he notices the knocking on my door, he pauses, the tip of his cock kissing the lips of my vulva, so plump I can feel my heartbeat down there. He smirks a soft smirk as if to say, *good timing, you gonna get that?* And I shake my head and pull his lips down to mine instead. He tastes like the ocean with a hint of salty earth. His lips are rough, and yet somehow soft. His hand cups my face and he caresses my cheek as he deepens into kissing me.

"Please," I beg him. "Please, Noah."

He looks me in the eye and penetrates me as swiftly and gracefully as he had lifted me onto the bed, lifting my body onto his again and holding me, now sitting on him, holding his gaze. We sit there like that, connected in every sense of the word, for what feels like hours. It could have been seconds or days and I wouldn't have known, the beating of my heart reverberated like the sound of a drum beating louder and louder. So loud that...

"Princess Ankhara, PLEASE!"

The voice of a young woman shocks me out of Noah's time warp embrace. *Who is that?* I look at Noah and then at the door, then back to him. He nods.

"She sounds afraid. What would you have me do?" He speaks like sweet honey, the fancy kind that comes in a too-fancy jar. *I wish you wouldn't be so formal with me.*

I sigh. I'm back in the reality of my mind, and in coming back to acknowledging my surroundings, I notice the fire flashing in the distance outside my window. I squeeze him, and gently slide off. I lick his cock, with my hand on his chest – my way of saying goodbye for now – and then kiss his lips one last time before moving to the window to take a proper look. *Bang, bang, bang!*

Anxiety kicks in as I begin to process what I see. The city below is on fire. People screaming and children crying. I can hear it all clear as day. *How had I missed this happening?* And my door. Someone is banging on my door. Something is wrong.

Not something. Someone.

Skavari.

"He's here." I turn to Noah, and see the fear in his eyes. "Get dressed. I have a feeling we're going to need to go." I didn't need to tell him, he is already dressing himself, with that worried look in his eyes. He isn't afraid for himself. I can tell. He is afraid for me, worried about what might happen to me.

He isn't the only one. I'd seen the look in father's and granny's eyes. Everyone is afraid of how I'll respond when I reunite with Skavari. And, fair enough. So am I. I have no idea what to expect. I haven't even seen a photo of him, but seeing this chaos now, I can feel him in my body. It is as though my energy is calling out to him, which makes no sense. *Nothing makes sense here, Ankhara,* I think to myself. *At least it's not fucking beige.*

"I'm coming through this door in three seconds if I don't—"

I wrap my gown around my body and open the bedroom door to see a small, elf-looking woman staring at me, exasperated and breathing heavily. Her demeanour quickly switches from annoyance to anger once she sees me, then she sees Noah behind me and awkwardly softens. *She knows.* Well, it'd be pretty hard to not put two and two together. Noah has buttoned his shirt back on himself and my robe is on, but this is not a typical setting for a guardian and a princess. If I've gathered anything since arriving here, it was that. Everything is hierarchy and an olden-day style of backwards and stuck. I usher our elf lady inside and she doesn't hesitate. Shutting the door behind her, I sit on the stool against the wall. Noah moves to stand beside me, ready to protect me, but I can tell he feels safe with this woman. He recognises her.

They recognise each other.

"I'm Katarina Vinelight, you can call me Kit," she begins. "I don't have time to explain everything and I'm sorry, I'm sure you're hearing too much of that lately for the mental health of any one human, witch or nymph. Your grandmother," she says, shaking her head, "Djen, she's been training me for this my entire life. Well, our entire lives. We've both been in training for this, just in different ways. I'm your guide through our lands. I have pledged my life to guide you so long as I can, on your quest to the dragon. I know you can't possibly be ready for this, but we truly must go."

I feel Noah's body stiffen beside me and it frightens me. We have no idea where I am going, what lies ahead of me or even if I will return. I have no idea if I am going to run into my brother along the way and fall to him or if I will even be able to do whatever was presented to me, but I know I have to try. In the short time I've known them again, I've felt the hearts of the people here.

"Your ways are twisted in shapes I don't believe in," I tell her. "Your world needs to change if you anticipate me sticking around this place, let alone being a member of the royal family. I understand the need for leadership, but the only people I am willing to lead are a people who are free. Free to leave. Free to make magic. Free to be who they were born to be. I don't know what I'm getting myself into here, but I like your style, and I'm as ready – and not ready – as I'll ever be."

Kit smiles. Noah melts. I can feel pride emanating from him and I give myself permission to calm my fear in it. I want to relish him while I still stand by him.

"What's the plan?" Noah looks to Kit, expectantly.

"Find Granny" and "Find Djen," Kit and I say simultaneously. *I knew I liked her.* I don't know if it is the green in her hair, or the fun of her pointy little ears, or the light-hearted fierceness I feel radiating off her, but something tells me Kit is going to be the truest friend I've ever had.

"Don't mind me," I announce as I disrobe (again) and nakedly find my way to my training clothes. I tie a belt with a scabbard for my dagger around my waist and braid my hair quickly before slipping on my boots ready for combat. "Now let's find this fucking dragon."

I know I can't go anywhere until I've seen Granny. I couldn't say why; I just know I have to see her before I go anywhere else. The palace is chaos. Guardians are running everywhere and so am I, Kit and Noah right on my tail. I run as directly as I can to Granny's chamber, only to find it empty. Panic hits me, but before I have the chance to really melt into it, someone grabs me from the side. I look up and remember to breathe again when I see who it is.

Grandma stands before me, breathing heavily but steadily,

with a stern look in her eyes. She looks me dead in the eyes, then looks to Kit and Noah and nods to each of them.

"Come." She speaks softly but fiercely. This is a woman you don't wanna fuck with. *Definitely my grandma.* "All three of you." And she turns and weaves her way through the chaos far more easily than anyone of her age and stature should be able to. I follow, struggling to keep up. Twice I'm hit in the face by someone rushing through the corridors past us. The guardians are all armed, some shooting arrows from windows, others gathering the civilians and housekeepers into more secure lockdown. It's a sight nothing short of a battle from Lord of the Rings. The only thing missing is the monsters. *Skavari has his own flavour of those.* I don't want to think about Skavari right now.

I recognise where we are by the huge painting we duck past. *Mum's chamber. Why are you bringing us here?*

Granny rushes inside and moves to the shelf in the back corner. She pulls several books in quick succession, not actually removing them from the shelf, and there is a series of clicks and cogs turning before the shelf sinks into the floor, opening a whole new world before our eyes. Right there, beyond this tiny secret door in my mother's ancient chamber, is a passageway that smells like forest. My body knows somehow that this passage will take us straight through the city and out to the forest at the border. I can feel it. I want to run through and hug the trees and paint myself with the dirt of the forest floor. I don't have that luxury, but I am definitely going to get the running part. Grandma flicks through the folds of her cloak, biting her lip. She is cute and awkward sometimes. It shows her age and personality and makes me wonder what she'd be like if the world was different for her. If her daughter hadn't died and her grandchildren hadn't been the core of our world's greatest prophecy. I can picture her cooking by a fire and telling tales that would rival those of the greatest storytellers that ever were. I can imagine her dancing and smiling and laughing at our naive silliness.

Instead, we are here, and she is reaching into her cloak to pull out a red-stoned dagger. It is beautiful – the shiniest silver I've ever seen with a large red ruby in a clasp on the handle. It's hers; I can feel it as soon as I touch it. My mother had fought with this weapon. The stone sings and buzzes as though it recognises me. *Weird, Megan. Weird. It's a stone. And your name isn't Megan.* I wonder how long it will take me to get used to that. A new name I knew nothing of.

"Your mother would have wanted you to have this. This stone was her most powerful ally and friend. When you need strength and comfort, draw from this stone. It has her force in it. She'll be with you always, wherever you are, and this will be a portal for you to tap into. A key, should we say, so that you may access the fullness of who you are. She wanted you to know who you were. She wanted you to meet yourself. This will guide you home."

"Guide me home? But–" I'm panicking now. This is all a bit too real. Tears fill my eyes and threaten to spill over my cheeks.

Grandma places the dagger in my right hand and her right hand on my heart. "Home," she says, calmly looking me in the eye, and I know in that moment we are saying goodbye. I couldn't tell how I know this; I just know. She won't be here when I return. *If you return.* Fuck off. Fuck of fuck off fuck off. I shake my mind and head to presence myself.

"I love you." It is all I can say to her. I have so many questions. There are so many answers I need. But in this moment, this is all I have. This is all I can say that won't stop me from walking through this doorway. She has to know. And my father. I have to know he knew too. "Tell him I love him too. Tell him thank you. Tell him I've got this and I'll see him soon."

I don't know if any of that last bit is true, but it feels right. I feel like I'm giving one of my usually reserved-for-myself inspirational speeches. I also feel like she may never pass the message on to him, but it doesn't matter. It isn't about that. It's about right now. About my heart remembering hers and my voice casting the spells I need cast on myself. Deep down, underneath it all, I know I can. I know I can do this if I keep choosing to. That's all I have. One more step in one more moment.

"Go love. I know. He knows. Your people know. Go. I am so proud of the woman you are." The tears spill and I see hers mirror mine like rain sliding down two sides of a mountain. She holds me in the tightest, warmest embrace of my life, the kind of embrace I imagined only came from grandmothers, but I've never had one to try with until now. Then she brushes herself off and turns to face Kit, then Noah.

"You both know." She nods at them and they nod in response, respect emanating from their bodies for this woman I know to be a warrior at heart. I've seen Noah fight, and I know what it means that he feels this much respect for her. It runs deeper than rank. "Noah, you will know where she is and what she's needing. Trust that. Kit, you will know when it's time and it will scare you. Do it anyway. You're ready." She takes a step back and looks over the three of us, taking us all in with her breath. "You all are."

Kit's eyes well up, a single tear escaping. Noah's bottom lip shakes with a grief that breaks my heart. They know too. We all know we are saying goodbye, and yet it is choiceless. We could hide in here and weep and pretend everything is going to be okay, but it isn't. Everything is definitely going to shit, and the only way to prevent the full-blown shit show is to run through that secret passageway. So I turn and run. There is only one way this can go, and it is definitely not going to be me giving up.

My breath grows sharper as I hear the hidden gateway close behind us, and fire licking at the walls. Our path is ignited before us and there is no turning back. My home is crumbling. My people, terrified. My heart, breaking, and yet all I can do is run. My feet hit the forest floor and I don't hesitate. I look back one last time. The palace is glowing with fire and fear, and Kit grabs my arm.

"Come. The time for tears has passed."

I blink and turn on my heel to begin running again. Within two minutes, the three of us are surrounded by Hoods.

Well. *Fuck.*

CHAPTER 18

NOAH

885 Hours Left

She is spinning, executing moves in ways I've never seen her move. With three days of training, Ankhara has become a weapon. It's supernatural. She moves more swiftly than Kit, who I have seen train her whole life.

Kit... that's an awkwardness to address in another moment. Right now, I have fifteen Hoods to myself and a mission to return to. Fighting is a meditation to me. I move quickly between my assailants, consistently taking them by surprise. One after the other, the bodies pile up on the floor as the three of us dance, Ankhara constantly a prickle in my mind. I can *feel* her. I know exactly where she is the whole time, even if she's behind me. I lunge forward to cut down two Hoods who are charging at me and I instinctively duck as I feel Ankhara flying down from a tree behind me. She lands on the third Hood, who had been charging at me from my right side. I hadn't seen the Hood, but I'd *felt* her, and I'd known. *Just like Djen said.* Ang's voice rings in my mind and immediately I know I just have to get Kit and Ankhara to that clearing. We'll be safe there, if even for a few hours sleep before our journey really begins. A quick head count tells me we have eleven Hoods left. Kit is making quick work of them. The way she blends into the trees and confuses them was better than watching TV. Kit is a nymph, at one with nature, the most connected of the hominid spe-cies. Humans being the most disconnected, the most forgot-ten, and witches the in-between. Witches remember, in part, but nymphs? Nymphs are connected to the land like no other creature. They see no separation between themselves and the trees, and it is easy to agree when you are with them. The way they dance between their physical and etheric form is fantasy-like. They make witches look like children of magic.

Not all of us. I'm sure she doesn't even know it, but Ankha-ra is doing the same. Floating her way up trees adds an element of surprise to her attack that baffles even me. I'm glad she is on my team.

The last of the Hoods falls under Ang's dagger. Ankhara wields it well, like an extension of herself, and she laughs.

"Did you guys actually see that shit?" she calls, seemingly high. She is. She is actually high from the thrill of it. *From magic.*

"It's your magic, Princess." Kit speaks confidently and clearly. I like that about her. "You're going to become more and more connected to it as those numbers tick down on your wrist."

I'd almost forgotten we were on a timer. *I can't lose time with her again.* If I am going to see Ankhara through this, I am going to need to be a pillar of focus. No more timewarp sex.

"Eight hundred and eighty-four hours. It still feels weird. Like it doesn't belong on my arm but it does. It's familiar and uncomfortable at the same time." She looks back up from her arm, straight at Kit. "What do you mean magic?"

"Ankhara— can I call you that?" Kit asks, and Ankhara nods. "Thanks. Princess is... weird on you. Anyway. Your magic. You are more connected to your essence than most. Firstly, be-cause of your birthrights and your blood. Your mother gifted that to you. Secondly, because of who you are. Your openness and your… Let's call it free will. It makes you unfathomably lethal and, quite frankly, a terrifying force to be reckoned with. I'm glad I'm on your side."

I agree with her wholeheartedly. That's what makes things so easy with Kit. We always agree. We always both follow what is right. We play by the rules. Ankhara has brought out a flavour in me I never felt with Kit. I like it.

"So you're saying, that because I'm uncontrollably myself, coupled with the whole royal family business, I'm a witch with magical superpowers. Like actual, float-up-a-tree kinda superpowers, not just dream walking and talking to dead mothers whilst sleeping?"

She really has a way with words.

I smile and look at my feet. I'm smitten, like a lovesick dog. *Get a grip, Noah.*

"Pretty much," Kit smiles. I can see they are going to get on like old friends. They were born for this. Literally.

I wonder how long that will last once Annie finds out Kit and I lost our virginity to each other.

CHAPTER 19

NOAH

884 Hours Left

It doesn't take much convincing to lead Kit and Annie to the clearing. Kit is always open to following the obvious guidance of where to move next. It's how she trained. Follow the obvious. Observe what's obvious and then take the obvious next action with an open heart. Me having a straight-up suggestion for what to do next is about as obvious as it gets. Ankhara on the other hand, is high as a kite, and more than ready to allow the two of us to ground her back into her body by leading the way, getting her taking some very real, one-foot-in-front-of-the-other steps. She's going to have to better manage her magic if she's going to do this.

Doubt is creeping in. Not only does she have a country of people to save, she has the whole world at her fingertips, even if they don't know it. Every living Being is depending upon her success, and she doesn't even understand the fullest extent of her power yet. Not even almost. *Trust in her path. She's got you for a reason.* I can feel the truth in those thoughts too. She really does have me, not just as a lover, or a love, but as a loyal friend and servant. I would give my life for her to lead. I really would. My only hesitation comes from the grief of a life ended without having ever been with her – like, *really* been with her. I want to show her how loyal a love could be. I shake my head. *You'll never be able to do your job and love her like that, even if the law allowed it.*

My focus needs to remain wholly on supporting her as the leader and warrior she is going to need to be in order for her to win this mission. This mission, the very first of her leadership and the very biggest that ever existed. It is a handful, just like she is, but that's part of why I feel she can do this. I'm afraid, sure – especially afraid as to how her feelings for me will affect her – but I also have faith, this sense in my stomach that she can do this. I just know it in my bones. Our ancestors wouldn't have chosen her if they didn't believe she could. Ang wouldn't have, and she was one of the greatest seers our city had ever known. Heck, she was one of the greatest seers our *species* had ever known. She was a legend in and of herself. *Another secret you've kept from her.* I know, as soon as we get to this clearing, that truths will come to the surface, and some of them I'm afraid to share with her, but it is time.

It is time Annie – *Princess Ankhara* – receives the full truth of who she is. Only from that place will she be able to complete this mission. Only from that place will I ever see her crowned Queen.

I look behind me to see Kit and Annie chatting away and laughing. Despite everything, these two women I hold so dearly in my heart are finding friendship and love and connection. This. This is what we are fighting for, true connection, and even as I have that thought, Annie's eyes catch mine. For a moment I forget anything else exists. I smile at her, a smile that maybe doesn't touch my eyes but definitely touches my soul. Then something hits me and everything goes black.

CHAPTER 20

ANKHARA

883 Hours Left

Fuck.

Fuckfuckfuck.

"Ankhara! Ankhara! Stop the bleeding!" Kit's scream rips through my shock like a bullet straight to my chest. *Come on Ankhara, deep breath, you can do this. What would you love?* Noah. I love Noah.

I trip out of my trance and run to him, skidding onto my knees beside his head. Kit is running around fighting another bunch of Hoods but she has my back, I can tell, and honestly I don't think I can have focus on anything other than him at that moment. Blood. There is blood everywhere. *Please let this be the kinda blood that doesn't stop when you cut your leg shaving.* I so want it to be a blood that means he is okay. I want it to be an over-reaction of the body. I want it to look way worse than it is, but I put my hands on his head to wipe it away and find it. A massive gouge in the back of his head that has blood gushing out of it. *I'm not trained for this. They didn't train me for this.*

"There's blood everywhere! What do I do?" I scream at Kit, beside myself with grief. "I'm not trained for this! This is too much, Kit, what do I do?"

Kit doesn't miss a beat in her battle, falling from a tree and taking three Hoods with her on her way down before landing perfectly on one knee. She looks at me for one second, and then ducks to miss a swipe from another Hood before flipping back onto her feet.

"You know exactly what to do, Princess!" This is the point at which I am sure she is on crack. *It would explain those moves.* "Deep breath," she says between blows. "Ask for guidance." She is weaving through trees and creating more confusion on that assailants' faces than I've ever seen, all the while remaining completely calm and guiding me. "Ask your heart. Ask your grandma." She's crazy, and I think she's my new hero.

"Here goes nothing." I shake my head and whisper to myself. "Come on, Ankhara you can do this. Take a deep breath." I do. "Grandma..? Granny, I need your help. Granny please, help me. Give me guidance. Give me something."

I feel a fire burn just above my belly button. It feels like a surge of energy coming straight from my centre.

And just like that I know. I know exactly what I need to do. I hover my hands above Noah's head and take another deep breath, closing my eyes. And start singing. Before I can even filter what I am doing, I'm singing to this wound in his head. Not with words, just... song. I am giving song to the pain in my heart at the thought of losing him, and, more than that, I am giving song to the love in my heart for him. I feel his heart open in response to mine; I feel his heart rate slow. I panic, and then realise this means the bleeding will slow down too. I open my eyes and my voice wavers briefly as I see my hands *glowing.* Bright, white-blue light is shining out of my hands and covering Noah's head, washing over him and spreading out over his body. The light falters, and I take a deep breath and keep singing. It intensifies. I can feel a warmth pulsing through my hands, coming straight up from the fire in my core and through to him. It is from me. No, it is coming *through* me.

I can feel my connection with the earth. I can feel Grandma standing behind me. And... Mum? I don't have the energy to look, I can't afford to move my focus from Noah, so I close my eyes again to eliminate distractions.

Faintly, as though in the distance, I can hear Kit grunting and growling as she continues to fight for our lives, but nothing compares to the sound of my voice reverberating through and out of me. I can feel his energy responding to mine, growing stronger. I feel more powerful than I've ever felt before, and all I can think to do is to focus on seeing him healed in my mind's eye. So I do. I sing and sing and picture him fully healed, sitting up and smiling at me with that love look he gives me. I feel the salty warmth of tears fall down my face, and they smell like him, like earth-soaked saltiness.

I am so immersed in my song and in my vision I haven't noticed everything else come to quiet stillness around me.

"Ankhara." I hear a faint whisper over my left shoulder that reminds me of...*Mum?* I open my eyes and turn and see Kit, kneeling beside me. She has blood smeared across her cheeks and a smile on her face. *A smile?* Why is she...

I turn to look at Noah.

"Noah, I..." He is sitting up in front of me, holding my hands, which I hadn't even noticed him grabbing. I look him up and down. There is blood and dirt all over him, but he seems... fine. "You... " I am lost for words. The rarest of occurrences. "How...?"

"You, Annie. You healed me. You willed it so." He is smiling and laughing as though he is chuffed that I'd do such a thing. *As if I wouldn't.* I just don't understand how I've done it.

"We have a lot of explaining to do, Ankhara." Kit speaks as though she is apologising. "A lot. It's going to be a bloody thrilling conversation but, right now, can we *please* get you to the safety of this clearing? You're awesome, and I'm not surprised you nailed that, but let's not put your newfound singing powers to the test." Kit is right. I like her. She is to the point. No filter.

"Come on. Let's get you safe." Noah stands up and holds his hand out to me. I accept and he helps me up, embracing me as I half trip into him. His body on mine sends a river of shivers down my spine that makes my lips tremble, so I bite them. I look up to him and I don't want to let go. Then he looks at Kit and coughs, and I pull myself back.

"Sorry, I'm a bit clumsy sometimes. Not sure what came over me there," I say to him, like I need an apology for wanting to touch him. *Him.* This freak between the sheets who has wandered into my world, and held me safely while it tipped upside down, only to nearly die on me, and then not want a hug.

His eyes are an apology I don't have space for. "Come on, lead us to this bloody clearing then." He looks like he wants to say something but can't. He just turns and nods, and leads the way. That was when I notice. Kit. She is looking at us with her jaw about to hit the floor, and a sadness in her eyes that only a pained lover could wear.

They've been together.

It hits me like a ton of bricks. These two people, the only two people I've ever been so exposed in front of, the only two people I have to help me on this ridiculous prophecy quest, have slept together. My dreamboat sex god and my newfound best friend. They've slept together. I roll my eyes and start walking.

Of course they have.

Nothing is ever easy when it comes to love. I decide at that moment to let him go.

I won't risk my life or yours, Noah, not by hurting the one person that seems even remotely equipped to get us through this. Not a chance on earth.

No doubt about it, it breaks my heart, but nothing would break my heart as much as either of them losing their life because of decisions I made with my vagina. And my heart... well. My heart will live to beat another day, and now isn't the time to break it open to the grief I can feel welling up in there, or to the anger I can feel stirring underneath. Those are feelings for another day. This minute requires one foot in front of the other, a breathing guardian and a living guide. That I can do. The rest will have to wait.

CHAPTER 21

KIT

882 Hours Left

*T*here is no mistaking it. None at all. I can see it in the way she caught her breath and the way he squirmed in her presence.

They love each other. Maybe even loved *each other.*

Noah and I haven't been together in months. And still it stings. We'd never been like that. Hell, I've never been like that with anyone, and I've never seen him like that either. Almost fragile, as though the world would stop for him if her heart ever did. *True love.* I can smell it in the air. Come to think of it, I'd smelt it earlier and hadn't had time to register it.

That is a gift of the nymphs. We could smell *everything*. And taste. And feel. It is a gift of being so connected. We are so in sync with our surroundings we experience them constantly in so many ways. It is difficult to describe, *smelling* someone's feelings. Imagine describing to a stranger to the world of magic that you can smell how they feel. It's a weird gift, I get that, but in other ways it also isn't weird at all. In fact, it makes perfect sense to me. It's all connected. All senses. All sensations. As an extension of that, it makes perfect sense to me that they would love each other. Him the greatest guardian our world had seen in centuries. Loyal to the depths of his heart, dedicated and fierce as any warrior must be, and yet still so connected to his feeling body. He wouldn't fight for a leader he didn't believe in. Despite his years of training and conditioning, his number one ruler is his integrity to his true cause. That is a gift they share. Her, the keeper of the greatest prophecy The People had ever seen. Clearly, also connected to her powers most truly through her heart. That's the only way she could have pulled what she pulled with him tonight. *If she couldn't, he'd be dead.* It makes sense. What doesn't make sense is how much it hurts .

We'd never been serious. We've never even seen each other consistently, and there's always been others in between, for both of us. That is the nature of our worlds. We could go a full year without even laying eyes on each other, let alone merging bodies. But this is different. This feels final. Like he actually doesn't want anybody else anymore, and that's what hurts. The finality. It's okay. I mean, I never thought I'd marry the guy, but it is certainly unexpected. *Trust that, that's how magic works, Kit. You know this.* Deep down I know that to be true, and holding that thread of thought is what will anchor me through this next few hours.

Best we rip the scab straight off.

That is my last thought as we finally walk into the clearing, though as soon as I see it I know I just can't. This can't be the place I speak of our past affairs. This place smells like her. Ang, Queen of The People. Wife of King Jate. Mother of Ankhara and Skavari. The most compassionate woman I'd ever met. The lioness heart I am certain she has passed on to Ankhara. She is *here.* I can't always see spirits. It isn't my strongest gift, but I feel certain that if it was, this is the place I would most clearly see her. The way Ankhara's posture shifts tells me she knows too. She can feel her. She is so much more deeply connected than she gives herself credit for. It is my task to tap her into that and help her listen to it. Something tells me this is the perfect training ground. I can feel the protection Ang has placed on this space. We'll be safe here, even if only for a short time.

As for her and Noah, when the moment comes, I will tell her everything, and I will tell her that her first priority needs to be this mission – after that, should the two of them survive, I'll have nothing negative to say about it. Nothing negative at all.

Just a little slice of heartbreak. Nothing a good dalliance can't fix.

That is when I see her, weaving between the branches in the distance. Her long blonde hair glows under the light of the moon and the stars. She is dancing. Either she is yet to notice our appearance in the clearing or she welcomes it. Noah and Ankhara haven't noticed her yet; they are awkwardly sitting next to – but not too close to – each other. I, on the other hand, can't take my eyes off her. I'm hypnotised by the shimmer of her moon-white blonde hair, and the glistening of the tears on her face as she laughs. Not tears, sweat. Her whole body is shimmering with the efforts of her most graceful, playful dance.

I look at Noah and Ankhara, peeling my eyes away from her, and, satisfied that Noah will keep her safe while I'm distracted – and also that he needs a moment with her here – I wander off towards the figure in the distance. Her hands swirling in the air are like a flag to me, and I begin dancing my way over to her, to meet her in the most heartbreaking, pain-dissolving dance I've ever danced. Her eyes open to meet mine and her hands slide across the edges of my arms, and I am lost to her. The world shimmers in the distance, blurry in the wake of our bodies colliding in a dance that would have mystified any spectators. Blending into the trees as we move, we fall into a chase of sorts through the branches and night flowers, and that was that. *The most perfect way to recharge.* Dancing the lovers' dance, breathing nature in through every fibre of my being; this is where the Holy Temple truly came to heal. This is where my heartbreak can be broken open to a deeper love of me, from me, through the presence of another, breaking open to herself, to her own heart and her own sex. Only from that place, completely broken open to ourselves and completely alone in the oneness of our magical dance. Only from there can our bodies meet in a dance that shatters my perception of all versions of love I've ever tasted before. Only from that place, of completely dissolving in another's embrace, in the presence of the realisation of my own deepest love, can I see that the heartbreak I feel is not the heartbreak of him leaving; it is the heartbreak of me seeing that a love I'd thought I'd needed wasn't available for me to breathe anymore. It was the heartbreak of me, seeing that the love I truly needed was the love of another with the body and magic the same as mine. The love of another who could blend with the trees and dance in the moonlight, becoming the sun. Tears cool down my flushed cheeks as I realise, for the first time in this life, that I love women, and the woman that I'd love to love was a nymph, a magical creature of nature, just like I can finally, wholly see that I am. No longer will I see myself as outcast or different. I am magic, and that connects us all.

Thank you.

I weep a silent prayer to myself. To the version of me that had loved him when I hadn't seen I was enough to love for me. To the version of him that had allowed himself to die to the love that must have shattered his world when he met her, because their love had gifted me the freedom to find this, to find my own.

I pause, on the ground on all fours, hands melting into the reeds of the river. I take a deep breath and look up to see her looking at me, but she isn't there.

All I see is a reflection of my own tear-stained face on the river surface. A face framed by my moon-white blonde hair. I smile. I sigh. I look myself in the eyes and I know. The woman I'd needed to dance with was myself, a gift my magic had known I'd needed before I'd seen it for myself. I laugh and, slowly and gently, I lower myself into the grass I had just made love to myself in, and cry myself to sleep.

CHAPTER 22

NOAH

882 Hours Left

It's a relief to see Kit wander off to dance with herself. That's a thing she does whenever she needs to come home to her own heart. I am glad to know her well enough to know to leave her to that. I'm especially glad to know I was welcome to stay here with Ankhara, though I'm not sure that welcome extends from the Princess herself.

"Talk to me. Please." I feel a little pathetic but I need to know what she is thinking. "I'm sorry I was so awkward, I just... I'm sorry." I'm exasperated. This is not the way I felt around ladies. *Ever.* But Ankhara isn't just another lady I'm seeing around bootcamp. Nope. Ankhara is a love I've never known. The moment I met her my desire to know her like I knew myself had been overwhelming, but not in my usual, must-rip-her-clothes-off kind of way. The lust is there, and the attraction – more so than I've ever felt before – but this is different. She is different. I want all of her, and I want her to have all of me. I don't want to filter myself. In fact. I can't. There is no hiding. It's a waste of time. She can feel me just as I feel her, I sense it. I don't have words for it, but my body just knows. Ankhara is the woman I am here to love. It feels clearer than anything else I've ever known. *Also illegal in about fifty different ways.* The perfect love story. I sigh as she stands up and moves away from me, which somehow actually feels better than her awkwardly sitting just beyond arm's reach.

She puts her hands on her head and walks a few more steps away from me before throwing her hands in the air and turning around.

"I won't do it, Noah. I won't do it! I can't do it." She is throwing her arms up and down like a crazy rag doll and pacing back and forth, not looking anywhere but where her feet are going next. "I won't risk it, I won't risk her and I won't risk you."

She turns and looks me in the eyes, her own eyes a flavour of broken I've only ever seen once before, in Ang's eyes the same day she brought me right here to this very clearing. *Weird.* And still, I can't help but see her beauty. *She's so much more beautiful than.... Well, anyone.* It is true. I've never seen more raw beauty than Ankhara has allowed me to bear witness to in her. It is a tragic gift, one my heart is proud to have received and yet one my heart breaks in response to, knowing that maybe, just maybe if after all this we survived and she still feels for me as I do her, I'll get to be with her again. We'll get to dance through life together. It is only after my brief disappearance down fantasy lane that I register what she is actually saying. *She won't risk what?*

She continues to pace up and down the clearing in front of me, hands wiping her forehead and weaving together anxiously. As though she hears my thoughts, she responds: "Kit. You and Kit. You've been together. I can see it... and it's fine, I mean, why wouldn't you, she's stunning and badass, and you're.. Well, you're *you*. But I can't risk it. I can't risk loving you and hurting her and confusing you and surrendering me when we have this prophecy to fulfil. I won't be the reason this team falters. I can't be. I can't have my own selfishness be the reason the world loses their true nature." Tears stream down her face and she crumples to her knees in defeat. "I just can't."

"You won't." Ankhara and I both start. I hadn't even noticed Kit come out of the trees. *And you're meant to be protecting her Noah. Good job.*

Ankhara stares at her blankly, clearly surprised to have been overheard by Kit. She'd thought she was just freaking out in front of me, which I know would feel to her simply as if she was freaking out in front of herself, whether she was able to see that in this moment or not. Freaking out in front of Kit, however, is a bit further beyond her comfort zone.

"You are the reason we will be re-connected to our true nature, Ankhara," she continues. "You are the reason we will each maintain – and, for many, reawaken – our gifts. Your triumph will mean the world reconnecting with themselves and each other and the natural world in ways that have been forgotten for a millennia. Your love, your own heart, your own hedonism, it can't be ignored. Your desire cannot be a reason you distract yourself from this mission, it's simply the point. Your fight, *our* fight, is for desire to be lived and breathed and felt freely." Kit is calmer than ever, her eyes as clear as quartz crystal. "I will admit, your connection with Noah" – she looks at me with a soft loving gaze before turning back to Ankhara – "it took me by surprise, but it is not a pain I choose to hold. It is obvious to me the love the two of you share, and more and more the messages your mother and grandmother have graciously passed to me are becoming clearer."

Ankhara swallows and takes a deep breath. I can tell she is doing so intentionally, focussing on grounding herself and receiving what Kit is saying to her. She laces her fingers through the grass and holds the dirt underneath them, the tension dissipating from her body. It is a relief to my eyes.

"You don't understand what you're talking about." Ankhara shakes her head, gentle tears falling down her face, "I don't have any control over it. I am completely overcome by it. This... magic? This fire. This feeling that moves through my body... I don't know what to do with it. I don't know how to healthily manage it. I don't do relationships. I do hot, passionate, wild love and then I leave because I am consumed by it. Tonight I ran up trees and healed Noah's head, but what if I angrily directed that elsewhere? What if I had an argument with the two of you and I lost myself to the flames of my... tools? I mean, look at me guys, I'm a mess. I don't even know what to call it. I don't even know what this is." She gestures at me before continuing.

"I don't even know if I want to be here. If I'd choose this if I really had a choice, and I definitely don't know what I'll choose when I see my brother. What if what he triggers in me *isn't* the leader you all so think I am? What if I'm actually the evil twin and he's right? What if I'm really just this out-of-control freak and you've all got me wrong? None of you would know, none of you even know me."

It shocks me to my core to hear her speak like this. She is devastating and devastated, and she has no idea. She has no idea how powerful she is. No idea how easy this could be for her if only she gives herself permission for her powers to rise through herself. No idea how much I have already seen of her. That I have seen the anger and despair that lie below the surface confidence and bravado. You can't make love to a woman – I mean *really* make love to a woman – without seeing it all. She won't let you, and, by the sun and the moon, had we made love. *I've seen it all and I would still choose you in a heartbeat.*

She looks at me with shocked eyes and a smile and I know she heard me. *You couldn't hear my thoughts if we weren't connected this deeply.* She nods, but I can still see the disbelief in her eyes.

Kit moves slowly to sit by her side and speaks.

"Princess Ankhara, it is time you knew the truth of who you are." Ankhara looks up at her like the scared child she is inside, and the fierce warrior I know her to be begins to rise. "The whole truth. Noah, I believe you have something to show our Princess?"

It takes me a moment to realise she is talking about Ang. Of course. The tree. I nod and hold my hand out, hoping Annie will reach out and take it. My hopes are met, and she rises to her feet to follow me, Kit not far behind. I lead them straight to the same tree Ang had brought me to those many years ago. Placing my hand against the trunk, I whisper, "She said I'd know exactly what to do." I turn around and take a deep breath as I see the woman I love before me. Ang's daughter. There is a sense of disbelief that I quickly shake off as I can feel my love for her emanating from my core. It is as pure as pure could be.

"When I was 12, your mother brought me here. She showed me this place and, though I didn't understand it at the time, she said that one day I would, and I was to bring you here as soon as I knew to." Annie is smiling; a confused smile, yes, but a smile I'll take. "We climbed up here," I gesture to the tree, which seems grander than ever with the broad opening in its trunk, "and we sat on that large branch over the river speaking. She was so at home in this place. She used to visit me in the stables and I'd think to myself how much I would've loved to have had a mother like her in the village. She seemed so happy and she was always so kind to me; and then, on that one day, she brought me here. She didn't say much. We sat up there above the river and watched as the world went by, and I got this feeling. It was like she knew she wasn't going to be here soon, like she knew she wasn't going to see you again, and she was very sad. Very beautiful, and powerful, but sad. She told me there was a gift and messages here for you that only you could receive, and we'd have everything we needed to figure out the rest." That is it. I wish I had more specifics to share with her but that is all I have. That is everything.

"What did she think I was meant to do with that? She knew I would love you? Know you? How could she possibly know?" She is becoming agitated again, her voice growing louder and breath shorter the more she speaks. Kit intervenes and, not for the first time, I feel a relief in her being there. We really are a good team, even if as friends.

"Your mother was the greatest seer of our time. She knew most before it happened. She knew for sure her death was near. She knew Noah would be a gift for you. She knew I would be a friend to you. She told me so, many years ago when I first began my training. She told me so much so I was so excited to meet you, as though I was going to be meeting a best friend." She is smiling. As if finally she can speak freely as she always wanted to.

"What do I do?" Ankhara asks. Her capacity to absorb information and focus on the task at hand astounds me. She truly is a leader in ways she doesn't even notice.

"It's obvious isn't it?" Kit laughs. "Climb the tree!" Almost immediately, Annie moves to the tree and all but floats up to the opening her mother had gestured to so fondly, and, as soon as she puts her hands on the wood inside the trunk, everything changes.

The tone of the air shifts as Ankhara loses consciousness and falls into the tree. Panic sweeps over me and instinctively I leap at the tree to climb it, jumping again as Kit's hand lands firmly on my left shoulder, stopping me.

"Stop, Noah." She pulls me down to the wet muddy ground and holds a knife to me. "This is the way it has to be."

And just like that, my whole world shatters.

CHAPTER 23

ANKHARA

881 Hours Left

*N*ever have I ever seen anything as beautiful as the way this place glows. Golden light floods my vision from all directions, but not in a painful, it's-too-much kinda way, more in a delicious, graceful, lush kinda way. The sounds of birds chirping and water dancing through the earth as this magical river fills my heart with a sense of peace I don't think I've ever felt prior to this moment.

Wait...

That's not true. I'd felt like this before. This was how I used to feel in my mother's chamber. In my dreams with her that had been dreams but also hadn't. This is how they had felt. This level of magic and bliss and peace. A joy creeps over me, into places that have been holding darkness for days, years, forever. I can feel it pulsing through me, cracking layers off and leaking into me while stale pain falls back to the earth where it belongs, where it can dissolve. I am sitting in the opening of the most wonderful tree. Just listening, as the heart of the clearing beats around me. It is stunning just to listen to, but the view takes it to a new level. I look out at the ledge my legs are spread across. It is a huge bough, with perfect footing, begging me to step out onto it. Everything feels safe here. Dancing along a branch like this in my normal life would have filled me with an adrenalin I've come to know and love. This, however. This fills me with peace. Walking along this particular branch feels like following a long-lived calling of my heart. I look down to the river flowing underneath me, and feel pure curiosity. There isn't any fear here; this is a knowing I have, like I am living the expression of my heart, and nothing can taint it.

At least, I thought nothing else could enter this space.

"You are more beautiful than I ever imagined you'd grow to be."

The most gentle yet powerful voice I've ever heard speaks quietly behind me and my heart skips a beat. I know this voice. My body responds with relaxation and openness. I am excited. Tears fall from my eyes as I turn to see her.

"Mum!" I run to her and hug her so tight I think the both of us might pop, but we don't. We hold each other for what seems like would never be long enough. I feel her tears clammy in the hair tucked behind my right ear. I feel her heartbeat in my chest. I smell her. I get to actually, really smell her again. Her hands hold me in such a tight grip it feels as though nothing can ever break it. "Oh Mum, I wish you were here. I so, so wish you were here." I sobbed. I am sobbing now. It catches me by surprise. I've never really given myself permission to mourn her. I haven't even given myself permission to miss her, and in this moment, I feel it all. I feel a pain like a knife through my chest, and I let myself. In her arms, it all feels possible. It all feels feelable. So I feel. I melt into the knife in my chest as it melts in me, and its shape shifts. Slowly, into a stone. A heaviness after the sharpness. A heaviness, evidence of a long-term holding, and I stay with it. I let her hold me as I cry for the heaviness, and the heaviness becomes an anger that scares me. I resist it, try to let her go and push her away, but she doesn't let me.

"You have to feel it, sweetheart." I push even more against this soft kindness that feels like the biggest lie I've ever heard. I don't have to do anything. I hate being told what to do. I push myself away from her with everything I have.

But nothing is enough to push me out of her arms, so I give in. I give into the anger that has been stirring underneath my heart this en-

tire time. I let it rip through me. My whole body. The flames of my rage lick every edge of me and I feel even her sweat dripping down my back and between my breasts. Sweat everywhere. I am in a trauma sauna. Finally, after all this time, I am making my powerlessness known, and then I start shaking as it changes shape again. This time, I find myself afraid. Completely and utterly terrified. Of losing her. Of having already lost her. Of losing my parents. Of losing my blood family. Of meeting my brother. Of loving. Of loving Noah. Of failing and letting down a People that I haven't even met yet. Of everything.

I feel the fear of all those who begged me to fail, and all those who begged me not to. I feel the fear of those who prayed, hoping with all their hearts for an answer but projecting with all their pain the fear that I would fail. I feel the fear rooted and birthed in my body and the fear that has been thrown and implanted by others. I shake. I shake like a scared animal as she holds me, solidly and safely, like everything was going to be okay despite the impossibility of that in the moment. The shaking rips through my body in what feels like hours but must be only seconds, and then starts to slow. I tremble, and twitch, and slowly fall into a stillness, occasionally broken by the sobs of me. A grief I didn't know I'd been holding breaks through the open space in my chest, and each sob leaves a new space inside me as the old pours out. My legs begin to give up on me but she doesn't. She won't. She never will. I can feel it. And it gives me all the permission I need to truly let go. Her container is the most solid that ever was. Warrior shields built by the love of a mother, birthed with my own flesh through her womb. I realise they've always been there. These shields. This protection she had placed on me. It has never not been there. It has followed me and held me and given me permission to be me in moments I'd not known I'd needed it.

My tears and sobs become those of joy and I dance into it. I allow the joy of her love for me to move through every cell of my being. I can feel the miracle she saw me as. I can feel the awe with which she had *brought us into the world. Us. I can feel him. Skavari. For the first time I can really feel him. I can feel the same love she had for him. Different. But the same. Expressed differently, but feeling the same for her. She loved us with everything. Every fibre of who she was, was bathed in love for us. And for Jate. Our father. King of the People, a way I can feel she was always proud of seeing him. He is a kind and gentle leader. He cares for every citizen as if they were his own responsibility, perhaps too much. I can feel every flavour of love she had for my grandmother, and other family members I hadn't met yet. And... Noah. I can feel the way she loved Noah, like a son.* She knew. *I can feel her knowing of our forbidden love, and I can feel her blessing. I can feel the rebel in her that wanted me to change the rules she hadn't had the time too. She was so fun. Dad is the more traditional one. Classic light masculine father vibes, trying to make sure everyone was okay, and he'll do it to his deathbed. Mum, however, she was like me.* I'm like her. *It is a joy to relish.*

I pull away, not letting go, but wanting to laugh and look at her. The laughter in my eyes is mirrored back at me through hers.

"That's how it's done, babe. Promise me that no matter what, you'll feel it all. Promise me, Ankhara." I don't fully understand what she means, but I nod yes. "You have to feel it all. It's the only way back here." She points to my heart and leaves her hand on my chest, tears filling her eyes again.

"Why, Mum? I promise I'll try, but why? Why aren't you here? And how do you know? Noah... and Kit?" She smiles and nods at me. She knew everything. *"You knew it all before you even left. Why didn't you change it? Why didn't you make it so you could stay?"*

"It was my time, Ankhara. And it's not yet yours. You must listen to me." She gestures to me to come sit with her, and we rest together on the thicker end of the branch, still hanging over the water. I swallow nervously, still taking her in, and nod. Whatever she has to tell me, I can tell our time was limited and I don't want to waste a second here.

"Kit. She is fierce and she will guide you wisely. There will come a time when you will have to say no to her. It will challenge you. Say no anyway." She pauses and looks at me as if checking that I've registered this. Slowly, I nod again. This is all too weird and it was almost catching up with me. The edges of my vision are fading, my pulse quickening. She notices and speaks more urgently.

"We don't have much time, baby, but know that I'm with you and I'll always be here if you let yourself be here too. Noah - love him. Let your love happen. Let yourself happen. Move mountains and shake our world to make it happen. The love the two of you share will heal our people in more ways than we could ever know." Tears are spilling everywhere, and everything is starting to blur. I can't tell if they are my tears or hers, or what is real or what isn't. It is becoming hard to focus, but she keeps speaking.

"Kit will teach you how to follow your heart - let her. She'll help even the most crazy of revelation make sense. It will seem strange, but let her train you. Know I trained her for this."

She is really fading now. I reach out but I can't touch her. She is transparent, like a ghost.

She is a ghost.

"Ankhara!" Noah's voice is screaming in the distance and it makes me look away from her.

When I looked back, she is gone.

"No! Mum!" I panic. I'm not done yet. She wasn't finished. "Mum, come back! Please, I—"

"And look to the tree, my sweet daughter."

Her voice reappears but she does not. As though the tree is whispering, her final words come.

"Your magic is hidden there."

"Ankhara, please!" Noah's voice is getting louder. "Please come back to me."

He sounds desperate. Just like I'd sounded calling out to Mum. I don't want to leave her, but even the tree is dissolving.

I stand, tears streaming down my face, and climb back into the hollow in the trunk. I take a deep breath and whisper to myself.

"Everything is gonna be okay, Annie. You got this."

I sigh and sink into the darkness of the wooden hideaway. My heart starts racing, and a cold sweat starts to shimmer over my body.

✦

Ankhara, Ankhara, Ankhara....

I blink and shoot straight up, smashing my head on the inside of a tree.

"Oh thank God." I feel Noah's sigh of relief in the distance as he hears me *fuck* around trying to staunch the blood flowing out the gash I've just created in my forehead. That's when I realise.

"I dreamt of her." I whisper under my breath. "I actually dreamed of her."

"You what?" Noah must have heard me, and I can hear him clattering up the tree towards me. I bend forward and look down at him just as his hands reach the opening of the hollow. I see Kit behind him smiling, her weapon drawn. *Strange.*

But nothing shocks me more than the stunned look on Noah's face. Well. Nothing, that is, until I turn to what he is looking at, which is, surprisingly, not my bleeding face. All around me, in every corner of the hollow of this tree, are tiny, rainbow coloured orbs flying around and touching me excitedly. It takes my eyes a moment to adjust but they do, and that's when I see it. A drawer has appeared, opening itself in the trunk ahead of me, holding a letter and a satchel. Not only that, but the inner wall of the trunk itself is covered in what have to be runes. It is stunning, perhaps the most beautiful sight I've ever seen. So much so, that I don't even immediately open the letter. I just reach out and hold Noah's hand, staring at the runes that I lack even the beginning of understanding but feel in every fibre of my being.

My magic.

This tree holds my magic, and I've just opened the portal.

And I'd seen my mum...

This was a good day.

This was a fucking good day indeed.

I choke back some more tears and take a deep breath. For the first time in days I feel no hurry to be anywhere or do anything. All I want to do is lie back and stare at the magic of these golden runes and rainbow orbs, and that is exactly what I do.

CHAPTER 24

Kit

878 Hours Left

Three hours.

They've been staring at those orbs and runes for three hours.

I have been sitting in the clearing under the tree, watching the magic unfold for Ankhara, after nearly having to slit Noah's throat to let Ang speak to her, but time is not a gift we have. I'm beginning to feel anxious. They need rest, that much I know to be true, but I need to train Ankhara more, and I don't have the luxury of giving them a full day to stare at pretty magic things.

Pretty magic things are about to become their new normal, and, if I have anything to do with it, they are about to become the new normal. The world is ready and waiting to wake up to this, while they are up there in a hole in a tree having a cuddle and a nap.

I've never felt so *old* before. But I have a job to do. And they are holding things up.

"Alright lovebirds," I yell as I make my way towards the trunk, ready to pull 'em out by the legs if I need to. "It's about time we go to—" I poke my head through the opening and abruptly stop speaking.

There is Ankhara, sitting up and a couple pages deep into a letter, written in a hand I know too well to be her mother's.

I smile, seeing Noah passed out beside her and resting in her lap. This really is an epic tree. Even the tree itself is magic in the way it opens up so comfortably. Not to mention the runes glowing on all it's inner surface. I gesture to Ankhara with a finger on my lips and motion for her to come out.

Those runes are going to be etched into her brain forever, she doesn't need to sit with them any longer, but we can afford to let Noah sleep. He'd only slow down our training with his protective interruptions, so this is perfect. I walk Ankhara over to the other side of the clearing where we can speak without concern of waking our sleeping beauty.

"Thank you."

The sound of Ankhara's voice is different and it shocks me. She is... wiser. I can feel the age that only wisdom brings to one's voice. She is changed. And she is thanking me?

I look at her with a question mark in my eyebrows.

"For letting me receive that the way I needed to. You were right, and so was she. My mother... I needed to find it for myself. I don't know that I even would have come here if any of you had told me the whole truth, and I think if Noah knew... well. I wouldn't have come here." She laughs as she says the last few words. I laugh too. She is right, he would have told her. He was like that. No secrets if he can do anything about it.

"You're welcome." I half bow to her. Then I laugh, "And you're right. He would have squawked."

We share the kind of laughter only lifelong friends share. The kind of laughter that reaches a depth that only exists when you've been in each other's pain. We'd both lost a mother when Ang had died, and we'd both gained a sister when Ankhara had come home. I am grateful for her presence, more than she knows.

"We've got to get you ready." I say, matter-of-factly.

"I know where to go."

Okay, you win. Wasn't expecting that.

"Like I know where, but I don't know where. And it doesn't make sense."

"Okay, give me a little bit more."

She sighs and speaks. "I know what it feels like. And I know what it looks like. A cave, with grey-orange walls, and I can see the dragon. I can *feel* her. How's that by the way. A female dragon. Is that even possible that I could know that? I mean, of course it isn't. But I do. I know it."

I smile.

She is better at this than I'd even expected. *Of course she is, she's the Princess. She was born for this.*

"It's your intuition. You're more connected than you think," I say to her with a smirk and a giggle. This magic excites me more than anything.

Now it is her turn to look at me with a question in her eyes. To her credit, she is nodding, and I can see a smile creeping in.

She's going to love this.

"Okay, Princess, let me tell you a little story about how you are connected to all time and space." There it is. Her full smile.

This is going to be fun.

CHAPTER 25

ANKHARA

878 Hours Left

"Okay, Princess, let me tell you a little story about how you are connected to all time and space." Kit speaks with a smug joy spread across her face. Joy. She is enjoying this. It's nice to see her like that. Not to mention, so am I.

This was going to be fun. I can sense it in my chest. I smiled. A real, full smile, for the first time in... maybe since I arrived in this place. I still don't even know what to call our 'world'.

"You, my friend, are an expression of pure creative spirit. Your very essence has unique qualities, and I bet you know them. I bet they're familiar. Perhaps hiding in plain sight. These are your gifts, your talents, your greatness. This is your flavour of magic. The flavour of joy and charisma and sass that you bring the world. You dig me?"

Holy moly am I digging her. I can feel her words vibrating through me. They resonate with my very essence, almost ironically.

"I dig it, but I'm not sure why that makes me so special. Aren't we all like that? Isn't that what yogis are talking about when they're vibing about their soul tribe?" I get it, for sure. What I don't get is the relevance to our mission. Quest. Prophecy. Whatever we are calling it.

"Well, let me get there. That's true in part, yes. We all have a genius creative spirit. We all have a magical essence that flows through us if we let it. And we all require a vehicle for it to flow through. You see, we can't all just be orbs of energy floating about, nothing would ever happen around here. There wouldn't be any point. So created were our bodies and minds, which, yes, can act upon genius instructions from our essence and, yes, perform miracles every day. I mean, you think about wiggling your finger and it wriggles; you don't think about breathing or your heart beating and that happens all by itself."

She continues to make good points, and it continues to ring true, so I hold my usually very interruptive tongue, and she goes on.

"We need that. We need a vehicle for our genius to pass through, but somewhere along the way people kept forgetting. More and more people relied on creations of the mind, creations from the vehicle, not from essence. As a result, people began to forget more and more their connection to their true nature and purpose. The spirit was forgotten. That natural essence that flowed through our genius – it was forgotten. It was undervalued and played down to be small. It was celebrated only in incomplete ways. Ways that weren't fully connected to the heart, and so, slowly but surely, magic became a myth. People forgot. Humans the most, but even the witches' lights were dimmed. So many stories and dogmas of magic not being real, planted seeds of doubt and numbness that grew so large and uncomfortable, magic was left in the category of tomfoolery and child's play.

"This is our people's greatest pain. Well, my people. I'm a nymph, Ankhara. A spirit of the forest and here, a spirit of the river too. I belong to the family of elementals that stayed connected. We didn't forget. Fairies. Dragons. Nymphs. Flowers.

We didn't forget. We stayed connected to each other. We kept listening, and so we kept our magic. Humans, on the other hand, forgot us and came to believe we weren't real."

Kit sighs. A sadness runs through her body and she looks at the ground.

"That was when we became invisible to you and humankind. You see, your focus creates your reality. Where you direct your flow of energy, and the beliefs in which you place the most power, become your reality. Thoughts of magic not being real, create emotion around magic not being real, which drives action around magic not being real, and *voila*, elemental spirits become invisible to the naked human eye."

I am shocked and yet not at all surprised as I sit listening to her. I don't even notice that I've sat down. I mean, it makes sense and I can feel it. I think that's why it doesn't completely surprise me. I can feel the truth of what she is saying in my being. Like it is familiar, even though it couldn't possibly be. *Well actually, genius, if you're connected to all time and space, it IS familiar.* I laugh at myself, though I still have questions.

"And what about witches? Why don't they remember magic like you do?"

She looks me in the eyes and responds with words that send shivers down my spine.

"Fear, Ankhara. They don't remember because of fear. Over the centuries, many different stories have been told – not a few of them about the predictions concerning you – and despite rituals and traditions clinging to family trees, the fear became louder than the calling of The People's hearts, and so their magic began to fade. They still see us, unlike the humans, but they're different. They don't... glow. They're dulled down to who they are and, just quietly, I dunno if you noticed, but they're miserable. Bless your parents and the ancestors of your royal family, they tried. Your mother's gifts alone were power-ful evidence of that, but one family is not enough, even if they are the leaders. Not with the prophecy about you and Skavari. The People were teetering on the edge of fear long before you were born. Your birth – and then your death – well, that tipped them over the edge. Ankhara, this is what your mother died for. To protect this knowing. I know she wrote you letters, but I'd hazard a guess that if you read all that she left you, you'd find she equipped you with the tools not only to remember, but to harness your gifts, because you, our fierce, sassy Princess, you are the only hope of magic coming back."

You are the only hope. Her words ring around my skull like a voice echoing in an empty football stadium. LOUD. No pressure.

"How is it all on me? If we all have gifts and magic, if we all have our own version of superpowers, how is it that I'm the one that has to undertake all this ridiculousness?" She almost looks offended that I've called it that. "Come on, Kit. A royal witch pretending to be human, not that she knows it, only so that she can come back to the world of half-magic and find out she has an evil twin brother, a dead mother, a depressed 'world on his shoulders' father, a kickass grandmother that I'm pretty sure is going to die soon if she hasn't already, and a prophecy to fulfil a quest of retrieving a dagger from a dragon's heart? I mean. It's not exactly Tolkien, but it isn't exactly original either."

This time she actually laughs. Like, head back, eyes rolling, holding her belly kinda laughed. The kind of laugh you can't help but laugh at.

"Come on, I'm serious!" I choke at her between belly rum-bles and giggles. "How is this my job?"

"Ahhh, Ankhara, you are such a gift to have home. I didn't think it was possible to miss someone you haven't officially 'met', but I missed you. I've waited my whole life to laugh with you."

This woman has a way of punching me in the heart with her words, nicely. *I've never realised how loudly the truth rung,*

"I don't know how, but I think I missed you too." I say back to her, enjoying the twinkle in her eye.

CHAPTER 26

NOAH

874 Hours Left

"And then she went on to tell me that we each had an inherent soul tension, that, when harnessed, would guide us on our personal holy mission. Or something like that. Honestly by this point my brain had reached my new information capacity, and she said she'd give me my next lesson after food and movement."

Listening to her speak is a magic I have never before known. I listen as I prepare stew over a fire I've made, stirring a number of plants Kit retrieved from the forest with the flesh and bones of a woodland animal she says had given itself over to the cause. I am thankful. Annie is telling me about her conversation with Kit, which I missed one hundred per cent of while I slept in Ang's magical river tree. She's also told me about the dream I had inadvertently pulled her out of, and it pains me that my fear robbed her of more precious time with her mother. It also sounds as though Ang knew that would happen, *of course*, and Annie isn't mad. Regardless, I'm going to need to accept my actions as they were and focus on moving forward. Annie is buzzing. I can't tell if she notices or not, but her skin is glowing with the force of her power, now fully awakened and pulsing inside her body.

"How are you feeling?" I am excited for her, for all that is moving through her, and I can also *feel* all that is moving through her. Intense would be an understatement.

She closes her eyes and takes a deep breath to answer, squishing her face up the way she does when she tries to focus on something.

"I feel.... Held. I feel like I'm going to be able to respond when he comes. When Skavari comes, I feel like I'm going to know what to do. I feel like... My mother... Mum. She knew, and now, I'm beginning to know. Not intellectually, I mean, from that perspective I feel ridiculous and confused; but in my body – more in my being – I feel the familiarity of my heart's mission, and like if I tried, I could almost *hear* it." She has a habit of sharing her thoughts rather than feelings. She also has a habit of catching herself.

"Grounded. I feel grounded. Connected. Spirited. Hopeful. Afraid. I still feel afraid, though now my fear is laced with hope it doesn't seem so bad. Now my fear is swimming in the familiarity of my heart, and I can feel it. I can *feel* where we are going. I don't know what it looks like or how we get there. But I can *feel* it. Like I'm connected to a version of reality where all my dreams come true, and with it, so do yours. And Kit's. And my father's. And, well, everyone should they so choose."

Her eyes trail off into the distance with her thoughts.

She really gets it. It's really her. Sometimes I have these moments of wondering if this is really going to work out, if she is really going to be able to re-awaken and grasp and harness a whole new reality in such a short time. A whole new world. A world where magic is *real*. And yet this happens every time she meets a new challenge. She rises to it like a remembering. Every time. She feels her fear. She feels her uncertainty. She feels the instability of it all and now even more so with the magic, and she chooses it anyway. Every single time, she chooses the calling of her heart.

And every single time, I'll choose her.

For the first time in a long time I have the feeling that maybe everything will actually be okay. In our little oasis, here in the clearing, nothing can touch us in any harmful way. Part of me wants to stay here forever, living off the earth and melting into Annie more and more each day. An even bigger part of me, however, is ready to save the world with her.

CHAPTER 27

ANKHARA

871 Hours Left

I am alone. For the first time in such a long time I am really, truly very alone. Kneeling in the centre of a clearing I don't recognise. Lost, in a world I've never called home. And, beyond the spirits of the trees and the birds, I am alone. I can hear birds tweeting in the near distance, and I start humming a melody in response. It soon moves into a tune.

Da dum da dum da dee...

It is self soothing, and from what I can tell the birds enjoyed it too. I don't feel alone when I connect with them, even though in reality I am. Noah is gone. Kit is nowhere to be found. All that is left is me, and the little rucksack I've been left with. How thoughtful. *I sigh. I've gone into my head now and that was the end of my tune. I lie back on the grass, catching my breath and a glimpse of the tree-filtered sky before closing my eyes and allowing my heart to break.*

Alone.

I am completely and utterly alone with no direction or way to go. I have no idea what to do. No idea where Noah or Kit are. I don't even know if they are alive.

Darkness sweeps over me and fear fills my body. I can feel a presence. Like I am no longer alone in the clearing, and I still feel such an emptiness in my heart. It is like a gaping hole has been carved out of me. When Noah left. Then when Kit left. And, finally, when I left my-

self and gave in to lying here. I can feel the surrender oozing through my chest, and this presence, though it frightens me, just gives me the excuse to follow through on the giving up.

I kneel. Getting up to my knees isn't as hard as I thought it would be. I can taste the end, it's right here. Tears streaming down my face. Loneliness tearing through my body. I open my arms and tilt my head back until I almost fall. And I cry. The biggest sobs I've ever allowed myself to sob. I howl. For the loss of my first family, and the loss of my second. For the pain of my brother, and birth father, and the missing of a life with grandparents. For the love I had felt and broken for Noah. And for the sister I'd found and lost in Kit. I cry and howl and sob for it all, until I can't take anymore and I scream.

"JUST KILL ME!" I scream so intensely it is like I can't breathe. "I'VE HAD IT! I'VE DONE IT! I'VE FAILED! JUST KILL MEEEE!"

It is a giving up of my spirit. I can't take one more breath of pain. No more.

"Please just make it stop..." my voice trails off as I whisper and bow my head, slumping forward in defeat.

I hear the soft, powerful footsteps of the presence entering the clearing before me. I smell the familiar scent of blueberries and grass. And I looked up just in time to see—

I jolt into wakefulness. Surprised to find Noah's arm draped over me. He nestles into his sleep as I disturb him with my movements. My heart rate is peaking. Blue eyes. All I can remember from the end of my dream is blue eyes and the smell of blueberries and grass. *Why had that awakened me?* I orient myself, looking around the clearing. Kit is on watch and Noah is deep enough in his sleep to tell me it is definitely my turn to watch over camp so the two of them can rest. I need rest too, but I also don't. I can feel my magic constantly recharging me. A source they haven't yet tapped into. A source I know I have to share with them when the time comes, but not a source I know how to share. *I'm pretty sure that would have been more use-ful than learning about plants in biology.* I shake off the thoughts of my old world. They aren't real anymore. None of it seems real. It all feels like escapism and illusion, hiding the truth of the real world from me. Concealing from me the potential of who I could truly become if only someone reminded me of the keys to unlock myself. A sadness fills my chest as the thought of Ang – *Mum* – enters my mind and I feel the pang of never hav-ing lived life with the education of her. *She would have taught me everything she'd known.*

"And she still will," I remind myself, forgetting to be mind-ful of not waking Noah by talking to myself. I slither my way out, not so stealthily, from underneath him and make my way over to Kit. Unsurprisingly, she speaks to me before there is any way she could have seen me coming.

"I should have known you'd never let us watch all night." She turns and smiles at me. That had been the plan, much to my disgust. That they'd trade places and I'd sleep through. I'd need as much rest as I could muster, they'd insisted, like they knew I'd be running the show alone at some point. The secret glances they kept making towards each other over dinner told me there was something they were afraid of mentioning but, unlike my usual self, I'd ignored it. I've had enough surprises for a lifetime this last week. Another not-very-fun looking sur-prise can wait.

"I'm not a Princess-y kind of Princess. You know that." She laughs and shakes her head.

"No one could know that better than me, I promise you." She has a sparkling glint in her eyes that holds such a familiar-ity that my breath deepens. "There's not a lot happening out here. The trees are calm. The birds are sleeping. Come. Sit for a minute."

I sit beside her, confused as to why she'd only invite me for a minute. Then I realise. She's been sitting in different places all around camp. As I trace the marks left in the grass by her backside, I see a circle around the clearing. Noah too, had moved around. His dents were deeper. *He has such a great ass.* My eyes dreamily wander over to him as I feel the fire stir in my loins. It has been days since he'd entered me. Longer still since I've felt the full sweetness of his bliss roll through me, and even though I haven't danced or loved him in that way for very long, I miss it. I long for him. Even my heart does, which is unfamiliar. This tugging in my chest makes me want to know every inch of him. That makes me want to breathe only with him.

"A-hem!" Kit coughs, noticing how swept away by him I've become. "You really are a beautiful fit, you and him."

I gasp, eyes widely staring at her. I'm surprised to hear her speak so calmly of my love for him, knowing that hers had so recently been the same.

"The way you look at him. The way he cares for you... he cared for me, sure, but never like that. You two are a match like I've only ever seen in your parents. It's beyond choosing. You'll find a way to be together. If anyone can change the laws of our world, it's Ang's daughter. If anyone can remind our people how to truly respect and love each other, it'll be you, Ankhara."

She speaks with such sincerity it pierces my heart. Again, Kit with the heart and throat punches. How she does it so gracefully I'll never know, but I am thankful. It is the first reassurance I've gained from anyone in the living world. From anyone in the world who knows of the intricacies I am only really now coming to see.

"Thank you." I don't really need to say it but it is all I have. Anything else would be a forceful push for something more, something that doesn't really need to be spoken. *I hope so.* I hope she is right. The beige version of me tells me this love is too vibrant and juicy to be anything I deserve to fight for, but my heart shares a different tale, and that was the one I was going to listen to.

"If you really want to keep watch, you'll—"

"I do." I cut her off. Her eyes are hanging out of her head and even though I know she'd move until she fell, I don't want her to. "I'll move around the clearing."

She looks at me with a question mark on her face. She had barely moved her arm to point when I cut her off.

"Oh, come on, I'd recognise those ass dents anywhere." I smirk at her cheekily, and she digs it.

"Of course. Only you." She nods and rises, placing a hand on my shoulder and looking me in the eye at a crouch before standing and walking to her bedroll. She hadn't needed to say it. Clear as day I've received her instruction through her eyes, almost as if I could hear her voice in my mind. *Focus.*

It is all I need. I turned my attention back to the trees of the forest before me, hearing Kit tuck herself away to sleep in the presence of the fire behind me. I can also hear the faint snores and sniffles of Noah and I smile. It is a small detail but a great comfort here in the middle of a forest I don't really know, to hear him breathe so deeply.

In the trees I feel a faint spark of hope. Like one day I'll look into them and see this place as mine. Not *mine* but me. A place I belong. A place I can connect to. *A place connected with my mother.* There isn't really anything to see other than tree trunks and darkness, and I stay, slowly moving my seat around the clearing in random directions and order, until I feel the dark power of a presence sweep over me.

I freeze, remembering. *I remember you.* I speak with my mind, wondering if she or it will hear me, just as Noah had come to. I don't know how, but I feel the presence is a she, and that she could hear me.

Come make yourself known to me, I think to 'it'.

I am afraid and curious. *Curiosity killed the fucking cat, you idiot.* Again with the inner dialogue abusing the spark of curiosity still trying to exist in me, louder than ever after the week I've just had with its ample evidence of curiosity being a bad and unwelcome thing. *Shut up, Megan.* I speak to myself. It feels somewhat satisfactory calling the old voices by her old name... my old name. They aren't really me anyway, just like she'd never been.

I'm not afraid to see you. It is true. I am, however, afraid of what she'll do to me *once* I've seen her.

A rustling sound in the trees up to my left gives me the hope of her imminent arrival, and just as I hear the deep thud of something landing down on the earth from the trees above, Noah wakes and notices my missing body.

"Ankhara!"

I scowl. When is this boy going to realise I can take care of myself, and will? I look over to him and, seeing the concern in his face, I soften. That *boy* loves me so much he can't breathe at the thought something might happen to me. He is darting over to Kit so I stop him before he wakes her unnecessarily.

"Over here, Noah, I'm fine. Look. Just... Shh, I'm trying to..." I turn back to the darkness between the trees but there is no sign of anything. The trees rustle gently in the breeze and the scent of blueberries and earth lingers, but she, my mysterious tree-climbing friend, is nowhere to be seen.

"What is it?" Noah arrives at my side, ever the silent and fierce warrior, standing at the ready for a surprise battle.

"Never mind. I thought I saw something but... I must be seeing things in the dark." I know I wasn't, but I don't feel ready to share with him yet. Could I really be imagining it, or was I almost about to meet the creature from my dreams just now? Dream walking. I know I do it, but I don't know the ins and outs of it. I wonder if there is anything in my mum's letter that might explain to me in greater detail what that gift is capable of. The spirit of this *she*, though powerful and terrifying, felt so familiar to me that I just know I don't have to be afraid of her. Even if she was here to do something to me, which feels true, I don't believe she was going to hurt me. I just sense this, knowing that it is going to be something uncomfortable for me. Another layer being stripped back to reveal a power of my own that I'd long forgotten. I sigh and lean into Noah as he sits beside me. "I'm glad you're here."

His body on mine is a sweet relief, regardless of what he'd potentially interrupted. We sit there for what seems like hours, until the sun slowly starts to lighten the sky on the horizon and the birds begin to wake with their songs. The eyes I'd seen in my dream bounce around my head the entire time. They remind me of the eyes of a cat Josie used to have. A seemingly sweet but fiercely temperamental creature that cat had been, my God.

That's when it strikes me. Amidst the guilt of having left my best friend in what was undoubtedly the shittest time of her life, the memory of her once-annoying cat floods my brain with the strangest idea.

"Noah, can I ask you something?" He looks at me with a happiness in his eye he only ever has for me.

"Of course. Though I can only maybe answer." Ever the gentleman. He makes my heart smile. I can see straight through to the part of him that is afraid he won't be able to help me. That all his training will have been for nothing if he lets me down.

But I'm not afraid of that at all. Right now, I am simply curious about the idea that has just occurred to me.

"Are spirit animals a thing? Like, they're obviously a thing. But here... are they a *real* thing?"

"I've always kinda hoped so. Horses are like that for me. Whenever I need some guidance, I never fail to receive it when I'm in the presence of those beautiful creatures. I think your mum was the same. She always loved coming down to see the horses, but every single time she came, so did a little black cat. Why do you ask?"

That was all the confirmation I needed. "No reason, really, just a strange thought I was having." I don't know why I lie to him, but it is like I just have to. Like this is a secret I want to keep to me, myself, until I've really figured it out. This could well be the only secret I have left, and I am going to figure it out myself.

He laughs and shrugs his shoulders as he stands and dusts himself off.

"Come on. Kit will be up soon, and she'll have you straight into training." He holds his hand out to me and helps me up. He is right. The day has come. My spirit animal quest is going to have to go in the 'worry about it later' box.

"Time for the most important meal of the day." I move so close to him when I speak I almost convince myself I'll have him for breakfast, and I like it. Judging from his body's response to mine, he likes it too. I wish there was time and space for me to rip his clothes off and climb onto him, but there isn't, so I kiss him on the cheek, nibble his ear, and run back to camp to start the fire for breakfast.

CHAPTER 28

ANKHARA

3 Days Later – 799 Hours Left

This is completely ridiculous.

That is all I could think as we start walking, literally in the direction I'd just *made up* that we should go in. I made it up. I don't know where we are meant to go. I don't know anything about this land at all, let alone how to find the only remaining dragon our people know of in this world. It is a ridiculous notion. That some part of me will somehow *know* just because it is my destiny. Just because some stupid light-up stupid crystal ball said so.

I stomp along the path with a stick I'd picked up as a brilliant staff I could slam and drag along the ground as we went.

"Is that really necessary?" Kit looks like she's ready to kill me. Like *I* am the crazy one.

I'm the one that just got kidnapped by a bunch of magical lunatics, Kit. Yes. It is necessary. Fuck's sake.

I look up at her and for a moment I'm glad looks can't kill. At least. If that was a superpower I had, I'm glad I haven't unlocked it yet. I am pissed, but I'm not ready to murder her.

"Is following the yellow brick road to fucking nowhere necessary?" I give such a bite to my words I even surprise myself. This is a tone I generally reserved for my parents and teachers on my bad days, yet here I am, throwing my attitude at this near stranger. *Come on, Ankhara, she's your sister and friend.* I don't care. I can hear this perspective telling me spiritual shit. Telling me to be open. Telling me to be loving and take some responsibility for my own emotions, but it's not as loud as what my nervous system is feeling. I am fuming at the ridiculousness of it, and pissed at the responsibility.

Make it up they'd said. *It'll be fun*, they'd said. Fuck that. I'm the one that is going to have to pay penance with my guilt if something happens to them. I'm the one expected to pull miracles out of my ass because I was born a twin witch to stupid people who forgot how to be decent fucking connected people. How is this my job? How is this my responsibility? I never wanted this. I never wanted to lead. I want to fuck. I want to throw Noah against the dirt and fuck my anger out. I want to fuck until I crumble into him. I want him to hold me. I want him to be allowed to touch me in the ways I so desperately need to be touched. I want Kit to leave. To give me some space to breathe. Really, I just want to breathe, and I know his cock is a gateway to that. I know, if I could just give myself permission to ride him, that he would touch me in all the places I need God to touch. I know, and yet I stumble down the path like a toddler battling with a stick that is too big for my own wrist torque. It hurts. In more ways than one. And I can feel Noah's infuriating, caring glance scraping against my back as we go.

Part of me is blown away by their faith in a cool way. Part of me is impressed. Inspired even, that they have such faith, such trust in me that they'll follow what I made up just because they believe my soul will guide us.

Part of me.

The most part is infuriated by the stupidity of it.

But they are right. We don't have anything else to go off. There isn't a map. It isn't like my bloody ancestors had been intelligent enough to write a note saying "By the way, the dragon we stuck a dagger in that you're gonna have to find in a thousand years is dot dot dot insert location". That would be too fucking genius. Or too simple. Or something.

I sigh.

This hatred isn't going to get you anywhere.

The voices in my head are confusing. Sometimes genius. Sometimes cruel. Always onto something. Not always right, but this one is. This *wasn't* going to get me anywhere.

I stop walking, silently hoping that Kit will keep going and Noah will know exactly what to say.

"What's your vision?"

Not what I'd expected but I'll play.

"My what?" I have no idea what he is talking about. All I can see in front of me is Kit's grey green muddy boots and fresh earth I plan to pummel my stick into.

"Your vision. Of where you're going. Of what you're aiming for."

It is a good question and it throws me. I haven't once stopped to consider what I actually *want* to happen. Do I *want* to 'defeat' my brother in a battle and find a dagger in a dragon and save the world it's magic? No. Well. Not that I know of.

"Who would want this? I don't *want* this, Noah. I've been thrown this. This... this mission. Prophecy. Whatever it is. How am I meant to have a vision of fighting my brother and pulling a dagger out of a dragon's heart that will probably, let's be reasonable, be so pissed off it was daggered in the first place that if by some miracle it does wake up again it will probably kill me immediately? How am I meant to get around that?"

He laughs. He actually laughs at me.

"I'm not talking about all of that." I stare at him blankly.

They're actually all crazy and I need to get myself out of here.

"I mean what you'd love, not your skewed version of your current reality."

Oh.

He says it with a gentleness that reaches my heart in ways that soften me and prevent me from staying mad. Only he can do that. And mum. My adoptive mother used to do that when I was mad. *I'd love to see my family again.*

"You really want me to answer that honestly?" I look at him, kinda afraid he'll say yes and I'll have to go there. I don't really want to. I'm afraid of what I'll find.

He nods and smiles and places his hand on my heart. His fingers brush over my breasts and my whole body tingles in response to his touch. I melt. Of course he does. He wants all of me. I can feel it as deeply as I feel how much I want him.

"You. I'd love you. I'd love to lock myself in a tower with you and make love to you until I couldn't walk anymore. I'd love to taste every corner of you and drink every flavour... and then, only then, when I've tasted it all and satiated my thirst for us, I'd like to meet this family. This royal family I'm supposed to save... I'd like to meet them properly, to really know them. And I'd like to find my parents. And maybe it's selfish but I just can't shake this desire I have for you." He is looking at me with the least judgemental eyes I've ever seen. His eyes ooze safety, and I forget about Kit and keep going. "I'd like to have a brother. Like. To actually have a brother. To meet him, and have a relationship with a brother who's missed me and longed for me my whole life. I'd like to meet my mother and father for real, as my mother and father, not as my dead mother and a loyal King. I'd like to be free."

He nods. "And when you've had all of that, and let everything else go, what would you love?"

I close my eyes and take a breath. I want to find the answer to this in my heart. I can feel it right there in my middle, just waiting for a voice to wriggle it out.

"I'd love to live in a world where magic is real." I really mean it, and I almost can't believe the words are coming out of my mouth. "I'd love to remind the world that their own innate wisdom breathes inside them so purely all they have to do is choose it for themselves and they'll have it. I'd love to live a life loving you, and have children one day. To have an ecstatic birth and redefine the world's meaning of orgasm. I'd love to normalise – no, *celebrate* – my pleasure and remind people that hedonism and magic aren't separate and aren't black. That they can be, but the blackest magic that exists is the suppressed magic that leaks out and rapes and tortures as it tries to breathe. I'd love to burn the systems that are burning our people, and I'd love to not so politely tell a certain few people in our society to shove some shit straight back up their ass and fuck off because what they've created is such disconnection. I'd like to dismantle the leadership of our people and create a new legacy to lead by. I'd like to eliminate arranged marriage and laws that bind love and fear that's written by ancient disciples. I'd replace it all with love and dance in the streets with the villagers' children and paint my face all sorts of colours with our kids and remind people that status isn't what matters, our nature is. I'd like to teach natural magic in school, to empower our children to be their own greatest teachers, healers, lovers and friends. I'd like to remind adults to play and allow children to teach us. I'd love to lead our people down a path of truth and wisdom that is guided primarily by their own free will. And you."

He is looking at me with the kind of pride I'd thought was reserved for the most doting of mothers. He has tears in his eyes, and knowing in his body. He feels so grounded and whole in that moment I want to stay here forever.

"You, Noah. I want it all to start and end with you."

He kisses me and knocks the air straight out of my body as he pushes me up against a tree. My rucksack slides off my body and I taste iron on my lips where he's bitten me. I bite him back and slip my fingers up his shirt to dig them into his body. I want him like I've never wanted anything before and I don't think anything can stop me. I don't care. I don't want it to. I want more. It is like I can't press myself into him enough and the bulge in his pants tells me he feels the same. I growl. Half because my animalistic desires are so alive I can't stop it and half because I realise I can't take my pants off with these ridiculous boots still on. I don't care. I'm going to try anyway. I undo my button on my pants and start ripping the drawstring open when I am interrupted and jerked away from Noah by a cough that damn near scares the life out of him.

Kit is standing just two metres away from us, arms crossed over her body, a smirk bigger than her face plastered all over it.

"Feeling better I see, Princess?"

I've not caught my breath yet, but looking at the appalled expression on Noah's face I suddenly throw my head back and laugh. I can't help it, he is hilarious. The most gentlemanly gentleman had completely forgotten we weren't alone. He had been completely swept up in the moment, as I had. The difference being I would have happily made love right then and there with Kit watching. The whole world can watch for all I care. Maybe they'll learn a thing or two about true connection if they did. Noah on the other hand... I think this may be his worst nightmare. He's flustered, throwing his hands everywhere trying to figure out what to do with his erection and how to bring his face back to a normal colour. It isn't happening. He's as red as a poppy.

"I'm not the only one."

I take one last indulgent look at Noah before doing up my pants and walking away. On one hand I am enlivened from his touch and having been caught in the almost-act. On the other, I'm disheartened. A sadness creeps over my heart that we've been interrupted yet again. Almost as though every time we succumb to the tempted bliss of one another something pulls us out. *At least this time it wasn't Hoods or danger.* I sigh and glance back at him.

His face has calmed down to its usual hue and his pants had softened out by the look of it. His heart feels less uncertain than mine, more reassured. He looks at me and smiles. *Our time will come.*

It is as though I actually hear the words in my mind. As though his voice actually intentionally responds to what I'd *thought* to myself just moments earlier.

Did you seriously just respond to my thoughts? I stare at him as I ask my internal question, begging him to answer me and prove I'm not being crazy at that a moment.

But he doesn't. Not in the way I thought he would. He laughs and shrugs, dusting himself off and shaking his head at the ground before walking back up to me.

A little deflated, I shake my head as if to throw the thought off. It isn't the wildest thing to have happened these past few days, but it might have been the most comforting had it been true. I comfort myself in the smell of him lingering on my clothes. Closing my eyes to breathe him in one last time before I keep walking, I am interrupted in my moment alone with the thought of him for a moment in time with the real him. He gently places his hand on my cheek, and tilts my head as he kisses my cheek and my chin.

"Yes, I did."

His whisper in my ear does more than send shivers down my spine. His every breath on my skin awakens the sacred fires within me, and I feel as though every time we kiss another of my gifts, another layer of my superpowers, is opened to me. It is as though every time I give myself permission to indulge in my love of him, another piece of my power switches on. Another part of my puzzle clicks together, and I like it. I like noticing it. I also like when he plays with me, and I play back.

I lean into his face, close enough to breathe him in, barely refraining from kissing, and look him in the eye to penetrate him with my thoughts.

The first opportunity I have to fill myself with you, I will love you for breakfast, lunch and dinner.

He gulps in a 'shit, I got the girl' kinda way. And I wink at him and nod. Because, yes, he got the girl. And the sooner I get this bloody dagger, the sooner I can go home and safely make being in love official.

CHAPTER 29

KIT

799 Hours Left

I'd never imagined that witnessing someone with an ex-lover of mine would be so amusing, but I love it. I love the way Noah squirms under the inhibitions of rank and I love the way Ankhara toys with him with her no fucks given humour. It is a match made for my entertainment. This terrain is boring. Normally I'd love the monotonous rhythm of it, but in the current circumstances I worry we'll be hypnotised and miss something – if something comes. I feel on edge and, as each step takes me further into the forest, I lean more and more into who I have to be to hold this vision. To take this mission to its actualisation I have to be the fear-filled warrior who chose it anyway, and I don't know what that looks like. *That's what's scary about it.*

I look back over my shoulder to see Ankhara has reclaimed her sooky stick, this time utilising it as a hiking tool.

"Nice to see you embracing the circumstances, Princess."

"I thought you weren't going to call me that anymore?" She scowls back at me and I laugh.

"I wasn't, but if you keep throwing tantrums like that, Princess is going to apply."

She laughs with me.

"Touché. I'm awful. A total princess brat. Perhaps I require some punishment?" She laughs more, turning around to wink at Noah. That is the tipping point. We all lose it, cackling in the woods about a lot of nothing. Really it just feels like a sweet relief. We've been in such intense energy, it's nice to relax a little.

That is about to end.

I feel myself freeze in my body as the wind sweeps over a cold chill and goosebumps sing down my back and up my arms. I lift my right forearm to eye level to see the hair standing on the tips at the end of my shivers, and I gulp. My heart sinks, and I close my eyes to gather my connection. The trees are panicking, talking to each other. They can feel them coming just as I can.

"Kit?" Annie's voice is half laughing, half flattening as she reacts to my reaction.

"It's them isn't it." Noah knows almost as much of this forest as I. We all do. We are trained for this. Our whole life we have trained for this, and even as I feel them coming, I know I can't possibly have been ready for any amount of training. I open my eyes and stare at Ankhara, not wanting to make eye contact with Noah and have my fears confirmed.

And yet I nod my head. I can feel it. They *are* coming. This isn't a drill. This isn't another training camp with images projected for us to conquer. It isn't mere images approaching on the cold wind.

"Guys? Come on, this ain't fair, ya can't just both freeze and nobody say anything. You'll have me in a panic." She is lighthearted in a way that shows she knows what's coming isn't light.

"Feel them." I want her to practice. If we make it through this, and if she ever has this 'opportunity' again, I want her to embrace her warning signals. "Close your eyes, choose to connect to the trees and the breeze and feel them coming."

She is a diligent student, I'll give her that. Never let anyone say she isn't willing. Thrown in any situation, she goes both feet first and dives straight into whatever is asked of her. Noah looks at her in admiration as she drops into herself and her energy probes outwards and beyond. He loves her. So much so I can see the crease of fear in his brow at what we are about to face. Probably at what Ankhara is about to uncover. This is the flavour of magic people feared. This is the stuff of all our children's nightmares. The stuff that has plagued our own. The way our parents had scared us into staying home at night and not wandering out in the streets alone. This, for nymphs and witches and humans alike, is the lone fear that kept night lights turned on and anxious glances cast at shadows. This is the manifestation of a nightmare we've been hoping our entire lives not to have.

And we are about to be in the thickest of thick of it.

Ankhara grunts, a cold sweat slipping off her forehead as she begins to shiver. Fear sinks into her body and as her lips start quivering, she opens her eyes. I see the most white I have ever seen in someone's eyes in that moment. She is petrified. She can feel it. She can't possibly understand it, but she can feel it.

"My whole life..." She trails off. Wanting to share the revelation she is living but unable to comprehend quickly enough. "I thought I was imagining it all."

"I wish." I gulp. She gets it. And with no training whatsoever in this realm, she is going to have to face it.

"How could we have been so stupid so as to not train her in this? How could the Royal Council have thought it was okay to throw us out here without teaching her how to survive this?"

Noah throws his arms in the air and paces back and forth, a moment of panic moving through him in response to the worst-case scenario that is no doubt running through both our heads.

Ankhara's panic increases in response. The connection between them is becoming more and more tangible and I can see the ways their physiologies react to one another. Someone needs to calm at least one of them down before the danger arrives and, seeing as there isn't really anyone else around, that someone is going to have to be me.

I walked straight up to Ankhara and kiss her. Straight on the mouth. Tongue and all.

Noah stops in his tracks and tenses into some deep breathing. Ankhara comes along for the ride and then slowly, we pull away.

"Woah," is all she has to say as she gathers herself. I feel her ground back into her body. She is calmer in seeing she doesn't need training for this. She is the living expression of it. "Can I do that?"

Noah is standing with a confused expression on his face. Sometimes he forgets the gifts of the nymphs. Our connection is so carnal, conversation and magic are often left out of it – unless, of course, you count the magic of orgasmic bliss. There is plenty of that. I smile at the thought, eagerly hoping my next lover will arrive soon.

Ankhara walks straight up to Noah and places a hand on his heart.

"May I?" she asks, and he nods, realisation dawning on his face, and so she kisses him. I watch the energy transfer from a metre away, fascinated. I very rarely get to witness as someone else lives the magic I am usually the one delivering. I was the only nymph in warrior school training for the guard, and thus, all my life have been the only one there with my gift. The seer's kiss. A gift of vision through connection. A gift of transference. When I kiss another, I am able to pass on information through the connection of breath. Visions of memories, premonitions and training can be transferred to another in an instant. In my brief encounter with Ankhara's lips, I have gifted her the memories of my basic entity training. The basics. Enough to survive. Enough to trigger her into remembering her own innate gifts, and now I watch her as she easily, without any effort, transfers the information into Noah.

Entity training isn't for everyone, and being the only nymph and the most connected to the forest, the responsibility had always largely been on my shoulders. I did more training than anyone else. As the transference slows down I see the relief and calm sink into both of their beings – partly from their kiss, saturated with such love, and partly from receiving so much information. They can't make sense of it at this moment. Rather, in the moment they need it, the memory required will occur to them. That is all that matters.

Noah glances at me and nods a silent thank you, then looks back at Ankhara, barely whispering the realisation he's just come to. "Because she doesn't need training, she just needs waking up."

The shocking realisation that Ankhara requires mere moments of preparation, in comparison to the years upon years we endured, is almost as insulting as it is exciting, but I don't care. In this moment and the moments we know are coming, it may be the difference between survival and death.

Ankhara takes a step towards me to stand directly in the centre of us. Shifting her gaze from Noah and I, back and forth and back and forth, graceful and steady in her stance.

"Remember what you love," she says to us both, and turns to the forest behind us just as the onslaught begins.

One last thought enters my mind as a battle cry exits my mouth.

She's going to make one hell of a queen.

And that is it. The next instant I cry the cry of battle and am lost to the storm of darkness that rains down on us like black tar pouring down from hell.

CHAPTER 30

ANKHARA

798 Hours Left

*I*n less than ten seconds we are completely overcome by these creatures. *Wait, no, they're spirits! What the? How do I know that?*

"I'll lead them away! Keep going! No matter what you hear, you have to keep going!"

I panic. Noah sacrificing himself is not how I wanted this to go down.

Neither is you failing. It's YOU Ankhara. You're the one that has to make it home from here.

His capacity to send me thoughts is getting stronger and stronger. I can hear him in my mind even as he fights his way away from me. Kit is to my left, swooping and diving through these *things*, but nothing is working. Every move she tries goes straight through them. They are literally intangible. I mean, we can *see* them, but that's where their realness seems to stop. *Other than the deadly fear they evoke inside me.*

"Don't be fooled by their transparency, Ankhara!" Kit screams at me as she dodges yet another lunging spirit. "They *can* and they *will* hurt you."

How that is even possible I don't know, but I don't have a lot of time to think about it. Every moment there is another strike to dodge. There is so much movement, so much confusion I can't even see Noah, although I can feel him pulling further and further away from me physically. Like an energetic anchor in my being, I can feel my heart tug with grief at his impending departure.

But then it shifts. Noah yells like an insane man in the distance and all the spirits turn to him. Noah's energy is palpable, and it seems as though that is what they feed on. Kit lunges at the opportunity to grab me in both arms and dissolve into the closest tree, literally, taking me with her.

"Woah." I let the word out involuntarily before immediately cringing to myself. *Lame, Ankhara. Super fucking lame.*

"Shh!" Kit smothers my mouth, and I slowly but assertively place my hand above hers and yank it off. I turned and glare at her, but soften the moment I see her face. Her eyes tell me the whole story. She is devastated at the thought of leaving Noah out there, perhaps just as much as me. I mean, she's known him way longer. He was her *first.* She loves him. It was a different love now but it was love all the same. And then she takes a step back, the grief and fear that were filling her eyes replaced by ferocity and courage. She puts her hand to her heart and bows, and then steps back through the tree.

Dread and rage rampage through my body. Dread at the danger they were in. Rage at how powerless I was to do anything about it. The rage wins.

"ARGHH!" I scream and crash my arms against the inside of the tree. Over and over again, blood spilling down my arms as the bark splinters and pierces my skin over and over. But it's not enough. The tree spirit is groaning, and was I more lucid I might appreciate how cool that is. But I'm not. I'm vibrating with an out-of-body-ready-to-kill-someone type of rage.

"There will come a time when you will have to say no to her." My mother's words ring in my head and pull me down to earth a

little. I still feel completely helpless, but I stop taking it out on the tree. It groans a sigh of relief as I take a step back. That is when I see the damage I've done. Thousands of splinters spilled out everywhere I look, sticking straight inwards towards me, and there are more upon more on the floor by my feet. Not to mention the ones sticking in my arms. Sadness fills me as I realise I've inflicted my own pain on this tree. Then a flash of memory of Noah's head split open in my hands runs through my vision like a lightbulb flickering on and off again.

That's it!

In a heartbeat I step forward and felt the tree tense in response. Sadness strikes me again, but I set it aside to focus on my breath. *Just breathe, Ankhara. Breathe and feel it.* And I do. I inhale and exhale as deeply and calmly as I can, and I visualise the tree in one piece again. I can feel my magic pulsing from my chest through my arms. My forehead feels like it is on fire, and it freaks me out a little, throwing me off balance, but the sound of the tree's song returning brings me back to myself and keeps me going. All it takes is three focused breaths.

I open my eyes and the tree is back how I'd found it. Glowing. Healed.

Fucking magic. I smile to myself. I could definitely get used to this.

Not a moment too soon I feel my heart tug and I remember why I am in the tree in the first place. *Noah! Kit! What do I do, what do I do, what do I do...* The words go round and round in my head until the rest of my mum's words hit me.

"It will challenge you. Say no anyway." She was talking about Kit. Just like seemingly everything else, she knew this was going to happen. That doesn't tell me how the hell to get out of this tree, though.

Think, Ankhara. You're the prophecy child of the most magical family alive right now. THINK. My hands are shaking and I resist the urge to hold them still.

Focus on the vision and you'll always find your way. I remember the words from Kit's lesson earlier this evening. Focus creates my reality. If I choose my magic, maybe I can walk through this tree, I decide. I walk to the inner edge and place my hands, now welcomingly, on the trunk. I close my eyes, and will my magic to be alive in my entire body.

"Come on." I whisper to myself in the shortest ever pep talk. There isn't time. They don't have time. I imagine walking straight through the tree and walking out. I feel it happen, and I opened my eyes. On the *outside* of the tree.

Fucking A.

My celebration is halted by the cold, wet feeling of a dagger sliding through my stomach. I scream in pain and look down, but there is nothing. Nothing except the sound of Noah's scream in the distance. My body was clear. I am feeling *him*.

I run.

"NOAH!!" I scream, but it is like no one hears me, not even the spirits. I can see them, just. Kit and Noah are both on their knees, completely surrounded. There are spirits *everywhere*. Somehow in the moments between me entering the tree and magicking myself out, the number of them had multiplied tenfold, but nothing is going to stop me from going to them. My surroundings blur and gain focus, and blur and re-focus again and again as I morph into the trees like Kit and shoot myself forward. Noah has bowed his head and Kit is sobbing. *They're giving up.* My chest tightens. *They're giving in to save me.* I almost hesitate. I almost stop at the thought of dying myself and not completing my quest, but something unknown moves me closer and closer and the rate I am gunning for them gives me no space to slow down.

"I LOVE YOUUUU!!!"

I scream at the top of my lungs. It is all I have. It is all I can do. All I can offer him is the molecule of peace in dying knowing that he was loved in all of his glory. All I can offer her in her last moments of this life is the love of the sister she'd never had. There is nothing else.

I watch as Noah braces himself for impact. *At least he won't have to see me die.* That is my last thought, and then something happens.

As though they'd heard me, the spirits pause. Each and every one of them, moments ago spitting cold black flames that cut flesh like knives, they just... Pause. And then turn on their floaty pivots to look at *me*.

Shit. Shitshitshit.

They are staring straight at me, with an innocence. No, somehow, it is hope. They have hope in their eyes, like that of a child looking up to their mother for the first time after a fall. My pulse throbs and races through my body. I freeze, looking back at them, relieved they were no longer aiming their deadly fire at my friends. Terrified that their focus is on me. I can feel the complete and utter dread moving through Noah, and I don't have to look at Kit to know she is feeling the same. We are powerless in this fight. There is no weapon we can use against them.

And it strikes me. We don't *need* a weapon against them. It isn't a weapon that turned their attacks into this frozen moment. It isn't fear being thrown against more fear. It isn't the two childish perspectives we've been projecting at each other that has stopped them in their tracks.

It is love.

Everything that happens from that moment forward is as if I have completely let myself go. Without a moment's hesitation I begin to walk forward. Every other being before me tenses as I walk, but I don't falter. One foot in front of the other, one step at a time, I walk all the way up to them, until I am an arm's length away from the spirit I deem their leader. The spirit that just minutes ago, had been about to kill my friends. I look him straight in the eye and take a deep breath, and tell him I love him.

"I love you." I repeat myself and slowly, he shapeshifts into a man. "I love you." I say it again, with more conviction this time, and the darkness in him begins to glow.

"I love you."

He seemingly melts down until his feet hit the ground, and he smiles.

"I love you."

I shift my attention to the other spirits around me and, somehow not to my surprise, I see faces. Smiling faces. Mothers. Fathers. Grandparents. Even a couple of kids.

"I love you."

Some start crying. Some laugh joyfully.

I look down at Noah and Kit and they nod at me, pride filling both of their eyes. I gesture for them to stand, and they join me.

"We love you." Kit speaks first, softly, partly in shock, and then Noah follows, slowly walking to stand by my side.

"I love you." His words melt over me and lick parts of me I didn't know existed. Even though he is directing his words at the spirits, I can feel them for myself too.

As each of us speaks, the whole clearing begins to glow. Literally. Everything starts to gleam` and if I hadn't had the week

I'd had, I wouldn't have believed it when the trees and flowers begin to *sing*.

My body is flooded in the remembrance of a level of connection I try to tell myself I've never felt, but that nonetheless feels familiar. In the eyes of the spirits, a reflection of my desire is beaming back at me.

They just want to go home.

I can feel it. With every fibre of my being I can *feel* it. I can't explain it, I can just feel it. That each and every one of them was just a child, just like us. They were lost children. Not children by age, not childish in spirit, but children of this planet who had lost their vehicles.

What happened to you?

I want to know and at the same time I don't. I don't want to know what awful thing killed each and every one of them, but when the leader walks up to me and makes a gesture as if to touch my forehead, I nod.

My mind is flooded with images of fire and screaming. The cries of these people fill my awareness and the smell of burning flesh sears my nostrils. I grimace, tears of frustration and helplessness spilling down my cheeks as I witness the terror that ripped through what must have been their village, their home. There is nothing I can do. He is showing me a moment from the past. *A moment that killed more than thirty people.* Witches. An image of a mother casting a protection bubble over her child flashes before me, and that's when I know. These were my people. Each and every one of them perished in the fires of... other witches. *What?* Snippets of witches in dark hooded capes casting shards of lightning into the homes and crops of *my* people enter my mind and a rage fills my body. *Who could do such a thing? Who could do this to their own people?* I am witnessing war. War between witches. War between people who surely just wanted happiness for themselves. And then I see it. A close-up flashes past my eyes and I see it. The witches casting fire... The witches creating all this havoc...

They were Hoods.

Hoods. The Forsaken. The followers of my brother...

I open my eyes and meet the tears of the man before me.

"Oh my..." Noah's choked whisper almost makes me jump.

This has been the most ridiculous, outrageous, fairytale-like, scary story week of my life, but nothing has prepared me for what I see next.

CHAPTER 31

NOAH

797 Hours Left

*M*other.

It isn't possible. At least, up until just a minute ago, I didn't think it could be, and yet there she is. Standing before me, the glowing picture of perfection and beauty I had always imagined her to be, is my mother.

I gaze in awe at the rise and fall of a chest I'd never thought I'd see again. The chest that held her heart in its cavity. The loss of which had created a cavity in my own that I'd never thought could be filled. One I'd never thought could possibly receive the answers it sought.

And yet here I am. Tears stream down my face as I stare at her in disbelief, and feel Ankhara's heart breaking open at the sight of mine being so vulnerable and undone.

What on earth can I say to her?

Nothing can make up for our lost time. Nothing can tell her how much I've missed her. Nothing. Nothing can ever communicate what life has been without her life in it. All I can do is stare and cry. All I can do...

She reaches an ethereal hand out and touches my cheek, pulling my gaze more deeply into hers. She rises, floating up into the air until she is 'standing' at my head height. Directly in front of me, her eyes glisten with a shine that I've only ever seen once else, in the eyes of Ang as she'd spoken to me of her daughter. The shine of a mother's love. The look in her eyes is a medicine I didn't know I'd needed, a healing I didn't think I could ever receive.

She nods and suddenly I can hear her. Clear as day, as soft and strong as I remembered, her voice appears in my mind as she holds her hand on my face, cupping my chin. I can imagine the glistening of my tears shining through the translucent image of her hand holding me, and I smile, listening. Feeling. Relishing the truth of her being here.

Noah, you are the only thing that mattered to me that night. Your survival. Your outliving of me. That was all I needed. I promise you that the pain of leaving you that night would have been nothing compared to the pain of leaving with you. There was no option where we both got to stay. I saw that. Ang had warned me. What she didn't tell you is that we were once dear friends. Sisters in spirit, and she saw our death. She prophesied it, and although we tried, there was no solution that resulted in anyone other than you surviving. Everything else we stepped through, every other vision, ended in the death of us all. And so I want you to know we knew, and we chose. We sacrificed all we were in the hopes that at least one of our children, that you, would live. It was a harsh reality for us to face. Many, losing children in the full awareness that there was nothing we could do to save them. We'd seen a moment, a flash, of this moment in time. Of a reunion with you, and we knew. This was our part in the Prophecy. The Prophecy that would bring magic back to our people. The prophecy that, should it be fulfilled, would bring the only possible vehicle for peace for our people. True power. Empowerment of heart. We saw Ankhara and her life with you, and we chose for you to survive in the hope of your heart holding hers through this journey.

I am so, so sorry I have not been with you.

I sob. Hearing the truth ring and reverberate through me, swiping away all the cobwebs of my heart that I had buried.

...though I promise, I have been with you every moment. In here.

Her other hand moves to find its resting place on my chest, and I feel as though all that is in my heart can no longer be held there. I cry. I drop to my knees and weep. Feeling her with me, feeling her hold me, this was the dream and wish of the boy inside me every day since that we had lost each other. Having her hold me, having her with me, had been all I had wanted since we had parted ways, and her being here sends a ripple of warmth and love through the entirety of my being. I can feel the shaking of my whole body as my nervous system, trained as an animal and a warrior, releases the fear I have held within me all this time. This fear, dissolving out of the system I have held together with pain since losing her. As though falling away like dust, my pain and tears begin to slow down as the shaking changes to a stillness, and I look back up to my mother's beauty.

She smiles. Actually smiles. The smile of a mother who has waited her whole afterlife for an opportunity to say goodbye to the son she left too early. The smile of a mother proud of the man her son is becoming. I can feel it. The knowing in her that I am stepping into the destiny that had been laid before me. Creating my own waves with my love and loyalty to Ankhara. Although it has only just begun and I don't even know what to call her – definitely not my girlfriend – I can feel in her the acknowledgment of the ripple effect our love will have on our people. I feel at peace knowing that she not only approves but applauds our love. She applauds our union.

She applauds me. A feeling I never thought I'd know, and I give it permission to wash over my entire system, replacing that which had shaken off like dust.

I love you.

The sound of her voice reverberates and a pain strikes my heart in the knowledge that the time has come to say goodbye. Briefly, I panic, wishing there was more time. Wishing there was more I could share with her, more stories she could share with me. But there isn't. I can feel there isn't. And, deep down, I can feel that there doesn't need to be.

Much as I struggle to admit it, I am ready for this.

I am ready to wipe away the cobwebs of my heart, binding me to tradition and holding me hostage to the fear of loving her. I am ready to step up, step forward and step into the man I know I want to become. A man who loves without succumbing to his fear. Not a man without fear, but a man full of fear in the awareness that falling in and choosing love was his choice, despite that fear.

That is when I hear her.

My gaze shifts to the sound of Annie's song. Her voice resonates through the clearing, dancing with the long grass and flowers and swaying in the gentle breeze through the leaves of the trees. She is on her knees in prayer, her eyes closed, her body offering an honouring of the spirits that stand before and around her. I can feel her heart pouring through her aura, reaching out to those around her, and each spirit in response becomes more full. Their colours take on a vibrancy that not even life could have given to them. Their faces fill with tears and smiles. Mothers embrace their children as they laugh and dance. Fathers and grandfathers weep their pride and joy. Her song, the song of her ancestors past and present, fills everyone's cup. Even Kit is sitting on the earth beside her, holding her hands in a prayer above her head, swaying and emoting to the sound as it moves through her.

It echoes, and as I open my heart for her song to echo through me, I look back to my mother. She is laughing. Dancing. Twirling in glee, completely elated. It is as though she is being given a freedom that even her living, breathing life hadn't granted her. And I see it. It clicks and lands in my awareness like a light being turned on.

Her spirit is free, and that is the greatest gift this journey could ever have given me. I watch her as a peace falls over my body, and I choose to etch this memory of her into the very fibres of my soul. I choose for this song and dance to be the memory of her that lives on in me, in my waking world and in the shifting tides of my dreams.

CHAPTER 32

ANKHARA

797 Hours Left

It is a prayer to my people. A prayer for all that has been and all that is coming. A prayer for all I've missed and all I have caused and all my brother has been through. It is a prayer for my family. For the families of my people. These people. Lost and alone for longer than I can imagine. Now found and at home. Tears fall down across my lips as I sing but it doesn't matter. The words move not only my mouth but my whole body.

Sitting in prayer, I sway. Twisting and turning to allow the melody to move through me. Rolling onto my back on the ground to feel the earth pour her message through my heart, I feel such painful joy. Like all the pain that has been locked away is having a light shone on it, melting away the crusted forgetting of what love is. I can't breathe, but I don't need to. The song is breathing for me and moving my body in ways I have no desire to control. I writhe around the ground, surely looking as though I am having a fit, and although I am aware that there are so many there to witness me, I am also unaware. I don't feel ashamed. I don't feel the embarrassment I have come to associate with this tone of my voice, with the nakedness of it. Instead, I feel connected. I feel so deeply connected to each and every being present. I feel the swaying of the leaves in the trees through my lungs. I feel the melting of the mothers' hearts inside my own. I feel the pride in the shoulders of every father no longer bearing the weight of the world, instead enlivened and enlightened in the joy of this song. This vibration that speaks through me is the essence of me. It is greater than anything my humanness could put together. It has a will and a motion of its own. All I need do is open to allow it through. My only job is to allow the breather of breath to breathe through me, and for the song to be sung as the breath escapes me. That is it. That is all I am here for and time is lost to it. It feels accelerated, in that the emotions move so swiftly, and yet there is a sense of timelessness, as though we could be here forever. A wave of calm washes over me that I've only ever before felt alone, but even then never to this depth. Never down to the very beat of my heart pulsing through each capillary. The smallest of my blood vessels is tingling with the aliveness of my essence. I am dancing this song now, weaving the web of words through the earth as I weave my body above her.

Standing, I open my eyes. Every single being is dancing. The clearing is a calamity. A beautiful calamity of light and laughter and love. Oh, my, the overwhelming sense of love I feel. Kit is laughing, weaving through a web of glowing children, showing them the tricks of her tree dancing, weaving in and out of trunks and teaching them to fly. Their laughter fills the air like the harmony I never knew I needed. This is the perfect song. The song sung of the heart of a singer and the song sung of the laughter of these kids. These kids who were once (and still are) my people. These kids who maybe would have grown up to be my friends and confidants. I'll never know. I've never even made the connection to the thought that if the Hoods have been around all this time, they've been murdering our people all this time. For as long as I've lived, since I was born and had spirited away to live a life of forgetting with humans while our people suffered.

I weep, still hearing the sounds of song echoing back to me from the spirits of the trees. For this moment I weep, and I allow the cracking open. For three breaths I kneel as I crack open and then I feel him. *Noah.* I've never seen him like he was watching her. He was different. Changed. Lighter. As though in re-meeting his mother he's been granted permission, from himself, to become a man. The child in him sleeping now, not fretting. I can feel it as much as I can see it, and it re-kindles my song. I bounce the rhythm off that of the trees and rise onto all fours, still watching him. I crawl towards him. Singing. Not softly. Not aggressively. Just singing this peaceful repetition to which the spirits coo to and the trees hum.

He doesn't see me coming, or so I think, until he reaches his arm out to grab mine just as I crawl into reach. He doesn't take his eyes off her, and I am not about to ask him to. Instead, I stand and pull him up with me, then turn and hold my hand out to his mother. I am following a call that has surfaced from somewhere deep inside me. I don't *know* what I am doing and yet, it feels like the most natural thing. Her eyes meet mine in the sweetest 'yes' and she floats and dances her way to us. Noah's left hand squeezing my right, I hold my left arm out to her until she hovers her hand above mine.

"It is time."

I haven't even thought the words before I speak them, and I don't know why I do. I don't need to. She already knows and, by the look of everyone else's faces, they do too. Kit and the children come to a panting, alive pause, and Kit stares, smiling happy tears now. I see the happiness in her eyes shift to grief then denial then acceptance in a heartbeat as she comes to realise too.

It is time.

She nods at me, as if her pride would give me permission, and it does. The feeling I have in response to her faith in me exceeds any sisterhood I've ever felt before. She gets me, more and more deeply to my core, than any other woman ever has. It is an honour to call her my friend and, really, teacher. I squeeze Noah's hand and let go, and without a second thought move forward with his mother in tow. I walk straight up to the man I'd decided was the leader. It is obvious to me that these people, his people, my people, they look to him as Kit and Noah have started to look at me. The weight of leadership had worn heavy upon his shoulders, but I can see now that, in sight of the end, the weight has lifted. His posture has shifted to an almost un-recognisable stance. He stands proud, relaxed and open. I can feel the essence of his heart pulsating out of him. And he nods to me as I hear his voice, somehow knowing, in my mind.

It is time.

I smile. Not knowing why, I simply can't help but smile. I take a moment to sweep my eyes to acknowledge each being that stands before me. Every single one of them knows, old and young, and I look at each as an acknowledgement of the time that has come, and still I sing my song. Last but not least, I look at Noah. A small frown of confusion has spread across his brow, and I caress his left cheek, right where I had seen his mother caress him. In an instant, his mother floats over to him and caresses him on the other cheek. He looks to her as if to soak in every inch of her one last time.

"I love you, Mum." His voice cracks through the melody of his tears and just as she nods, he looks at me and does the same.

Letting go of his warm face, I step forward and open the door. The door to the other side, peeking through a veil I'd never thought really existed. It is like drawing a curtain of lace from a window. It feels smooth and soft and almost transparent in my fingers. Silky, like shimmers of water on duckling feathers, and almost unseen, like the web of a spider without the stickiness. It feels powerful, yet malleable to my touch. My fingers brush through it, and it parts to what could have been a door, to what I had thought was going to be a door, but rather, becomes a bright white light. Looking in I feel nothing but the urge to look away. It is too bright for my focus, and so instead, I watch as each and every one of the spirits gracefully floats through. First the man, who parts from me with one final salute. He is followed by three children, ushered gently by the most bubbly mother. She is followed by someone I assume to be her husband, and the rest of the spirit army. One by one, they file through. Some pause to say goodbye. Some race through so fast I wonder what is on the other side. They are joyous. Each and every one of them. None is sad or afraid or doesn't want to go. It fascinates me, until finally it is her turn. I feel Noah's breath bring my body to ground as he fights to see through his tears and I breathe with him, knowing that even if he isn't right next to me, he'll feel it.

Thank you. I feel his body speaking to me, as if grateful to be drawn more closely to the earth by the breath.

I look at him and smile through the mists of tears.

You're welcome.

Communicating with him in this way is fun, and for a moment my focus drifts as I wonder what this will look like a few weeks from now if it has already grown to this.

Her movement towards me brings me back to the present. She gestures, seeking permission, and I nod as she leans towards me and brings her forehead to mine. When our energies touch, I gasp. Just as Kit's kiss had poured memories into me, Noah's mother is giving me a vision with her mind.

A small boy, perhaps four years old, runs through a muddy, yet somehow dusty, field, laughing, being chased by what seemed like his father. No. His uncle. His mother's brother. They are playing in this muddy, dusty field, until the little boy, little Noah, becomes tired and declares it is time he has a nap. He high-fives and thanks his uncle, turning to walk inside before hesitating, then running back to give his uncle a bear-sized hug.

"I love you Uncle Jon." The man smiles and his eyes well up.

"I love you too, little man." He picks him up and gives him a big squeeze. "Your father would have been so proud of the way you love."

The man I now knew to be Uncle Jon slowly puts little Noah down on the ground and tousles his hair as he turns to walk back inside.

Little Noah walks towards the hut where his mother stands at the entrance, the image of natural beauty, and he pauses to let her cup his face and kiss his cheek before he goes inside, seemingly to his bed for a nap.

"He will miss you so much." Painfully looking away from young Noah, she looks back to Jon, her face hardening.

"He will meet me again." He speaks softly and surely, before walking forward to embrace her in a hug that he knows is their goodbye. "I'm so sorry we couldn't find a way."

She pulls out of his embrace and grabs him by the shoulders.

"I'm not." Her eyes are focused and piercing. "Because of this, he will live. Because of this, our whole village will not be lost, just a number of destined people. This is our part to play. One day, it will come full circle, and he will understand why it had to be this way. One day, he will know far more than I do, and on that day, I hope he finds you."

They embrace again, this time melting into one another, burying their heads into whatever nook they could find.

"You are the bravest woman I've ever met, Annalise. I am proud to know, love and serve you."

"Bravery requires fear, dear brother. I do not fear leaving this life now so that my child may live a full one. He will help her bring us all home."

Uncle Jon nods and steps away, and the image dissolves. As quick as it had entered my mind, it is gone.

I open my eyes and I am here now with just Kit, Noah and… Annalise. She blows a kiss and waves her fingers as if to send a kiss to all of us; then, with one last glance at Noah, she turns and moves through the veil. The light makes a popping sound and I wave my hands through the lace to close whatever it was I had opened. I turn to see Kit nestled under Noah's right arm, and I make myself comfortable under his other. I'm not sure how long we stand here, but the three of us are still arm in arm, staring at the place Noah's mother had gone, when the sound of footsteps behind us jolts us back to the here and now.

Turning around, we are confronted by a dozen or more Hoods. Shocked, my heart sinks, and as I pull my weapon out of my belt, I hear him for the first time.

"It's about time we were reunited, Ankhara."

His voice travels down from the branches of the tree above us but before I have the chance to look up, a figure dressed entirely in black drops down in front of us. There, standing in the centre of a clearing that has just been host to the most beautiful ceremony I've ever witnessed, he stands. His black hood matching the hoods of those who stood around him, he smiles. Nothing I've seen in my entire life matches the chills that run down my spine at the look in his eyes as he smiles.

"Hello, Skavari."

My world flips upside down in an instant and the last thing I see as a wave of pain rises from the back of my head is his smile as Noah and Kit's bodies drop to the ground beside me.

This is how I re-meet my brother.

CHAPTER 33

ANKHARA

786 Hours Left

I awaken with my head absolutely thumping. Immediately, I try to raise my hand to the back of my head where I can feel a throbbing lump growing, but my movement is restricted by whatever is tying my hands behind my back. *What?* Completely disoriented, I try to open my eyes, but the light pierces me with such sharpness I immediately close them.

Where the fuck am I?

Then I remember. Skavari. Skavari had been here. Not only had he been here, one of his henchmen had knocked me out. *Cunts.* A searing rage moves through my body and I start shaking and breathing raggedly.

"Ankhara? Are you okay?" Noah's voice whispers frantically, coming from the direction of my left shoulder. His voice immediately calms me down, and reminds me to take a deep breath. *He's okay. I'm okay. We're okay.*

"I'm fine. I have a fucking headache and I'm going to kill my cunt of a brother, but I'm fine. Where's Kit? Can you see anything? The light hurts my eyes."

I *feel* him frown, after he gasps at my language. He hasn't quite gotten used to that yet and it amuses me.

"Noah. I swear. Get over it and help me figure out how to get out of here."

He laughs, almost silently.

"Okay. Kit is over to your right. She hasn't woken up yet. Skavari is here somewhere, I doubt he'd leave you, but I haven't seen him since I woke up, only heard him. I've counted fourteen Hoods. Two of them won't leave his side. Two won't leave ours, though they have no trouble napping outside our tent. We're in a tent, by the way. I'm not sure how long I was out, but if I could see your arm we could get an idea. Can you twist it?"

I'd actually completely forgotten about the magical moving time bomb on my arm. Between finding Mum's tree cave of codes, training with Kit, hiking, being bombarded by spirits and then running into my brother, the small tickling sensation on my arm had completely left my brain. I twist my arm to see if it helps.

"A little more to your left." Noah speaks and I twist my arm the way I think will show him. "A little more." I twist until I am certain any more twisting will snap my arm right off.

"Ah, there." *Thank God.* "Perfect."

"Perfect if you want my arm to snap," I quip.

He laughs. Standard. Then says nothing. I wait impatiently for, well, anything.

"Are you going to tell me what it says?"

"Oh. Sorry. 7-8-6. There's seven hundred and eighty-six hours left." Even when I am annoyed his voice melts me.

Quick maths tells me that we have lost eleven hours.

"Eleven hours? What the hell have they been doing with our bodies for eleven hours?" It seems like a stupidly long time for someone to be knocked out.

"I don't know. That's what I'm worried about. Though it can't be my focus. We have to focus on getting you out of here. Kit's a nymph, so whatever they drugged us with, it'll last longer for her. She's hyper-sensitive to any unnatural chemicals, even plastic irritates her. They must have drugged us once they knocked us out. Or cast a spell, but I don't know any spells like this. This is not the kind of magic we learn at school. This is... Dark. That or drugs. They have a similar sense of emptiness about them."

"Can you see okay?" I'm a bit nervous about my eyes. Not being able to see makes me feel so out of control. Plus I want to see that perfect face of his, and see Kit's body breathing.

"Yes. Perfectly. And so can you. I think you just opened your eyes looking straight into the torchlight. The sun's gone down but the tallest guy left the lantern shining straight on you. I think he's the leader, next to... Skavari."

"You mean my brother." I sigh. It scares me too. But fear of a name only increases fear of the thing itself. "You can say it. It scares me too, but it's the truth, and that's the only thing that will set us free from this place."

"You are wise beyond your years, my love."

"Don't kiss her ass with your comments until she wises a way out of here and takes us with her." Kit pipes up beside me, just as I turn my head away from the torchlight and open my eyes a bit. The embarrassment of my stupidity with the light washes away in seeing her wake up, especially seeing as she wakes up with her sass intact.

"I think your head bump landed you with extra sass!" I like it.

"Not quite, Princess. I've just gotten over the formalities. I think being tied to a pole will do that to a group."

She has a point, and though I don't love the circumstances or the Princess-calling, I do like the abandoning of formality. The way she said "princess" was more playful than formal, and I want her to be that way with me. *I want everyone to be that way with me.*

"Any ideas as to how we get out of here?" Noah enjoys the banter, but our situation challenges the soldier in him; he is a man on a mission, and it reminds me to stick to mine. Get out. Escape this tent. Get the dagger from the dragon. I'm not sure how Skavari fits into that.

"I think they're waking up, boss." We can faintly hear someone I assume to be our guarding Hood.

Fuck. Well-played team.

The sound of footsteps approaching makes my head pulse again with a fresh wave of anger.

What the fuck do they want with us?

The tent flap is flicked up and six Hoods pile in, two standing on either side of each of us. It is super intimidating. Never have I been in a situation like this before. I mean, yeah, Noah and I were attacked by Hoods in his room, and loads of times since then, but this is different. We are completely incapacitated. It lights a rage at our powerlessness in me that scares even myself. I am nearly at boiling point in an instant. I can feel my hands shaking against the ropes that bind them behind my back, my tummy pressing frantically against the many loops of rope that hold me back against what I assume is a pole the same as Noah's. Kit's is different. While Noah is tied to a standard wooden stake, Kit's pole looks man-made, like it has black rubbish bags stuck all over it. I wonder if that has something to do with her nymph magic. It made sense that a barrier of plastic between her and the tree might disconnect her slightly, but it seems strange to me to go to such extreme efforts. From what I've seen they don't even use plastic in this... world. Perhaps they stole it from humans? *I guess I'll find out.*

I shift my attention back to the tent flap just as his feet come into view. He is wearing worn-out tanned leather boots, scuffed, from all his tree climbing no doubt, and yet laced up with brand new laces. He has on the tightest black pants I've ever seen on a guy. Let alone a guy who still wants to run and jump out of the sky. *Impractical idiot.* I'd be out of here in a jiffy if silent insults set me free. Funnily enough, they don't. Slowly, I force myself to look up from his bottom half and meet his face with my gaze. It shocks me, seeing the familiarity in his features. His jaw is identical to our fathers, but his eyes somehow remind me of our mother despite the pain they carry and right there, above them, is the scar our grandmother told me about. That scar could very well be the reason we are here, having grown through separate lives and lifestyles. That scar started the avalanche that had our parents send me away. His whole demeanour and image confront me, and yet I hold my nerve and look him straight in the eye.

"Well, well. Lovely to see you awake my sister." He speaks as if familiar with me. As if we've known each other our whole lives, *well.* Not just distantly.

"You barely have any right to call me that." I growl at him, struggling to remove my restraints.

"They will only get tighter the more you struggle. You see, they're charmed, and you'll feed them with every bit of energy you put into shaking them off." He smirks, proud of himself. "Isn't that brilliant? See what we can do, Annie?" I shiver at the sound of his voice using my lover's pet name for me. It makes me feel sick.

He spreads his arms out and gestures at the three of us and his Hoods.

"And that's just me. Imagine if we combined our energy, sister. Imagine what we could do in this world if we combined our magic. We'd be unstoppable. Not even our rich little father would be able to buy his way out of that one."

He continues as though I'll hear what he is saying and leap to take his hand.

"Ankhara, they've been numbing you to your magic your whole life, and now you're back you get to choose. You've been back a matter of days, and already they've sent you on some life-threatening mission. They don't care for you like I do. Don't you see?"

It is at this point that I realise he is crazy. I would have thought that would make me more eager to get away, but it makes me sad. I feel this deep sadness creep through my heart and body, and a longing. Like maybe, if I give it everything I have, I can convince him to see differently. Maybe, just maybe, if I go with him, I'll be able to bring him home. We can be a family again.

"What happened to you, Skavari?"

I want to help him. I want to stand up and walk over to him and hold him. I want to take him in my arms and tell him everything is over and it is going to be okay. Sympathy oozes through every fibre of me.

"They didn't tell you?" He looks shocked at first and then his eyes darken. "No, of course not. Of course. I bet they told you some sob story about how I ran away because everyone missed you and I felt like I wasn't good enough. Didn't they? They told you I left because I was weaker than you. Annie? TELL ME WHAT THEY SAID!" He stands up so fast he is yelling in my face before I've registered he is moving. His breath smells like a rabbit or dog cooked on the fire. It is disgusting, and so is his attitude. I have no interest in telling him anything he wants to hear.

"ANSWER ME!"

"Okay dog breath, if you're expecting any sort of answer from me, you're going to have to pause from the sound of your own voice for a moment and actually give me a moment. Do you think you can do that?"

He recoils, horrified. As if I've slain his only pet, he crosses his arm over his body and leans away from me. If I wasn't the one tied up, anyone looking at him might think he was protecting himself from me.

"Skavari. I'm not here to hurt you. You're the one that knocked me and my friends out and tied us up, remember?" He settles and sits on the floor in front of me, just a metre away. It is bizarre. My twin, who until little more than a week ago I hadn't known existed, now sits within arm's reach and I can't touch him. Not even physically.

"You are here to hurt me. Isn't that why they sent you? I know they brainwashed you against me. You would have attacked me if I'd tried talking to you. That's why you have these ones with you. A warrior and a mage. To hurt me."

My heart breaks. He really believes what he is saying. I can feel it. If I couldn't feel Noah just as strongly, I'd say maybe it was a twin thing. *Maybe it's a me thing.* I shake the thoughts off. It doesn't matter *how* I feel him, the fact is that he is in so much pain. He really believes his family, even his twin, is out to get him. Every time I look in his eyes I want to go to him. This innate desire in me floods my senses and tells me to care for him.

A memory of my mum's letter flashes through my mind. *"He is your heart's poison and will be the key to your undoing if you let him."* She'd written it. She was right. Even just being around him is making me want to go to him, to forget any plans and abandon our mission so I can be with him. *Focus, Ankhara.* All I have to do was get through to him enough that we can get out of here. I have to make him see I am his friend, even if it makes my skin crawl.

Be careful, my love. His influence on you is stronger than you think. I can feel him in you.

Noah's voice reverberates in my mind and I gasp. *Why did I always forget we can do that?* I turn and look at him, and my brother jumps at it.

"What! What did he do? Did he say something to you? Is he controlling your mind? He's controlling your mind isn't he?" He crawls over to Noah like a creature out of a cave. "Stop it! Stop doing that to her! Don't do anything to her!" It's like watching a horror movie where the main character has a psychotic break and splits into different characters. Noah braces himself at his approach.

"No! No, Skavari. I promise. He's not doing anything, I promise." I am so desperate for him to believe me, for him to not do anything more to hurt Noah, that I think I convince myself so he'll believe me. I have tears in my eyes as I look at my brother, begging him to stop, but it feels like bartering with a child who is playing a different game to me. None of his moves make any sense.

He reaches out and strokes Noah's face. Sadness flashes in his eyes as he caresses the man I love. Noah stiffens, almost holding his breath entirely. Tears fill Skavari's eyes.

"My family is mean. Sorry, warrior. My family is very mean." Skavari's words are the creepiest shiver-inspiring words I've ever heard. It is just *weird*. I expected him to be this scary, magical fighter. Instead what makes him scary is his insanity. You don't have any clue what he will do next.

Skavari turns his gaze back to me. Then, as though a clog turned in his brain, he stands up and his gaze softens. His face returns into the angry glare I remember from my first sight of him and when he speaks he seems totally different.

"Dear sister. Don't treat me like an imbecile. I know the two of you love one another. I can see it in his puppy dog eyes. Hell, I can feel it leaking out of you. It's almost cute. Mostly disgusting. He's a peasant. A warrior, of a different class to us. To you. My sister, you and I were made to rule, not fight. You and I were made for something more than what this life has offered us so far. More than what our family has offered us - to cast me out and to send you away from me? I mean, that was cruel. Don't you agree?"

He sits and crosses one of his long skinny legs over the other, then folds his arms over his knee, bending one arm up to flick something out from underneath one of his fingernails. It is like he wants to entice me but at the same time show me he is bored by this. None of this makes any sense. All that makes sense to me are two things - his brain is messed up and we need to get out of here and away from him as quickly as possible.

"It does seem quite cruel, yes." Perhaps agreeing with him is a shortcut out of here. My pulse quickens. Agreeing with insanity seems like a false safety. I know the truth. Even if I doubted their decision, I know my parent's intentions were pure. They'd sent me away because they wanted to give me a normal life. What confuses me was that they hadn't offered him the same gift. Maybe he'd be different if he'd grown up forgetting I existed too. Maybe the prophecy wouldn't have ended like this. *Maybe I should stop thinking about maybe's and stay focused.*

"Would you like to tell me your version of the story?" I ask him, tentative and curious.

Skavari looks at me, his eyes scrolling up and down over my body. He is trying to figure out if I mean it. I guess he sees the part of me that does, because he settles in to tell a story that is very different from anything I've heard before.

"Okay, sister." He shifts posture and brings his elbow to his knees to lean on. "Let me tell you a story that will knock some sense into that pretty head of yours."

He looks around at everyone else in the room, giving me an opportunity to do the same. All six Hoods stand motionless, unwavering in the presence of Skavari's craziness. Kit is hunched over, a cold sweat on her forehead and dark red and grey rings under her eyes. She looks like death. Literally. She needs to get out of here and my gut tells me she doesn't have much time to do it.

Noah is stiff in his seat, tied up just as I am, and other than his obvious frustration and probably a headache like mine, he seems fine. His forehead tells a different story. I know the furrows in his brow mean he is worried. One look at his face when he glances at Kit is all I need to confirm why.

She'll die if we don't get her out of here, Annie.

This time I make sure not to react to the sound of his voice in my mind.

How? What have they done to her?

He looks away from me and I do the same, not wanting to draw any attention to our communication.

Plastic. Nymphs are an extension of the forest. Anything chemically based.. Well. It kills them. Poisons their blood. She won't have more than hours.

Skavari brings his eyes back to me and waves at his Hoods.

"Untie my sister immediately. I won't have her locked in here with peasants."

The two Hoods on either side of me utter some words in a language I've never heard and the ropes loosen. I feel the pulling stop as the energy leaches out of the bindings.

"Come, sister." Skavari rises and extends a hand to me. "We have much to catch up on. Let us do so alone."

Internally, I gulp. I don't want to leave Noah and I especially don't want to leave Kit here in the state she is in. I wriggle my hands and free them from the ropes, reaching out my hand to allow my brother to help me up.

We'll get her out of here tonight. Be ready. I whisper to Noah in my head, afraid that if I think it too loudly someone will sense it. These people are gifted in magic. I feel sure they'd be able to taste it around me, if they haven't already felt or seen it.

"Let me tell you the story of how I came to be me." I nod to Skavari as I stand, now right before him. He is taller than me. I imagine if we were to hug my head would tuck well under his chin. He is taller than Noah even, but much thinner.

"Okay, I'm ready to hear your truth," I tell him, and I mean it. I am ready. I want to hear both sides. It is something my dad had taught me. He always used to say, *"Megan, there's always three truths - your truth, their truth, and THE truth. If you are truly wise, you will always connect to all three."* In my whole life he's never been proven wrong. Every time we had a family conflict, he'd make us look at both perspectives, then imagine we were floating above the conversation, taking the angel's perspective from above. Having all three perspectives makes the truth obvious. Just as Kit had said the next step would always be.

I love you. His voice is balm in my mind. *We'll be ready.* I steal no last glances at Noah or Kit. I want to keep my focus on Skavari, to show him I am listening. I want him to know I care. Whether or not I intend to stick around here, that part at least is true.

"Return to your usual posts," Skavari calls over his shoulder to his Hoods and they respond, moving silently and immediately. They are diligent warriors. I'll give them that.

A quick count tells me three of them left the tent and three stayed. As we walk outside we are greeted by two extra bodies, who I assume to be the two who stay close to Skavari. I hadn't even realised they'd been standing by the door this whole time. *Shit. Focus Ankhara.* I am going to need to be more diligent myself if I want any chance of getting out of here.

"Leave us," Skavari says to his B1 and B2. I wonder which of them was the asshole that left the lantern shining in my face.

It is dark outside, and cold. I haven't even thought about our packs since we'd woken up here, but now I really want my jacket and a snack to warm me up.

"Can I get my jumper? It's chilly out here." I speak tentatively, with no idea how he'll react, and smile at him. *Come on, love me enough to respond to my basic needs please.*

"Of course. We'll go get your bag for you. You can bring it on our walk and use it as a cushion." My hopes heighten. Maybe this will be easier than I thought. If he gives me my bag, I'll have access to everything I need to incapacitate him.

"Thank you." I smile even more widely, oozing smileyness in his direction in the hope that it will catch on.

"And don't get any ideas. My men have already been through your bag. I know all you have is old letters and some snacks, and your weapons have been confiscated for obvious reasons." He drapes his long skinny arm around my shoulder and, to my surprise, it is a comfort. It helps that he is warm. "I want to get to know you and I won't hurt you, but you have to know you can't go back to them."

I look at him with an expression that asks the question for me. Back to whom?

"Back to our people. Back to the clues that might lead you to fulfil our so-called destiny." He reaches further around me and lifts my arm, looking at my magical time-keeping tattoo.

"You aren't leaving my sight for the next... seven hundred and eighty-four hours. After that, you can do what you like." He pauses and smiles, looking me in the eye. His insanity washes over him like waves over the sand of a beach. "If you try to leave any earlier... Well. I'll start with killing your nymph and your boyfriend, and you won't much like what I'll do after that."

He smiles and takes a deep breath, seemingly quite happy with himself as he turns and puts his arm around my shoulder again. In contrast to every other moment of my life, I have no words. I feel completely and utterly under his control.

"Now, let's get to know each other, shall we? Starting with your jacket and a nice night-time tour."

Maybe it isn't going to be as easy as I thought.

Maybe I've already failed.

Kit is going to die, and it is going to be my fault.

CHAPTER 34

ANKHARA

783 Hours Left

All I have to do is wait for an obvious moment to strike.

At least, that's what I keep telling myself as Skavari speaks. And speaks. An hour has passed and I've stopped listening in detail, having noticed that listening to him has the same hypnotic effect on me as meditation. His voice dulls my focus, so I have to keep my attention elsewhere. I am staring at the uneven patch of stubble on his chin when I suddenly hear my name.

"Ankhara? Are you even listening to me?" He angers every time he notices my attention drift away, but I don't have any other option. I need to keep myself separate, focussed.

"Yes, brother, of course. I'm thrilled to be finally listening to you" I only half lie. "I'm just really tired. If you talk to me much more tonight, I'm afraid you're going to have to repeat it all to my tired brain tomorrow morning." *And I'm afraid I'll run out of time to save my friend's life.* I repeat the word 'yawn' in my mind until it triggers a real physical yawn, which I embellish with everything I have.

Skavari leaps up, playing the role of caring brother he is desperate for me to believe. I would, maybe, if he weren't holding Kit and Noah's lives to ransom.

"Let's get you to bed. I'll show you your tent. We can continue over breakfast. You'll be thrilled to see your tent is right next to mine, so my best men can watch you too." He seems genuinely thrilled. I'm not.

My heart sinks as I give another well-executed yawn and he guides me to a cluster of tents.

"This is you and this is me." He gestures first to a small beige teepee, for me, then – *fucking of course* – to his brown tent to the right. It must be at least four times the size of mine. "You'll find your clothes inside, and my men just by your door should you need anything."

"Thank you," I say to him softly. And part of me means it. He is my long-lost brother. He is the twin I never knew I had. It is a strange sense of relief to finally be near him again. To feel him. To hear him speak. And if, I'm honest, when I look at him I can see the resemblance. He really does look like me. And yet, he really does have a darkness in him that I don't want to acknowledge as familiar.

CHAPTER 35

ANKHARA

780 Hours Left

*M*y eyes fly open.

Shit. When did I fall asleep?

Somehow, in the anxiety and boredom of tracking the routine of the guards outside my tent, I have dozed off. My head bobbing into my chest jerks me back to the present, my heart racing.

Kit.

She doesn't have much time, and I can't afford to fuck around wasting any of it. I had no idea plastic poisoning was a thing, but it makes sense. Nymphs are an expression of nature, as we all are, but they are so much more connected to that than us. We human-folk seem to have developed a knack for poisoning ourselves with disconnection and surviving it. It seems like reverse evolution if you ask me, but right now I am just grateful that Noah isn't sick as well. One of us is going to have to carry her out if we have any hope of getting her out of here. I doubt she is going to be able to fly through the trees in her current state, and I've never seen any evidence to suggest she'll heal quickly like supernatural creatures did on telly.

I am completely in the dark. I had blown out all the candles inside my tent at the first opportunity; I wanted the guards to settle into the thought of me being asleep, and I definitely didn't want them watching my shadows. I have my bag packed ready to go, under my blanket in the event someone should walk in, but evidence so far suggests that they aren't going to do that. They do, however, walk laps around the entire tent, which rules out my most basic escape plan of digging or cutting my way out. No. I am going to have to come up with something else.

Well, if there's ever a time for practising magic, Ankhara, here it is.
I think back to all I've learned in the last few weeks.

Spirit communication is probably not the trick for getting out of here. Neither is walking through trees, seeing as I am surrounded by some sort of plastic canvas. *Think again, Ankhara.*

Dream walking? Irrelevant. I need to be awake.

My mind flashes to the symbols, the golden runes I'd seen in my mother's tree. I close my eyes to envision them more clearly. They were spells. Intentions. Pieces of potions to be put together. None of them applied to breaking out of one tent, then into another, then out again.

I start to panic. Doubt rises in my mind. *What if I can't actually do this?* Kit's life is hanging by a thread and none of my training has been stealth-like. Nothing applies to this. Frustration starts to ooze through my system and dance with the fear that was already flooding me.

"Dammit, Kit, why didn't you teach me how to break free from something like this? Why teach me about visioning and seeing the truth and stepping into magic when I can't even create my own freedom when your life depends on it?" I whisper under my breath, berating her for her seemingly irrelevant teachings. Then it strikes me. Magic. Magic isn't just walking through trees and dreams and talking to things other people haven't seen yet; it is everywhere. It is unexpected happenings and pieces coming together in ways you couldn't even have imagined. It is having awareness and focus, and letting go so that you can be guided to your end result. End result. *What's my end result?* I close my eyes and take myself back to the clearing with Kit. I want to hear her again. To allow her voice to ground me back into her steps. If I am truly connected to all time and space, I know I'll remember the pieces to get out of here. She wouldn't have trained me for nothing. This is definitely unexpected and that's what she'd been preparing me for. *"Expect the unexpected, Ankhara. That way there will always be space for magic."* Her words reverberate in my mind.

Everyone's voices seemed to have a habit of doing that recently. There is something about the essence of someone's soul that sticks with me, and I can hear it in certain people when they speak. Not always, but usually there are moments where someone's voice will pierce through me to release a deep memory.

This is one of those moments. Kit had been so connected to herself in the sharing of those teachings that I've naturally harmonised into my own self connection, and, by extension, my connection to her and the information she had gifted me.

First step. Choose.

I close my eyes and take a deep breath in a meditative pose. Feeling my feet on the earth I give myself an internal pep talk, not wanting to speak out loud in case someone hears me and comes in to see what I am doing.

"Okay, Ankhara, what do you choose? I choose the highest good. I choose to be of service to that. Pretty sure that's where I start. And keep breathing and opening." My body immediately begins to relax just from recognising that intention, and I feel my frequency shift as I choose a different playing field. A more connected playing field is where I am going to be able to kick the goals I needed to kick – namely, rescue Noah and Kit and get out of this place alive ASAP – and so I let myself float there. I focus on a golden ball of light that I tell myself is my greatness, the expression of my magic, and I visualise it coming closer and closer to my body until it completely washes over me. I feel calm, excited, grounded, alive, energised. A sense of inner peace and warmth sweeps over me and is met by the fire of my determination.

"I choose to get the benefit of this practice, and to formulate useful information about getting out of here unseen." I feel openness and clarity sweep over me as my mind begins to empty out.

"I choose to come from the perspective of my connection to all time and space. To allow a free flow of focused information to fall through me. To see truth, choose love and follow wisdom." And then I stand up, take another deep breath and ask myself what I'd love.

Answers and emotions flood me. Visions appear in my mind's eye of the three of us free in the forest. Kit lying on the earth, injured and sickly but refuelling and healing through her connection to the plants. Me hearing the singing of trees, and Noah holding his hands around mine. We are safe. There is urgency in the air, but we are free and able to choose for ourselves where to go next. It feels intimidating but in a good way. Like the stepping-stones had been created for me to choose my destiny, and it is time for me to live in that. I feel inspired by it.

I shake my body and let that vision go. Now I have clarity about my goal I need a greater perspective on my current situation so I can fully inform myself. I ask my higher self to show me the truth of my situation and I take a deep breath and empty my mind to allow the information in. I see darkness. Shadows. A sense of being locked in a dungeon with no escape, and yet there are tiny holes of white light in the vision too. As though there were actually little exit points to the outside world that I am just missing because I've been staring into the darkness. It is frightening, and I feel incapable of changing anything, and yet there is also an undertone of possibility if I allow myself to see it.

I shake that off as well, very ready to let go of the shadow side of myself that wants me to stay here with Skavari. It is real, that part of me that wants to hide away in the forest with him and allow the time to tick down and take any and all of my responsibilities with it. The rebel in me loves the idea of it, and of him. The little girl in me too, just wants moments in time with her twin brother. They are all parts of me that are afraid of losing him again, just when I've found him. And there is also a part of me that just wishes I could save him, and almost believes I can.

I take some more deep breaths, giving myself permission to acknowledge everything there as a piece of the truth, and then step back into the vision of the clearing with Kit and Noah, out and safely away from Skavari. At least in that moment of my vision we are. Kit healing brings relief and joy to my heart. Noah by my side feels like home. I feel grounded and easy in the thought that anything is possible with both of them by my side. The three amigos. Throw a mission at us and we've got it in the bag. Inspiration and power sweeps over me and I ask myself the final question.

What's my next step to getting there?

Immediately an image of me putting cloth over my guard's face floods into my mind. I am knocking him out with something, lowering him softly and quickly to the floor while the other one makes his lap around my tent.

I open my eyes.

Okay, okay, okay, cloth, cloth, cloth.

I look around the room and see a small cupboard pantry. I race over as quietly as I could, feet skimming softly and effortlessly over the dirt-covered rug on the floor. It is a horrible rug, sharp under my feet, but it does have the bonus of muffling sound, so I feel a moment of gratitude for Skavari's shitty taste in decor.

I open the cupboard and started sniffing what I can from of the little glass jars clustered within, opening them and waving my hand over the top like they teach you in science class. Mr Price's sharp voice echoes in my ears as I am transported back to high school. *"Never straight-up sniff anything if you don't know what it is. That's asking for a chemical disaster. Investigate, then act."* Thank you Mr Price. Perhaps science wasn't so useless after all.

I figure this was meant to be a tent for his guards to use in the night. There are loads of supplies in here and, to be honest, if I hadn't spent those hours sitting in my mother's tree reading her notes, I wouldn't know what I was looking for. Sniffing my way carefully through the jars, her discussion of valerian rings in my mind and I pray I'll find some. According to her notes, valerian, also known as all-heal, is like a natural anaesthetic. Enough of that beauty on a cloth and anyone will fall into a deep but harmless stupor.

As soon as I open the seventh jar I smell it. *Thank the freaking angel.* It seems a weird thing to be here, alongside chamomile and lavender in a tent I imagine was meant for the guards, but I am too elated to care. I grab a handful of the white flowers and leaves and wrap them up in my scarf, then wet one side of the cloth from the hot water bottle they'd left for me. Sweet, really, all things considered. I put the rest of the jar in my backpack for good measure. I have no idea how strong this stuff is but if it works I could maybe use it again at the other tent.

With no concept of how long this might knock someone out for, I creep up next to the tent entrance and squat. My bag tightly strapped to my back and my weapons in hand, I am going to be ready as soon as the next guard round comes. I crouch there for what feels like forever, silently aware of time ticking away thanks to my time-bomb tattoo, I can feel my heart pulsing in my ears and the tickling on my arm as the time passes.

As I feel a rush of warmth move though my hands, an idea occurs to me. I could sit with this concoction in my scarf and lace it with intentional magic while I wait. I feed the plants with my life force, giving them my energy to amplify their natural gifts. I stop only when the heat grows so intense it starts to burn and the smell begins to waft up towards me. The last thing I need is to knock myself out.

Finally, I hear B2 say he is going to patrol, and I rise, patiently waiting for him to be far enough away for me to strike. I have no idea if there is anyone else around the nearby tents, but there is no way to check and Kit doesn't have any time for me to waste second-guessing myself. I picture myself subduing the remaining guard and lowering him to the ground, then take a deep breath and pull aside the tent flap.

CHAPTER 36

ANKHARA

778 Hours Left

At first nothing happens. It's like everything is in some sort of slow motion. I somehow manage to not make any sound with the flap, and B1 is standing at his post, bopping his head around happy as Larry. The idiot has earmuffs on.

Perfect.

I relax, thinking he can't hear me, and immediately step on a stick that snaps under my foot. I freeze, cringing. In my panic it sounds louder than a gunshot. B1 freezes briefly, then sighs and returns to his bopping. It takes every ounce of self-control to not let out my own sigh of relief. I can't risk it. I look around me and hear B2's footsteps come to a stop at the back of the tent, and then smile at the sound of urine splashing.

Thank you thank you thank you. Here goes nothing.

I leap forward and smother B1's mouth and nose with my flower potion, patting his hair soothingly as I hold the cloth to his face. I don't know why, but somehow it seems like a good idea. And it is; almost instinctively he nuzzles into my hand and passes out as I gently lower him to the ground. It is a sweet combination of magic and mummy issues that I am happy to take advantage of.

I give in to instinct, and creep around the tent in the same direction B2 had travelled. This time watching for sticks more diligently. If I can hear his footsteps, there is nothing to say he can't hear mine if he is at least half focused. I can hear him whistling as he packs his pants and ties the drawstring, enjoying the finer moments of life. I let him. I want to catch him by surprise, and the longer he stands there the more he seems to relax. I'm in a hurry, sure, but not in such a hurry that I want to tip off the whole camp with a loud scuffle.

The fingers holding the scarf buzz and I look down to see the decoction soaking it doesn't appear vibrant anymore. *Fuck.* Somehow I just know. I can't explain it, but I realise it isn't going to be so easy this time. The dose has worn off and there is no way I can get more potion out of my bag without alerting B2 to my presence. Then something buzzes against my shin in the same way my finger had just been zapped, and a tingling sensation spreads up my left arm and leg. I look down to see my dagger handle glowing on the inside of my boot. In my panic I hadn't even realised it was still tucked away in there. This is the dagger that belonged to my mother. I hadn't thought of it earlier. In fact, stupidly, I'd forgotten all about it, but Noah had mentioned to me in passing that it was thought to have magical powers. Perhaps it had somehow shielded itself from our captors.

However it came to still be there, I'm grateful. But I'm not grateful for the thought of using it.

Him or Kit, Ankhara. You can't save both. You can't save everyone. I know it isn't my job to save everyone but I don't want to kill anyone either. I take a deep breath and feel my light within. My guidance. And I cry. Briefly, silently, as I crouch in the moments before striking down this man, I let my heart shed its tear, and then I pounce. It is swift and easy. So easy it frightens me. *Life is so goddamn precious.* I slit his throat and muffle his sounds with the scarf as if I'd done it a thousand times. Gently, I lower his body and take a moment to place a hand on his forehead before anger fills me.

Anger at this blood that stains my hands. Anger at all the death I've encountered these past weeks. Mrs Jo. My parent's identity. My birth mother. The spirits in the forest. And now B2, at my own hand. Later I will wish I'd known the name of the first man I ever murdered in cold blood. I have killed before but this feels different. He didn't attack me first. He didn't even see me coming. I can feel a cocktail of grief and anger boiling up inside me. In this moment, however, I need all the fuel of anger to propel me forward. I place my scarf over his face and drag him over next to the tent so that he is less out in the open, then take a deep breath, and run, cursing myself for not taking the scarf with me, but forcing myself forward. I don't know how much time I have. It is a race between Kit's life and B1 either waking up or being found. I have to get my skates on.

I run up through the trees like Kit had shown me. It is the swiftest, most natural way for me to move, and the only sounds I make are the same as the breeze makes in the leaves; nothing flinches in camp as I move through. Nothing, that is, until I finally land in the branches of the tree hanging over the front of the hostage tent.

My stomach drops as I look below me. Nobody sees me, but that isn't what I am worried about. I am in the trees now; no one will catch me from here. No, it isn't me that I fear for. I looked down expecting to see two men standing out the front of the tent, just as there had been outside mine, but that isn't what I see.

Below me, in the light of a campfire and a lantern hanging by the door, are not two but three guards. It isn't their numbers that scare me, however; it is the sight of a fourth Hood dragging a lifeless blonde body out of the tent as though it were a rag doll.

My hand shoots to my mouth to stop any sound coming out as I cry.

"Boss ain't gonna be too happy with this. Especially not if we wake him up in the middle of the night and tell him." The Hood who dragged her out speaks in a relaxed, country voice. *Evil bastard.*

My heart feels like it has been ripped out of my chest. Kit's body rests completely still on the earth. No plants lean towards her as they usually did. Instead, the grass actually droops. It is like the death is seeping out of her.

"She must have been more connected than we thought. What a waste. Let's wake him. He'll be more pissed if she's been dead half the night and nobody felt the urge to let him know. We either tell him or we'll all be dead come morning."

They nod in agreement as the biggest of them speaks. He is obviously the leader of the group, 'cause they all stare at him like evil puppies waiting to be told what to do. There is fear leaking off them all and I can see that they are all just scared kids too. Following my scared kid of a brother. *This is how idiots run the world.* I make a mental note to request emotional intelligence be added to our school curriculum as soon as I got back. *Maybe if we weren't all so scared and voiceless all the time, leaders couldn't lead people through fear.* It helps, thinking of how I could somehow possibly make a difference in this world in a moment when I've failed in the worst way possible. It softens the blow, but nothing dulls the pain in my heart when I look down at the emptiness in Kit's face, the sunken eyes. Nothing can stop the cold that creeps over my heart as I watch her lifeless form stretched out on the ground while they argue over who will go break the news to my brother.

I can't take my eyes off her. I trace every inch of her body. I don't know what I am looking for. Maybe I'm saying goodbye. Maybe I want to soak in every last piece of her before never seeing her again. It almost seems counterintuitive to embed such an image into my mind, but I can't help it. I let my eyes fill with tears as I sear every inch of her into my vision. I etch her brow, her soft, warrior hands, her badass outfit, all of it, into my mind. I am just about to pull myself away when I see it.

Her right index finger, splayed out in the dirt, twitches. I blink and catch myself before stupidly jumping out of the tree, and will myself to stay focused on her finger.

Twitch.

There it is again!

Tears fall from my face in relief just as I realise the smallest of the Hoods had been nominated to tell my brother. Classic.

A teardrop lands on the shoulder of the big guy, and he brings his hand to the back of his neck to investigate what has splashed there. I curse and move, flying into the next tree just as he looks up. I don't wait to see what happens next. I have a new target.

There is no way in hell I'm letting anyone get anywhere near waking up my brother. The small Hood has taken a shortcut, walking around the camp past the back of everyone's tents. His laziness affords me the perfect opportunity to pounce on him in the darkness where nobody will see us.

In a matter of moments, my death toll for the evening is almost two. I land on the grass behind him like a cat, and he doesn't even notice. My tree-running gift is next level. That, coupled with my newfound hope of saving Kit's life, means he has no chance of getting out of this alive.

Unless...

Something irks me.

This Hood is just a kid. He must be a couple years younger than me, even, and he's obviously terrified of my brother.

He hadn't laughed at Kit's body like the others had. In fact, he'd looked sad. Something about the kink at the top of his ears and the slump in his shoulders as he walks tells me he has more in common with Kit than I'd cared to have thought.

Maybe...

No, Ankhara. No mercy.

He might be able to help us.

He also might kill you.

He clearly doesn't want to be here.

That doesn't mean he wants to be with you.

The voices in my head are having a fucking field day, and that is something I don't have time for.

No festival debates today my internal friends I think to myself before taking a breath and clearing my mind.

I imagine my mother in the tree above the river in the clearing. The picture of her immediately brings me ease. *She'd know what to do.* I smile at the vision of her and she reaches out to me, touches my forehead, and nods.

It is all the confirmation I need. I open my eyes and leap forward, covering my new friend's mouth and kicking his legs out from underneath him. I spin myself around and land on top of him, wrapping my legs around his hips to lock him down, with one hand holding his hands above his head and the other still over his mouth. His eyes stare at me in horror and I bring my face-smothering hand to my mouth in a 'shh' symbol before he can make so much as a peep.

I stare him straight in the eye and take a deep breath while I allow him to panic underneath me. I want him to see that I am calm, and not as scary as I seem.

"I'm not going to hurt you. I need your help."

I feel his chest tighten and his body relax underneath me. I simultaneously make it worse and better for him with my words.

"If I let you go, will you sit with me? I just want to speak." He nods, and I feel a sudden desire to make my power known to him.

"I'll have you know I am a certified badass, and if you pull anything, I won't hesitate to kill you if it means saving my friends."

He nods again, more vigorously this time, and I slowly let go, leaning back into a crouch.

For what seems a really long moment we just stare at each other. Two kids caught up on opposite sides of a fucked-up world. Both of us failed by the education that brought us here. Both of us, I imagined, failed by our families. Mine in letting me live without my magic. His in letting him live here. This is no place for a kid to find any happiness. Not even my brother feels that in this place. I don't imagine any of his Hoods do.

"Are you going to kill me?" His voice is shaking as he quietly asks his fate.

"I don't want to." I decide honesty is the best policy here. The law of my dad. "Can I tell you the truth as I see it?"

I ask and he nods, looking hopeful and confused.

"Thanks." *Not like he has a lot of choice, beige babe.* I force my mind to shut up and I speak. "The way I see it, you and I are just two kids that have been thrown down opposite sides of a fucked-up track. Do you know who I am?" He nods, and I decide to speak from my heart to his. I want to get through to him. I have hope that this can be a small light in a very, very dark tunnel. There have been multiple lights in my vision after all, and Kit still being alive is definitely one of them.

"Good. Then you know I think my brother is an absolute asshole, probably as much as you do." He sheepishly laughs. *Good sign.* "Well, I need to get my friends out of here."

Sadness creeps over his face.

"She's not dead. Just. She's barely alive, I saw it. Her finger moved. I saw her finger move twice. There isn't much time but at least she's on the earth now. That actually buys us a minute." He looks relieved and a light sparks in his eyes at this news. I don't know how much of it is relief at not having to impart bad news to my brother, but it is genuine.

"You could help us. You could help us get out of here, and if you do, truly, I promise you, I will have a place for you with my people. Help us get out of here and I will repay our debt to you with your freedom."

I look at him and wait. It is as though clockwork is ticking over in his brain as he sits there, contemplating his destiny.

"It would be an honour, Princess. You are everything my mother said you would be and more." His words shock me. I had expected his dislike of my brother, but I definitely hadn't expected to find anything but dishonourable affection for me in this place. *Magic.* Yes, this is unexpected indeed.

"Thank you... ah—"

"Simon." He smiles and holds his hand out to me, and I shake it.

"Right. Simon. Thank you." I stand up and dust myself off and he rises to stand before me. He isn't much smaller than me, but he is definitely in that awkward teenager phase. I feel relief flood over me that I hadn't had to kill him. *Yet.*

I shake off my doubt and fear and I focus, looking him dead in the eye.

"Right. Here's the plan."

He listens with everything he has, and then I jump back up into the trees and run back towards Skavari.

CHAPTER 37

NOAH

780 Hours Left

"Kit! Kit, please, wake up! Just say something, move, breathe, just show me you're still here, Kit!" I have never felt so helpless in my entire life as I sit here tied to a pole watching the life drain from my best friend.

She hasn't moved in what I think has been over an hour. She hasn't spoken in much longer. Her breath has come sharp and ragged for quite some time, and the guards rewarded me with a punch to the face when I told them she was running out of time.

I'd begged. And they'd shown no mercy. The anger that rages in me at their lack of compassion, their lack of common connectedness, is so strong I am shaking. In fact, I don't know how long it has been since I wasn't shaking. I'd been shaking when they'd taken Ankhara. My heart fills with dread at the thought of what they may have put her through. Of what they could be doing, right now, to the woman I love. But the reality of watching Kit die is what tips me over the edge.

"What's all the fuss about in here?" It's the large guard again. He is a *big* guy. Not one I'd usually like to fight but, given the circumstances, I can't be choosy about the opportunity.

She said she'll come. Be ready.

Ankhara's arrival is my only solace.

"She's dead." I spit at him. "She's dead because your fellow henchmen didn't listen to me. I told them she was on the edge and…" I can't speak any more. Sobs wrack my body as the devastation of this reality hits me. She isn't dead. Not yet. She is so very close, but I am connected to her faint little life force. I can feel the tiniest pulse of energy coming off her auric field. This is all I could think to do to help her. Get her off the plastic. If they at least drag her body over to the earth, it will feed her. I know it will.

He laughs and then swears. "Well fuck. What a waste of time that whole connection business is then, eh? Dying within hours of touching plastic. Seriously." He shakes his head as if it were a baffling joke. My friend's life. Nothing but a joke to him. I cry out in disbelief.

"She deserves better than this, you piece of beef!" Not the best insult I've ever come up with but it is accurate and I am emotionally depleted.

He laughs again at my insult, which is almost fair enough, but that is well besides the point. I need to get Kit out of here.

"Is that so princess boy?" He strolls over to me and kneels in front of me before almost gently slapping my face, the way friends and warriors sometimes do. It is an insult to our code that he feels able to do that. A complete insult.

"When Skavari and Ankhara find out what you've done they'll have your head." It's the only card I have left to play. Scare him into action. "If you leave her here Ankhara will interpret that as a direct disrespect. How do you think the almighty Skavari will respond to his sister being disrespected like that? On the first night of their reunion, no less?"

I have him thinking. It almost didn't seem possible for him. The way his eyes roll around his head as he taps his chin makes it obvious he is all brawn, no brain. This man is incredibly mentally slow. At least he'll be easy to bait.

"Uh, you might be right actually. Our Lord can have a bit of a temper... as you've seen."

"I have. And I doubt he'll take well to insults directed at his sister. Or to direct failure to carry out his direct orders. Maim us all you like but don't kill us. That was his instruction."

"Fuck." Now I have him right where I want him.

"It is possible..."

His gaze snaps to me as though I hold the golden key to unlock the trap he's found himself in. He grabs my shoulders and shakes me.

"What? What? Spit it out, you idiot!!" It's rich, him calling me an idiot, but it is perfect.

"Well, I thought it was just a myth but... you might be able to revive her spirit. She's a nymph."

He looks at me as if I am crazy, so I take it upon myself to continue, lowering my voice as if I am telling him some personal secret. Which I guess I am. It's just a secret that I am totally making up.

"Nymphs are connected to the earth, right? So there's this myth, that if you bury them in a shallow grave shortly after their death, they can be revived." In all honesty, it isn't a myth. It's something I know to be very true – if she isn't already dead yet when they place her there, and she doesn't have much time.

He looks at me as if contemplating what could be true. And then he frowns, shakes his head and growls.

"Look, I'll drag her out there and I'll let the boss know, but I'm not going to believe your mystical dumb-ass shit just because you want free labour for your friend's funeral. It was an accident. He won't kill all of us over an accident like this – probably just the messenger." He stands up, looking confused that we'd just had a semi-decent conversation.

"Thank you." I say to him. Despite my best efforts to keep control of myself, tears stream down my cheeks. Dragging her outside is all she needs. I just wanted him to think it was his own idea, but whether dirt or grass, any living thing will feed her as much energy as it can to support her continued breathing. And that is all I need, to buy Kit some time until Ankhara arrives to get us out of here.

I watched helplessly but hopefully as Big Guy moves over and unties Kit. He grabs her by the foot and starts dragging her, a sign of profound disrespect. It would be simple for him to pick her up and carry her. She is tiny compared to him, but part of me is grateful. I can't imagine he'd put her down gently, and I'm not sure she could survive a fall from twice her height in her condition. She needs earth, and he is dragging her against it. I feel a spike in her energy as her body slid against the ground. It is slight, but it's there, and it reminds me to breathe again.

Focus, Noah. Kit has some time now and Annie will be here soon.

This is what I tell myself as they squabble over what to do about Kit's death.

I close my eyes and take a deep breath as anger and overwhelm flood through me. My mind fights me with the images of Kit's pale, lifeless body and my heart aches from not knowing Ankhara's whereabouts.

That is when I feel her. Ankhara's energy is like a breath of fresh air to my being, but then she breaks my heart. I can feel the moment she sees Kit's body and I immediately try to send a message to her mind, to let her know that Kit still has some time, but before I can form the thought, she is gone. I feel her leave and it rips something out of my body as she goes.

She's been through so much in such a short time. More than anyone should have to bear. My only hope for her now is that this will not be the straw to break her back, because if her will breaks now, if she flees in despair, it will not only mean the death of Kit and myself. If she runs now, in the face of all that she has lost, if she chooses to forsake us and all that comes with us, then magic is lost to the world forever.

I sigh and force myself not to strain against the magicked ropes that hold me in place. If I am going to be ready when Ankhara returns to me, as I have to believe she will, I can't throw away my spare energy on this piece of rope.

Come on, Ankhara. You were born for this. Choose your heart.

I silently will her to come back to me as I sit in stillness with my eyes closed. All I can do now was focus on my end result - our freedom. The rest is up to her.

CHAPTER 38

ANKHARA

777 Hours Left

It is one hell of a risk but I have to take it. I'd felt the heartbreak in Noah when I left Kit's body, and I feel his call pulling on me now.

I'm coming, hot stuff.

What I wouldn't do to be able to run straight to him at that moment. My body begs me to, but something greater than me tells me I have to go back, and I lean into that. Simon will do his bit. I have to believe it. I have to and I do.

I arrived at the trees behind Skavari's tent and hide in their shelter, waiting. I want to see if anything had exposed my escape yet. I can just see the body of B2, tucked right against the base of the tent. My mission is simple. It occurs to me as soon as I look at him. Grab my scarf. Finish off B1. Leave.

Slowly, keeping low to ground once I come down from the tree, I make my way over to his body. My eyes have adjusted to the darkness now and everything feels so bright to me that I'm sure anyone could see me if they looked. *Don't think about that, just keep moving.*

I reach the corpse, drenched in a pool of cooling blood, and retrieve my blood-soaked scarf. I can still smell the valerian on it, just, and I quickly empty the flowers and cast a spell over a fresh batch from my backpack, grateful I'd had the wit to pack the rest. If I don't have to, I'd rather not kill someone else – but Kit has barely any time, and I'm not taking any chances. Slowly, I make my way around the tent and crouch to peer around the side to the opening of the tent, right where I expect B1's comatose body to be. The ground, however, is bare. There is no one to be seen. A quick glance at Skavari's tent tells me his lights are still out, and I can feel him sleeping. That means B1, having regained consciousness, has decided to try to solve the problem of my escape without incurring Skavari's wrath. I imagine he hasn't found B2 yet or he would surely have raised an alarm.

"Well, what do you think you're doing?" His voice comes from behind me, so close I can feel his breath on my neck. *How did I not notice him approaching?* I'd been so focused forward I hadn't even heard him coming. I throw my scarf and dagger on the ground, holding my hands in the air in surrender as I slowly turn around so I can pinpoint his location.

"Okay. Fair's fair. You caught me." I speak matter-of-factly. As if I'm going to go down without a fight.

He looks me up and down and underestimates me. I can see it in his eyes, the way he judges me as a piece of meat. He doesn't see the warrior in me at all, and he laughs. His chuckle closes his eyes and he reaches his hand out as if to usher me back into the tent.

"Get back inside and I'll tie you— eh!"

He doesn't see it coming at all. I drop to the ground, pulling his hand down with me and kicking his feet out from underneath him. Before he's even registered what is happening, I've slipped the dagger straight through the side of his neck, and placed my scarf of death over his face to smother his choking.

Two people. I've killed two people in the space of an hour. *At least this one was attacking you.* I'm happy, for now, to tell myself that makes it better. But despite my best efforts at silencing his death struggle, someone has heard us. There's torchlight coming from around the corner and I can hear a Hood quietly calling out to the guard so as to not wake Skavari. I desperately want to run, to race back to the other tent in the hope that Simon will be ready to have my back, but I can't. I can't risk my brother waking up. He'll feel me. I just know he'll be able to feel me as though I was part of him. I have to get as far away from him as possible before he wakes up. So I hide, behind the tent around which I can see the light approaching, and as swiftly as a cat, before he even sees me coming, I've pounced upon him, slit his throat, stifled his death throes and dragged him to lie with his brothers in death.

Make that three.

I don't even take a breath to gather myself. I just keep moving. As though in a trance I gather my things, wiping my dagger on my now-ragged scarf, and run. Into the trees I sprint as fast as I can and I feel like I am flying. My heart sings at the prospect of seeing Noah and my blood pounds in my ears as I frantically and magically approach. I arrive at the same branch I'd perched on as Big Guy had dragged Kit's body out not an hour earlier, and gasp. I haven't even had the chance to gather my breath before I am forced into holding it again.

Kit's body is still below me, but lying now in the centre of an entire clearing of dead grass. Literally the entire clearing has given its life in an attempt to sustain her. Simon is standing with the other Hoods, laughing sheepishly at a joke one of them has made. I can see nervous sweat dripping from his forehead and he wipes it with his sleeve as he gulps from a tankard.

But none of that is what shocks me. There, across the clearing between the trees, float a pair of large, fluorescent blue eyes. I don't know whether to be excited or terrified at the presence of this creature, but I could swear, on my life, that it just winked at me. *She.* Whatever it is, it's a she, and even though I can't see anything else other than her eyes, huge and luminous, two metres above the ground, I jump. As if jumping onto a bunch of Hoods isn't scary enough, I do so knowing full well a mysterious creature stands in the trees watching. But somehow, I have no idea why, this knowledge makes me feel better. More powerful. She feels familiar, and the sheer power of her presence reminds me of that same power within me. It also makes clear the stark contrast with these three dim-witted, half-drunk Hoods. Simon is there too, of course, although I am counting on him doubling my numbers with his own sword.

He does. As soon as he sees me falling from the tree, headed straight for Big Guy, he slides his dagger into the guts of the guy standing next to him. I hadn't even seen the knife in his hand and I gulp at the thought of him doing that to someone who not long ago had been on his team, but also, with one glance at Kit, I get it.

I crash-land onto Big Guy and we roll over. Everything becomes a mess so quickly and all I can think about is getting inside that tent to see the state of him, the man I love.

"Noah. Can you hear me?"

I fight to stay focused enough to think to him as Big Guy pins me down and blood drips down my face from a cut on my forehead. My eyes fill with red and I can barely see. I can hear, though, what sounds like Simon arguing with the third Hood. Distracted by my jump, it sounded like he hadn't seen Simon's handiwork, and Simon is now blaming him for it, telling him to back off or he'll report his traitorous actions to Skavari.

Sneaky lil genius. I like him.

"I can hear you, Annie. She's alive. We need to get her out of here." Noah's voice is a sweet melody amongst the chaos.

"Trying over here. I saw her move." I respond and it distracts me.

Big Guy punches me across the face and the world starts spinning. We haven't made so much noise that anyone else is coming yet, but I am getting absolutely raped by this huge dude and with him pinning me to the ground, my arms pinioned above me, I have no leverage to do anything about it.

Raped. The word triggers a memory in me and I know exactly what to do.

I don't give myself the chance to talk myself out of it before I kiss him. Shocked, he releases his grip on my arms and I don't hesitate. I wrap my left ankle around his right leg, locking it against the side of my body, and do the same with his right arm. Before I know it I have pushed him up with my hip, having created enough leverage by unbalancing him to the side that I flip on top of him.

Thank you self-defence class. Fuck you rapey world. Ten points for me, motherfucker.

I smile and slit his throat. I don't know where or when I picked up the knife, or how I even found his neck through my bloodshot eyes, but I do it, making my official murder toll for the evening four. Four human lives I'll grieve for later.

I look over to the trees where I'd seen the blue eyes before to find only an empty clearing staring back at me. What isn't empty is the campsite. The fight has been loud, and people all around are waking up.

I'm coming, Noah. Brace yourself.

I steal a quick glance at Simon only to see him fall as his opponent slices his face.

"No!" I run towards him, not wasting any time, and stab his opponent in the back of his shoulder. He cries out loudly and falls to his knees, where I gracefully grab his hair and finish him off. *They're gonna call me the neck knifer.* I shake my head. I don't have time to worry about the serial killer name I'm going to be labelled with. Simon is hurt. I crouch beside him and he shakes his head.

"Get them out." He is gasping for air. I can't see if he is hurt anywhere else, but he's not in good shape. "Get them out of here. I'll do my best to cover you."

"No. I won't leave you." There is no way I am breaking my promise when he's put his life on the line for me. "I made a promise to you. I keep my word."

He grabs my hand and pushes me back, touching his hand to my heart with mine. "I see your honour, Ankhara." It feels nice that he's left out the formalities. "I'll take you up on your promise one day. Let me do this for you, Princess." *Almost.*

I gaze at him briefly, distraught at the thought of leaving him behind but certain I am running out of time.

"I will come back for you. This won't be forgotten."

With a squeeze of his hand, I let go, and run inside the tent. I have to free Noah first. He can carry Kit and I can't. I just hope his arms aren't numb. *And that that huge creature isn't out there where we're about to go running.*

Seeing him for the first time again sends electricity firing through my entire being. He looks perfect. Somehow, in the middle of a hostage breakout situation, I find a moment to admire the beauty of him.

"You're alive."

I smile.

"You knew I was alive, you pretty idiot, I was talking to you whilst becoming a murderer for the fourth and fifth time this evening."

He looks at me with a shocked and saddened expression that quickly hardens.

"We don't have much time, Annie, you've gotta get me out of here."

"Right. Sometimes I think I'd be a lot more efficient if you weren't so busy making me weak at the knees." It is a nicety to be joking with him. An eye in the middle of a murderous storm. My dagger slices easily through the ropes and the magic in them hisses, dissolving into the ground in a white foam. It gives me the creeps, but at least there is a sense of nature in its returning to the earth.

"Okay new plan. Can you carry Kit while I help Simon?" I ask him.

"Who the hell is Simon?" I shrug off explanation and run back out to the sound of shrieks in the encampment. Scream after scream echoes through the night as Hoods fall in the distance. Once glance is enough to show that the blue-eyed winky creature has stormed the camp and we have a brief window of opportunity to make a run for it.

"Ankhara, I've got her, let's go!" Noah yells at me from behind as I run back towards Simon.

"Leave!" I call out to Noah over my shoulder. It is agony feeling his hatred of pulling away from me, but it is necessary. Kit doesn't have the time for any detours. I am pushing it myself, and even though I can run through the tops of the trees, it won't help if Simon can't.

I reach him and he shoots up into a sitting position from where he'd been lying on the ground.

"Drag me into the bush and knock me out," he begs.

"What?"

"You have to knock me out. If Skavari or any of the others find me here awake they'll know. Or at the very least they'll kill me for being the waste-of-space warrior that I am. At least if you knock me out, they'll see I tried. And if you drag me into the brush, that thing just might not eat me."

I look at him, distraught. I hadn't really meant it when I'd left him earlier. Not if I could help it, and whatever that creature is, it's buying me the time to get him out of here.

"When Skavari wakes he won't fight for his men. He will hunt *you*. He doesn't care about us, and I'll only slow you down."

He is right. My brother has shown me no evidence that he cares for anything other than his own agenda, and if he catches me I don't think he'll be as "welcoming" as he'd been earlier. Not after the trail of bodies I've left behind in the last few hours.

I have no words. It was rare, but real. *This is becoming a regular thing.*

"Win this war," he says between gasps. "Find the dagger. Then all of this death will have been worth it. I can stay alive until then, and, who knows, it might help you knowing there's someone on your side in here if you ever get caught again."

There is no arguing with that, and I can feel Noah's pull on the back of my heart. It is time for me to leave.

"I'm sorry," is all I could squeeze out of my mouth before I whack him in the head with the pommel of my dagger, drag him into the bushes with his leg sticking out and his sword in his hand so he looks like he's gone down fighting, and run.

CHAPTER 39

ANKHARA

772 Hours Left

We've been running for over three hours when the sun starts to come up. I'd quickly caught up to Noah and run with him, moving from tree to tree to keep a watchful eye over the two of them, and behind us. So far, it seems we've managed to get away with no one on our tail, but we aren't keen to stop and find out – and I'm definitely not keen to meet that creature when we have a whole body to carry.

Kit is groaning. It seems as though she is gaining energy from Noah, which would be great if it didn't mean she was wearing him out. We have to do something.

"Noah, stop!" I gasp. Even magically running between trees is exhausting after three hours. I'm dripping with sweat and my muscles ache with untrained fatigue. "We can't keep going like this."

"*You* can." He puts Kit down to rest on a patch of long green grass that immediately starts feeding energy to her. Colour is starting to return to her pale pink cheeks. It provides a pleasant distraction from the alien language coming out of Noah's mouth.

"Correct me if I'm wrong, please, but I could have sworn I'd just heard you say *You can*. Meaning *I can*. Meaning *Go on without me Ankhara and leave Kit and I to possibly die*. So obviously I'm crazy because you'd never say that. Tell me again, what did you just say?" I'm babbling in exhaustion and disbelief, but I know from the sinking feeling in my gut that I'd heard him correctly.

"You can," he all but whispers as he slowly walks up to me and clasps my hands. "We always knew there would come a time. Kit and I... we were just here to help you while we still could." Tears well in his eyes as they do mine, but he holds his ground. "We all knew. You are the one who has to fulfil the prophecy, and if Kit and I keep moving like this, she'll die and you'll probably get caught."

"That doesn't mean this is okay. I'm not okay with leaving you when she's like this. I'm not okay with not knowing if you're okay. I don't want to be so far away from you that I can't hear your thoughts. I don't want to be far away from you at all. I need you. Both of you. Especially you. Noah, you can't just expect me to leave you out here. How would I even know where to go?"

He smiles a sad, proud smile, and points to the centre of my chest. *My heart.*

"This."

He says it as if that is the end of the conversation. I don't want it to be. I want to know where he'll go, where he'll take her. I want to know where I should go, and how long I should go there for. I want answers. Any answers other than the one he is giving me.

I look up at him and everything melts away. Everything melts into a blur around the edges of his face, and I am lost in a puddle of salty tears and sexual energy as he kisses me. His lips taste like the salt of the earth, and his hands feel rough yet smooth on my skin. Immediately I press my body into his and I feel myself open to him. Energy and emotions flood my body. I sob. Somehow, kissing him and sobbing at the same time is possible. In the fires of our passion he manages to push me up against a tree. I feel my rucksack press against the bark and his hands slide down to my belt and fasten something to it. I pull myself away and look down to see he's hooked his water bottle and key chain.

You'll need these more than me.

His voice tickles my mind like velvet as I drink him in. I want to soak in every last inch of him. I can feel the truth in it. Me leaving. I knew it was coming. Grandma and mother had both prepared me for it in their own ways. But I don't have to like it.

I wrap my arms around him and kiss his neck in a bear hug. Tasting my tears on his skin, I trace my lips back up to his jaw, and kiss his cheek back to his mouth where I pause, moments away from him, feeling his breath on mine. Our tears fall at the same time as we look at each other, our mirrors. I feel my heart crack open and am about to kiss him one last time when I hear movement behind him and panic. We both spin around, braced ready in a fighting position.

We are met with laughter.

"You two are always in need of a little cool down."

Kit is leaning against her elbow in the grass, smiling a strained smile at the both of us.

"Well done team. You did good."

"Kit!" we exclaim in unison and fly to her side.

"Lay back down," Noah orders her straight, and not without a grimace of disgust, she complies. She is evidently still very much worse for wear.

"How are you feeling?" In hindsight it is probably a stupid thing to ask. "You look like shit." I smile at her, not wanting to filter our usual banter for her current condition. She is a badass. She doesn't need me to cushion her.

"I'm fine." She looks up at me. "And he's right, Ankhara." She doesn't need to say anything else. I know exactly what she means.

We are all thinking the same thing.

Somehow, it is obvious.

I'm starting to hate-love that word, I think to myself, and they both laugh, letting me know the thought wasn't actually kept to myself. I blush.

"You guys..."

"There's nothing else we can do that you aren't ready to do without us." Noah cuts me off before I can even make my case for staying, and I nod.

He's right. I don't know exactly what it is telling me to, but I have to do this. I have to complete the next step on my own.

I close my eyes and take a moment to gather myself. I see a golden ball of light and feel its warmth. It radiates kindness, charisma and strength. I feel loyalty, honour and creative inspiration bleed through my veins as my power comes back into my centre. My desire flows through my body like lava through the veins of a mountain, and I let it. My body is alive and I am free. It is time for me to fulfil the prophecy. All I have to do is run.

I open my eyes, drinking them in. Kit, alive and on her way to recovery. I can rest easy in the knowledge that at least she is going to survive. All she needs is a safe place to hide for a few days and she will be completely fine.

And Noah. Oh my word, Noah. Looking at his chiselled face switches a light on inside me, but nothing compares to the way my heart skips a beat when his eye catches mine. I can feel him in every cell of my body just looking at him.

You'll still be able to feel me if you try.

I nod to acknowledge that I've heard him.

I squeeze both their hands as tight as I can, and I look down at Kit.

"Look after him," I say to her, and we all smile. Mostly because I am funny but also because all three of us are doing our best not to cry. I look back up to Noah, "and don't you dare stop running until you're certain neither of you will die."

He looks amused at my seriousness, but his face softens in response to my glare and he promises me with his eyes as only he can.

It is all I need. Certainty. Security in the knowledge that both of them will be safe.

"We'll make a trail away from you. Stick to the trees as you move, and don't stop until you can't feel him anymore." He makes a good point. I'd forgotten I'll be able to *feel* Skavari's hunt approaching me.

"Run."

✢

CHAPTER 40

ANKHARA

770 Hours Left

Kit's voice echoes inside my head for the next eight hours as I run non-stop, the image of Noah's eyes in the fore of my mind and my heartbeat pulsing outwards, energetically attuned to my surroundings. For the first time since I'd left them, when I push out with my magic, I feel nothing.

I am alone. In the middle of a forest I know nothing about, I am completely and utterly alone. It is the most hollow, isolating feeling of my entire life. I don't know where I am going, and I don't know what lies between now and the end of this road, but I know what I want, I know where I've been, and I know how to figure out my next step to get exactly where I need to be.

Magic will guide you home.

A voice I don't recognise speaks to me and I feel a buzzing in my lower leg. My boot... *the dagger.* I pull it out and stare at the stone in the hilt. Bright ruby red, it is humming and glowing. I brush over it with my thumb, and a beam of light shoots from the end of the blade, catching me completely off guard.

"Woah!" I throw the dagger up in the air in shock and, again to my amazement, I see it land *in the air* and spin, the red gem casting its beam of light out in circles. I feel it begging me for instruction, so I push aside the part of me that still thinks all of this is crazy. I have had enough evidence now to know to follow my senses, crazy or not.

"Take me to the dragon's den," I command my mother's tiny but fierce sword, and it spins to a stop, pointing between the archway of two trees. "Well. I figure I have nothing else to lose."

I pluck the dagger from the air and hold it, figuring I'd best keep it on hand in case the light moves. A pang shoots through my heart, knowing that running that way is steering me further and further away from Noah.

I look down at the ticking time bomb on my arm.

Seven hundred and sixty-two hours.

Just over a month.

"A lifetime away from you, Noah Morgan. A blink in the eye of time to save magic for the world. No pressure."

I wonder how long it will take for speaking to myself to turn to insanity, hoping a month isn't long enough to tip me over the edge, and then the urge wells up in me to throw the knife out in front of myself. As it flies through the air it rises, and I mimic its motion, moving up the trees to the height of the path my mystical knife is tracing.

I fucking love magic, I think to myself and I run through the treetops.

Time to slay a fucking dragon.

I'd be lying if I said it hasn't crossed my mind that the sooner I slay that dragon, the sooner I'll be on the receiving end of a different kind of fully consensual slaying.

I'm pretty sure it makes me run faster.

TO BE CONTINUED...

SNEAK-PEEK
ANKHARA CODES; BOOK 2

I didn't think it would come to this. I'd dreamt it. I'd felt it. I'd been suspicious of it. I'd even feared it... but I didn't think it would *actually* come to this. I didn't want it to. I didn't want this to be my reality. My world. *My world, what a joke.* Everything I'd known to be my world had been flipped on it's head. You know yourself better than anyone else, they'd said. Yeah, right. No one even told me my real name. *But I had known. I knew Megan wasn't who I was.* I sighed. I guess it was true. I guess I did know, and maybe forgetting, maybe feeling like everything was wrong was part of the process. Who knew.

Not me.

Maybe me.

I sighed again, and lay back on the grass. I gave my heart to the earth. A practice Kit had shown me. *Oh, Kit.* A tear rolled down my face. I'd known her less than a few weeks and I felt such a gap in her absence. I missed her like you would miss someone you'd known your whole life. But I guess even that.... I *had* known her my whole life. I'd just buried the memory of it.

"Imagine the earth is holding your heart, imagine she has your back, and she can take from you everything that isn't serving. Imagine she can remind you to find your power in your heart, and to use your will to access it. Imagine. Just imagine that the earth is supporting you, and you're connected deeply to that support. Imagine, as you lay on the earth, that you can feel your innate connection to all time and space, and as you lay there for longer and longer, she brings you closer and closer to the remembering of who you truly are. Just imagine." That's what she'd said and she was right. If I gave myself the freedom to imagine it I could feel it. I could feel everything

shifting as though it were shapeshifting, even though all that was truly shifting was my mode of awareness. The longer I lay there and the more focused I was, I felt myself slip out of perception and into my intuitive state of being. Into my frame of mindlessness where I could see the connection between all things and beings, where nothing was separate truly, and everything was just experiencing an illusion of separation through identity. And I could see the genius in that. I could see the gift of all the different puzzle pieces each of us brought to the table. Each species. Each plant. Each member of each species. Each bringing our own gifts. I melted into it and I felt the earth shift. Birds flew from the trees, and the air changed pace. My eyes flew open and I began to notice how my surroundings had shifted. The once alive clearing I'd stopped in felt dead, the aliveness replaced with a silence that sent chills down my spine and made me question.

The birds are gone.

Danger has come.

Something had scared the birds away, and it wasn't me connecting to nature that had done it. It wasn't the aliveness of my being clearing the way. Something else had joined me here. Something... big. Powerful and large. I could *feel* it and if I focused I could hear it. Just. I could hear the faint pants of breath, as though this giant creature had been racing to arrive here, and was now trying to suppress its oxygen thirsty pants. I sat upwards and looked around, slowly, not wanting to make any sudden movements and draw any unnecessary attention. Well. I was 99% certain I had already drawn this creature's attention. What I didn't want was to draw it's attack.

"It's okay, I can feel you." I said into the trees, hoping that the creature would at least feel my intention if not speak my language. "I mean you no harm. I'm simply here to connect with you." It felt true despite feeling like a really strange thing to say. *Connect with it? I just don't want it to kill me.* My identity was running riot, but my heart felt calm, and I believed in my heart more powerfully.

Slowly but surely I stood up, facing the direction I could most strongly sense it, and held my hand out.

"Please, show yourself to me. I promise I won't hurt you."

I looked up, feeling pretty awkward to be honest. This seemed ridiculous, talking to the forest on a hunch that there was some creature out there who could not only hear me, but understand the words I was saying, or *feel* the energy of my spirit and intention. Wild. And if I'd learnt anything in the last few weeks... it was that wild didn't make it untrue. My definition of crazy, didn't make something untrue. In fact, I'd kinda learnt that everything I thought to be crazy was sane and natural. *Natural.* I was born for this.

I felt my shoulders arch back and my heart open, and that's when I caught my first glimpse of her. A giant, black, paw stepped out from the brush of the long grass, and paused. All I could see was this paw. It was *huge*. At least the size of my face. I swallowed, and took a deep breath to calm myself. If this thing wanted to kill me there wasn't much I could do about it other than run and hide in a tree trunk, which, judging by the size of those paws, she'd peel open like a piece of fruit and gobble me up as swiftly as a human might gobble up a peach.

There would be no running here today.

I stood my ground and bowed. *Just like the dream.* First I kneeled, and as I felt the air soften, I bowed on all fours, arms outstretched to this creature I could only imagine to be the magnificent beast of my dreams. One who had never hurt me, and turned out to be my friend. *Focus on your end result, Ankhara. Love and honour this creature and it will love and honour you.* I heard the footsteps of great big black paws and focused on my breath and my energy. I imagined the light of the soul of this creature, and stayed connected to her. I connected with her gifts, her strengths, her magic, and holy fuck I was blown away. This creature was seductive. She was sensual and powerful and majestic in ways beyond that of a human or a big cat. She was the embodiment of mystic magic with a hedonistic twist. I could feel her desire in my loins and her heartbeat in my throat. I wanted to growl. And I did. Before I could contain myself I was growling what was more of a moan, and it only made me feel her more deeply. That's when I heard her growl in response. It wasn't an angry growl like one might expect, more so a primal meeting. Our sounds were introducing us in a way words couldn't. Her spirit was dancing with mine, a magical form of handshake I wished was the norm. I made a note to myself to recommend that to my people if I ever got home.

A soft, firm pressure built on my forehead, and I felt the tickle of her breath down the side of my cheeks, twinkling in my loose wisps of hair.

"Hi." I didn't even mean to speak out loud but her touch felt so familiar it slipped out. It felt as though I was meeting myself in a different form. Like I was remembering a version of myself I'd been or getting a glimpse of a version of me I'd become. I *was* her. I don't know how I knew it but I just did. I couldn't explain it to you if I tried. You'd think I was crazy, but if you felt it, you'd see, it was the most natural thing ever.

Her left paw gently rested on my right hand, and her nuzzle into my neck told me she was ready to say hello too. Part of me, my mind I suppose, was telling me I should be nervous, but there wasn't an inkling of that in my being. I was excited and I smiled to show her. She purred and nuzzled into me further, so much so that I rolled over onto my back, laughing. She *licked* me. From my forehead down my face she actually licked me. But it wasn't scary or gross. It felt soft and innocent, like the lick of a kitten meeting you for the first time and wanting a taste of your flavour. I gave myself the opening of my eyes and drank her in for the first time. She was stunningly beautiful in a way that yup, I'll say it, she intimidated me with her good looks. That doesn't happen often. Her eyes were the most piercing blue I'd ever seen and they had an ethereal essence to them, like they were seeing *me.* Like the full, magical-can-walk-through-trees-and-open-portals, me. She could see it all and all I could do was stare at her. It was like an instinct had taken over my body and I was taking her in like a mate, even though that's not what she was for me. I flipped into a primal state of being, and I rolled over, wanting to dance with her. I wanted to honour her. To bow to her again, now in the full seeing of her in both the feeling realm and the visual.

Standing up, I finally grasped a picture of how truly magnificent she was. Her long, silky midnight black body glistened in the sun like silk, and it was all I could do to walk beside her and run my fingers through her skin cloak. It was like touching magic. My fingers tingled and felt everything and nothing at once. A similar essence to what touching the veil had felt like, but more electricity. I wanted more and I could feel her yes. I felt so strangely connected to her. I ran my hands through the full width of her and wrapped my arms around to hold her. Pressing my ear against her body I could hear her heartbeat. A soft, slow humming drum at the base of the rhythm of the forest. *Holy wow.* It was hypnotic. Like I didn't have a choice to leave and I was okay with it, I'd listen to her heart forever. I would have, except she dropped her body down and slid me off of her, taking a step back from me. I saddened, my heart aching to be with her. I desperately wanted her to stay. I didn't want her to leave. Not like everyone else. *Please stay with me.* I silently begged.

I cannot leave you. It is not possible, Ankhara.

Her voice ricocheted in my mind just as Noah's had. *That feels like a lifetime ago.* Sadness crept in at the missing of him, and yet I was so intrigued by this creature's voice I forgot. *She called me by my first name.* Her voice was old and thick, full of wisdom that only comes with time and life. It echoed, like the voices of many speaking through her at once. It was as though she was the culmination of my ancestors, before me and to come. I could feel such familiarity in the song.

She locked eyes with me and roared, the most fierce, throat tingling, heart racing sound I'd ever been witness to. It freaked me the fuck out, and I squinted my eyes and body tight on the ground. *Maybe she's here to eat me and that's why she can't leave...* A panic almost set in, but didn't. I couldn't tell you why. I just felt... numb. Afraid maybe. Safe maybe. I didn't know how I felt. I opened my left eye to peak at her, and quickly followed with my right to see that she was bowing to me. This big, magical, mystical creature of a thousand years of wisdom was bowing down to me. She was honouring me and I could feel it. My skin began to glow as a flame of orange gold light shot out of her forehead and into the earth at my feet. Every inch of my skin was glowing so brightly I could see it through all my clothing. Even the mesh between the laces of my boots leaked streams of the golden light I was coming to know as the purest form of me. *This is what it feels like to be seen in my greatness.* I felt soft, grounded in my truth. I felt my heart, beating steadily in my chest, and I felt connected to the spirit of my inner flame. I felt powerful yet humble. I felt open yet fiercely protected. I felt funny, hilarious actually, and deeply wise. I felt all of me. All of the beauty and gifts and talents and weirdness and for the first time in my life, I saw it as my own. I saw it as my unique flavour of God and greatness and magic and all of these words people use to decorate ourselves in our purest form: Love.

I felt the core essence of love. Above and underneath all else, at the edges of my fingers and the tips of my soul, I felt love. And just as I realised, just as I came to this true meeting and knowing of myself. I opened my hands to her, and she rose from her bow, a tear in her eye bigger than one of my mouthfuls. Reflexively, I raced and caught her tear in a leaf, quickly bottling it in one of the tincture bottles Kit had left me with. She'd said I'd never guess how I'd need them, and she was right. Never did I ever imagine this could be happening. Never did I ever give myself permission to drink in the fullness of myself like I had in this moment. And never did I ever want to forget it. I smiled and looked to her with a thank you that required no words.

Shiviera.

I heard the word in my mind a thousand times before I realised what it was. *Shi-veer-ah. Shiviera?*

Yes, Ankhara. Shiviera is my name.

And I cried. I cried a thousand tears for all the times I had forgotten her, and for all the times I'd wished for her, not knowing. And I smiled, in the joy of having the family of my soul back by my side.

"It's an honour to have you by my side, my friend." I spoke to her not because I needed to. She would have heard my thoughts, I knew that to be true. I spoke to her to cement the magic woven by my words as spells. So that the forest may hear my respect for her, and the birds may see her as my friend. I spoke to her aloud because this forest was my Kingdom, and I wanted her to be known by everyone in it.

My thoughts flashed to Noah as she bent her shoulder to me, gesturing for me to climb onto her back. *I can't wait to tell you she's real.* My first thought as I climbed onto her and transferred a portion of her tear into a locket mixed with mine. This giant, black, tree loving cat. The spirit of the jaguar. *The spirit of my heart.* My guide. Ready and willing. Here, I hoped, to take me home. I took a deep breath as I settled into my place on her back, and melted into the air with her as she took off, with no idea where she would be going, and every idea that wherever it may be would be just right.

ANKHARA CODES: AN ADVENTURE TO ESSENCE
BOOK 2: ALLIES OF THE SOUL
COMING 2021

ABOUT THE AUTHOR

*E*llie Deighton is a teacher of magic. A keeper of wisdom, she is gifted in guiding other's home to their own creative genius. Ellie has now turned her skillset into story form, creating a platform where every day people can journey towards the remembering of themselves, much like her clients do. Ellie runs online masterminds and trainings in support of others expressing their highest potential, and teaches, writes and speaks as an expression of her own. Based in Bunbury, Western Australia, she has travelled the world in pursuit of her heart and teachings and is now home where her journey began, filling her days with creation in the form of music, mentorship and other magical musings.

PHOTO: LAUREN COUANON

AUTHOR'S NOTE

I live in Bunbury, Western Australia, having returned home after years of not having one. Earth has felt like my home for the last phase of my life and yet I am completely lit up to be back where I was born.

I used to play basketball at a competitive, national level in my teens. I was a high achiever. Sports captain. Prefect. Straight A student (except in year 12 maths, something just happened). I was an early bloomer. I dated and fell in love young and have never regretted following love around the world.

After school I lived at Trinity Residential College in Perth while I studied at UWA for four years and despite being on track with a vision to become an emergency surgeon, my heart was whispering to me that there was something more.

I didn't know what it was, but this 'more' had me upheaval my whole life and I left university and the life I knew in pursuit of a life of it, whatever it was going to be.

I found 'more' to be magic.

I created love and travel and business and delved into full time entrepreneurship at the age of twenty-two.

I haven't looked back. There have been moments that have terrified me, friends that have torn at my heart, and yet nothing frightens me more than a life of not listening to my hearts whispers.

I live intuitively. Unexpectedly, my family call it. That is how this book was born. My heart whispered 'write a book' and I said 'okay'.

Becoming an author has been a lifelong dream of mine and although *Ankhara Codes* was not at all what I expected, I now know that the magic lies in the unexpected.

I am forever grateful for that day I chose to follow my heart and for every day I have chosen that since.

If I had one nugget of wisdom to share with you it would be that - follow your heart and allow yourself to remember that you already know. You already know what you love, who you love and how you'd love to feel.

Go out there and pursue it like nothing else matters, because really, it doesn't.

All else will fade and one day, when you close your eyes for the final time, your essence will linger in the ways it has stamped the world with your blueprint. I hope you leave behind the essence of your magic so that our children may live in a world born of it.

I'll see you soon, I hope. Come say hey online somewhere. Who knows, maybe we'll grab a cuppa.

In Love,
Ellie

Connect with me online:
https://www.instagram.com/ellieanndeighton/
https://www.facebook.com/ellieanndeighton
www.ellieanndeighton.com
hello@elliedeighton.com

MAGIC IS REAL
ARE YOU READY TO UNLOCK YOURS?

Turn the page for a sneak peak of the magic Ellie offers in her online world and use the code 'ANKHARA' on her websites to redeem your readers discount and free gift.

www.ankharacodes.com

AWAKENED CREATIVITY
Genius Activation

Awakened Creativity is an online journey of elemental magic that has been put together for those who are ready to taste, share and live their essence in this world that is begging for it. It is high time to activate your genius and unleash your true gifts. This is a portal for you to do so alongside a community of geniuses who live their magic and want to see you live yours too.

"This whole journey was more than I expected it would be. It felt like a guided deep dive into my essence and my magic that I had forgotten and disconnected from. The structure that Ellie has put together for this course feels like a remembering. Seeing how everyone connected with their own magic... I don't have the vocab to describe how amazing this has been. It is worth it, worth it, worth it. "
\- RYDEEANNA,MALAYSIA

"This course itself has been completely transformational experience for me. I love the way Ellie presents the information to you and let's you go along your own journey with no judgement."
\- BEN, AUSTRALIA

Join Us
www.ankharacodes.com

THE REMEMBERING
Genius Witch Collective

Where the spirit of the witch comes to earth to take up space in your body. Where you live the fullest expression of you. Where you unite with brothers, sisters as teachers and allies. That is The Remembering. The Genius Witch Collective is a global community that welcomes all those who feel the call.

"The Remembering is a gorgeous community that came to me in the right time of my life. It has given me access to beautiful souls who connect with magic in many different ways. The Remembering has helped me feel normal in having these conversations in such a way that magic becomes just a normal way of being."
\- MARIYA, BULGARIA

"The Remembering is you in an ocean of people who get you and celebrate you and do it with you. This is for you if you love being present to that glowing, ooey gooey magic that is every day."
\- SELINA, AUSTRALIA

JOIN THE COVEN
www.ankharacodes.com

Thank you

www.ingramcontent.com/pod-product-compliance
Lightning Source LLC
Chambersburg PA
CBHW070554120726
47909CB00007B/2340